I0526433

SEX IN SOUTHEAST

First Edition

Published by The Nazca Plains Corporation
Las Vegas, Nevada
2010

ISBN: 978-1-935509-75-2

Published by

The Nazca Plains Corporation ®
4640 Paradise Rd, Suite 141
Las Vegas NV 89109-8000

PUBLISHER'S NOTE
Sex in Southeast is a work of fiction created wholly by *Billy Jay Dee*'s imagination. All characters are fictional and any resemblance to any persons living or deceased is purely by accident. No portion of this book reflects any real person or events.

Cover Photos
Jecka and Ken Pilon

Art Director
Blake Stephens

SEX IN SOUTHEAST

First Edition

Billy Jay Dee

CONTENTS

BEFORE SEATTLE 1

A BIPEDAL TOUR OF THE EMERALD CITY 9

ANOTHER NIGHT IN SEATTLE 17

COMING TO GRIEF 23

DEFINITELY NOT A VIRGIN ANYMORE 27

ER, GREG 33

THE GRAND SLAM 37

HI, LAX 41

CARLOS 49

I DON'T THINK SO 53

TESTOSTERONE TRIO; MOUNTAIN MAN 59

TESTOSTERONE TRIO; NORTHWEST PASSAGE 63

TESTOSTERONE TRIO; A REALLY HOT TUB 67

IF THAT'S REJECTION… 69

A NIGHT IN THE TIJUANA OF SOUTHEAST 75

ANOTHER NIGHT IN TIJUANA 77

KEN 81

LAYOVER AT THE AIRPORT 85

LODGE THAT GRAND ROD 89

NOT IN MY NATURE 97

ON THE WAY TO SEATTLE 114

PRIAPUS: SEVEN SHORT ADVENTURES 116

RENDEZVOUS WITH RUSS 141

SATURDAY NIGHT HOT 143

TARRYING WITH TERRY BEAR 147

THEIR FIRST TIME 153

THREE TIMES IN THE COUNTY SEAT 159

TRAILER TRIO: F'CKIN' 167

UH, BUDDY 173

CARLOS IN THE VALLEY OF THE SUN 179

A WALK IN THE PARK 185

A NICE THING 187

WOOD CHIPS 191

ABOUT THE AUTHOR 197

BEFORE SEATTLE

I looked forward to flying to Seattle. I live in a fishing village on a island surrounded by federal wilderness areas in central "Southeast". It had been a long time since I'd seen any man-on-man action. Probably a month since Chubby-Ray had asked me to whip it out. "Watch the video," he encouraged as he rolled the head of my cock around in his mouth. How hot is that? Brazilian porn stars performing for me while a volunteer fireman blows me. But, that had been a while ago.

I never make dates the first night in town because you can't depend on Southeastern weather to cooperate with travel plans. So, that left me free to run to the Hawk for a quick beer. Not a whole lot going on there on a Thursday night. So, I was off to Club A. What a great night. It was non-stop action. I barely got out of the locker room before things started happening.

When I first walked into the locker room, I was surprised at the number of guys there this early in the evening. The ones that particularly caught my attention as I stripped were an older guy and two friends. The older guy was probably 60, average build and appearance. A head of white hair and black eyebrows. He seemed friendly, but not particularly interested in me.

Meanwhile the two friends were dressing near me. Bronzed, beefy guys enjoying the easy conversation of good friends. It made me miss my red head buddy Drew. We haven't had a chance to hang out much lately. They also made me think of my date for Saturday. Mike and Dave were a pair of carrot-topped tops I was supposed to meet at Sprags on Saturday.

My dick was starting to twitch.

I hit the showers. To cut the chill afterwards, I took advantage of the sauna. I passed the older guy with the black eyebrows on the way. In the sauna was a guy about 50, friendly, privates barely concealed by his towel, fine body covered in a light layer of blonde hair. His smiling face was crowned in pompadour style with a pile of blonde hair.

He started stroking himself as soon as we began to talk. So, you can probably understand how I didn't notice when the Old-Guy-with-Black-Eyebrows snuck in. I finally had to ask blondie if I could help him with that.

"Sure!" he said. And the weekend began! "Sure!" He said tossing his towel aside. He scooted forward on the cedar bench as I leaned over to suck his cock. He had a nice seven-incher with a big head and a strong lean to the left. I went to deep-throating him as my right hand slid along his six-pack belly. I love the feel of a fuzzy body.

My left hand found my own dick beneath my towel. Blondie was starting to ride in and out of my mouth, lifting his hips off the bench and scooting his balls ever closer to my mouth. Whenever he popped from between my lips, I'd ask if he was enjoying himself.

"Oh yeah," he replied with ever increasing enthusiasm.

At one point I turned my head to see if we had an appreciative audience and discovered the Old-Guy-with-Black-Eyebrows was watching from close by. Blondie's oversized cockhead found its way back into my mouth. His long narrow shaft was wet, smooth, and clean. He slid it in and out of me with ever increasing rapidity. The middle finger of my right hand honed in on his hole and started moving in.

In response he moved his well-muscled ass off the bench and spread his thighs further. Someone lifted the towel up off my loins. Blondie panted heavily now, with ever more appreciative phrases slipping from his lips. I braced myself against the bench and he gently held my head in place with his right hand while he fucked my suctioning mouth.

I felt a cold breeze slide across my exposed bottom just as Blondie came in almost tasteless warm spurts. He thanked me profusely as he hurried from the sauna. I turned to see if the Old-Guy-with-Black-Eyebrows was ready and stared into Mitch's black eyes instead.

I'd encountered Mitch here before. He was crouched on the bench above my ass. The Old-Guy-with-Black-Eyebrows watched from the door. Mitch is built like a god. "BLACK" is tattooed above one perfect pec, "WHITE" above the other. Beneath, his sides, which flank a perfect abdomen and narrowing torso, are tattooed with the heavily engraved gates of Heaven. And there lies something worth worshiping – his ever hard, ever ready, thick greased eight-inch cock.

"Hi," he said.

"Hi," I replied leaving my mouth agape.

Old-Guy-with-Black-Eyebrows saw the look on my face and apparently detected no hope for him. He turned to leave.

"Nice ass," Mitch declared from on high. That stopped him.

"I've got a room. How about you guys come up?" Mitch said. He has eyes more earth brown than black that race from intense seriousness to unfettered delight as quickly as a lightning bolt flashes across a storm-darkened sky. Of course, I said yes. Old-Guy-with-Black-Eyebrows passed. Can you believe that?

Mitch locked the door behind us as we entered his room. He dropped his towel and bounced across the bed landing with his back against the wall, arms supported by pillows, legs sprawled across the sheet. His stiff rod bobbed somewhat upward. Those expressionless night-clad eyes gazed upon his throbbing cock and then rose to my blue eyes.

I threw myself down between his perfect thighs and began to worship his golden idol. He had the body of a Greek god cast in polished bronzes.

"God, you have a great body!" I exclaimed as my hands explored his well-muscled body-scape.

Delight flashed across his face. "You too," he lied. Then his eyes returned to that darkened shade as cold and black as the eternal night of space.

I sucked both of his perfect hairless balls into my mouth. Mitch liked that. I licked his cock to gleaming. My hands flowed up this firm belly and rippled abdomen – as flat and hard as polished marble.

"Nice belly."

"You, too."

He leaned from above my prostrate form and squeezed my small pot belly twice, pulled at my little six inch cock, rolled one leg over so he could examine my asshole and then leaned back again. It's not that I believed I had a great body, but to hear him say it assured me I was good enough to meet his standards.

He pulled my head back onto his cock and gently started face-fucking me again. Occasionally, I lifted his balls to my mouth when pushing my chin back to the mattress. I could see delight flash across his face. For the most part his assault was eerily silent except for the slurping noises my mouth made around his drooling cock and his heavy breathing. The time before in Seattle, I'd been with my boy friend, Ken. He's loud in his appreciation, affectionate to a fault, and always loving and intimate, even when he's hammering me hard.

At some point in the forced feeding of my 48-year-old face, Mitch's hands let up the pressure on the nape of my neck. I looked up to the Olympian heights of his face and found his eyes upon me as stern as Jove's between lightning strikes in a night sky. Without acknowledging my presence, his stare turned to something else.

I followed his gaze to the mirrored wall. There Mitch reclined like a river god of antiquity. Powerful, beautiful, manly, rippled abdomen, massive shoulders, bulging muscles, thighs like a hero. I lay at his feet wallowing like a beached whale. That was it! I was going to suck that shaft so hard he'd beg me to impale myself. My head rose over his lap and I plunged my mouth down onto his cock. A finger reaches for his squeaky clean ass.

His hands gripped the back of my head and forced the thick mushroom of his cock far to the back of my throat. Too far.

What happen next wasn't erotic and didn't involve him cumming. It did require us to shower together. And, though I apologized and he said it was all right, I declined when he wanted me to return to his room.

"I'll walk around first and let my stomach settle. Then I'll be up." Which I was eventually.

I walked all the floors and peeked in all the doors, but kept moving so my stomach would have a chance to settle. I eventually planted my ass on the carpeted bench in the video room for a breather. That was pretty boring after a while so I headed to the recreation room. The darkened maze appeared to be empty so I swung around into the blow job alley. Empty also. I turned back and there in my arms was the Old-Guy-with-Black- Eyebrows.

"Hi."

"Hi, yourself" I responded.

His hand slipped beneath my towel and started stroking my six-incher. I tried to return the favor, but he explained he'd just cum.

"You look tense," he noted as he grabbed my shoulders and started massaging the ache out of them.

I hadn't noticed I was tense until that moment. There is no boyfriend in Seattle any more to help ease my tension, no chance to be with my best friend in a while. I guess, a lot of tension had been building up. I was putty in Old-Guy-with-Black-Eyebrows' hands when he started massaging my temples.

"Here, turn around."

He leaned me towards the blow job wall and started rubbing my back and shoulders. The towel wrapped around my waist was lifted high off my ass. I responded by shoving my butt out and sighing loudly.

"Turn around again," the old guy ordered.

A Filipino guy had been fondling my ass.

"Come over here," Old-Guy-with-Black-Eyebrows directed, "so you can blow this guy. Stand up on the bench," he said to the Filipino.

For a little guy he sure had a big dick. A big brown dick with smooth petite features. He mounted the bench. My mouth mounted his cock. Hands stripped off my towel. Hands bent me into position. Hands started playing with my ass. A big blonde kid with a little dick snuck in next to me, eyeing my aching hardon. We exchanged a smile and his hand started stroking me. The Filipino guy wanted me to lick his hole clean, but my stomach still wasn't ready for that. Blondie slid between him and the wall and went to it, eagerly wedging his tongue between the smooth brown ass cheeks. I kept working that Asian phallus until it was time for another rest.

"Sorry, guys."

I slipped away. Or so I thought. The blonde kid caught up with me, whipped out his cock and shoved it in my face. He was a big boy, but his cock was short and thin, less than five inches, I'd guess. I like that. I started rolling the head in my mouth while jerking the shaft, but he was short enough that soon he could freely face-fuck me without discomfort to my sensitive throat.

"That's great. That's great!" he murmured. His hands reached for my cock, reached for my ass, clasped my shoulders, and caressed my head. "That's great! I love that!" His hips began driving faster, his breath came more rapidly. "I love that!" He was fingering my hole and lifting my ass up in the air. He slipped from my mouth and positioned himself at my behind, then jumped back to my mouth. "I'm going to cum. I love this." Back to my rear and then, "I'm going to cum. Can I cum on you?" He came in shattered globs of scorching hot jizm.

The guy next to me didn't seem to notice. I loved it. When the shower of youthful semen ended, I started cleaning myself up and turned to thank the kid. He was gone. Instead I found myself staring into the bottomless pit of Mitch's eyes. Wordlessly he was nodding for me to follow. You know I did.

Well you know Mitch – the expressionless night-clad eyes, throbbing perfect rod and then the body of a Greek god cast in polished bronze. But the best part this time around was he wanted me! Again! But, maybe more cautiously.

Once the door locked, he swung me on my back and perched over my chest. He slid the bulbous head of his cock within range of my lips and tongue, but saved the shaft to stroke himself. He hunkered over me, his angelic frame swaying sensuously. Each long twisting stroke or drop of precum would make his face burst into a smile that faded before his storming eye as he gazed down at me trying to decide what to do next.

He pinched precum off the head of his dick and smeared it like battle paint high on the right cheek below my eye. He stuffed the head of his rod in the gaping abyss of my mouth. A sigh, so giant, escaped his lips that it forced his shoulders back and jet black eyes up. His free hand followed the sigh heavenward, stroking his rippled belly, chiseled frame and perfectly round pecs. He was panting.

His little round mouth formed what was almost a smile. His black orbs drilled into my blues as he stroked his cock downward into my face. He pulled it out, stained my face with precum again. He was jerking hard now. His breathe coming in spasms.

"You going to fuck me now?" I asked, as I began rolling my cock across my abdomen.

His flint-black eyes gazed down upon me from on high. His knees and marbled thighs pinned my shoulders to the bed. His free hand reached into the steaming pit of my left arm. He brought the acrid scent to his nostrils.

"Want to fuck me?" I asked breathlessly, as my six incher started ache with the need for more friction from my hand.

Wordless, he shoved his cock back into my waiting mouth. He leaned back, moved my right leg to the side and shoved a finger halfway into my tangy ass. That too rose to his nostrils.

"Nah. I'm gonna shoot a load into your mouth."

He spread more precum on my forehead, then his left hand held my helpless face in place while the right pumped load after load of creamy tasting cum into my waiting mouth. He fell back into the wall. Fell back into his river god pose. He watched me shoot all over my belly without word or expression. His cell phone rang. He started talking. I wrapped my towel around me. He shook my hand, called me by name, locked the door behind me and I assume went back to talking on the phone.

I'd had fun at the Club, but my ass still ached for a rod in it. Fortunately, the next night the bears met. The bears of Seattle met the first Saturday of every month. I always try to be there. "Wall to wall fur," as they say. I had several people to say "hi" to – old acquaintances and new pen pals. So, I awkwardly worked the room and finagled introductions out of folks who'd just met me to their friends. Awkward at first, but the beer was cheap and the bears were friendly, so I (as usual) had a good time. Then I ran into the pair of carrot-tops I'd been e-mailing.

"Let us buy you a drink."

"A Budweiser?"

"Don't you want a man's drink?"

"Jose Cuervo?"

"Make it two, barkeep!"

I was led around by a ruddy hand. I was introduced to everyone. Got left to guard the beers. Got introduced to their out of town guys. Got dragged to the bar to help carry the next round back to our table.

"Hey, while we are standing here, let me introduce you to our friend, the legendary Dan."

Husky Dan stood right behind me, breathing down my neck. Breathing DOWN my neck; which means he's tall. I like that. He wasn't as tall as my boyfriend, but he was at least 6 feet. All I saw was a killer smile framed in a brunette goatee. I don't know what we talked about, maybe the tequila had taken effect. I only remember wanting to kiss those lips. Dan seemed to like that idea.

His kisses were warm and wet and tender, passionate yet controlled. I didn't remember a make-out session like that since my best friend and I took a drunken trip to the state capital. We wandered around a bit then hung out with his friends.

"Does he like tequila?" I asked one of the red heads.

"What do you think makes him legendary?" We left soon after that. Got to his place and got naked. We made out again. Made out like I haven't, well, since that trip to the state capitol. As we kissed my left hand reached beneath his belly and found a long dick. Not nearly as big as my boyfriend's, but nice! Almost hard

enough, too! I started stroking and to help the cause I asked again. "So why are you legendary?"

Bashfully he told of a dinner party at his friend's house. Everything was fine until he got left alone with one of the guests. When dinner was served and the hosts came looking for him, Dan was butt-banging a perfect stranger in the middle of their living room. Next thing I know, my ankles are hoisted in the air and I'm getting butt banged by Dan, who is on his knees in the middle of the bed. He came quickly in a healthy quantity and we fell asleep. I woke early and roughly stroked his semi hard cock to arouse him.

"Why don't you climb up on that thing?" he grunted, groggily.

I obliged, alternating pounding up and down with grinding my butt into his groin. He liked the latter and came quickly again. Another healthy load, too, that leaked out of my ass onto his hairy pubes and balls. I cuddled in his arms and jerked off as he asked me arousing questions. Apparently, Dan liked that, too, because he came again.

I had fun in the Emerald City, but I was glad to be headed home to my wife's bed and my best friend's company. Home will be good, but so will Dan next time I'm down. I got his phone number.

A BIPEDAL TOUR OF THE EMERALD CITY

The cuter one checked me out.

I sat in front of the Triton's fake fireplace. This made my third stop on a walking tour of Seattle. The Bond's website provided the map. I felt more at ease here than during happy hour at the mortuary-like, Bunnies. Dudes played darts, pool, and pinball. The burly bartender keeps the lights up and the walls covered with rough cut lumber clean. And that sandy haired stud was still checking me out.

Jack and his buddy came in fifteen minutes after me. They sat two barstools away. They shared a similar stocky frame – both almost as tall as me at 6'1", but with sandy and blond hair. Jack looked the cuter of the two, with those damn light blue eyes and a sensuous smirk common to good-looking men. Not that I'd kick Jack's best friend out of bed! His chin sported several days' growth of a blonde beard. He smiled a lot. And made me laugh out loud.

They talked and joked up a storm in a fast paced witty banter. So why did Jack check me out every time I looked around? (Okay, actually every time I looked over there to check him out.) But, my beer mug stood empty and plenty of bars on the list needed me to visit.

As I left, Jack said, "I noticed the Concho belt. You got the boots to go with it?" I lifted a booted foot to show them. An engrossing fast-paced conversation about their vacation through the Southwest followed. Ends up we had a lot in common. A three-way could sound good to me. Jack's best friend told me about

their transfer to San Diego and about buying a new house. That's when it came out that they were former lovers and best friends.

Behind me, I heard Jack say, "It's about time he got here", followed by the smacking of two sets of lips in greeting.

Jack's best friend and I rose. Jim introduced his date. The date was unbelievably beautiful. His body appeared dark and muscled all over. Broad brown shoulders narrowed to a small waist and flat belly. His butt looked to be round and firm. His pleated tan slacks left his crotch to the imagination, but his shear t-shirt clung to an amazing chest as tightly as I wanted to. His little nipples stood at sharp-pointed attention with excitement. He shook our hands and said our names with the desperate effort to make a good impression on his date's friends. Jim called him "Beefcake" to his face. So, maybe Jack hit up on me so that his best friend would have a date, too. That wasn't a bad thing either.

We decided to walk to Sprags. The conversation returned to their routine of: wit, finishing one another's sentences, and private jokes. It sounded like me and my best friend (and former lover), so I joined right in. Jack's date sort of got lost in the dust.

When we got there, we were all hither and yon for a while. The two buddies and I said "Hello" to the bear-bartender that used to work at Spags. We wandered around deciding where to sit. Jack and his date hit the bathroom. Jack's best friend made a comment that he hoped this worked out for Jack. He'd been through four lovers since moving here.

"Which one were you?" I asked

"Number 2," he answered as Jack's date joined us.

The look on his face! And my wife feels threatened by my best friend! Jack's best friend assumed that the date knew and I didn't see him approach. Ugh! Jack's date recovered before Jack returned.

"Where are you going on this walking tour?" Jack asked

"Probably Neighbors next."

"How about the Hawk?"

"I was there last night."

"Isn't that place wild?" he interjected, "I was there last week. Bottoms lined up on the balcony to suck off some stud with a foot-long dick."

"Well, you know that partition behind the back patio. Last night a bunch of boys crowded in behind it. I said to the Marlboro man next to me, what's going on back there? Only one way to fine out, he says. So, I go check. They've got a Latino pretty well naked, one's sucking his cock, some are playing with his nipples, and one's fingering his ass. That's when I noticed that the crowd watching had their dicks out and were stroking one another off."

Jack's best friend leaned over my shoulder to listen. Jack and his date stared in rapt interest.

"Did you?" Jack asked encouragingly.

"Well…yeah! It was wild. A dozen men back there taking turns sucking one another off. At one point, three of us knelt with our backs to the wall slurping on a friend's cock. When I stood up for my turn, the cocksucker on my right kept sucking his partner and the stud two over started butt fucking his. The second time I went back, the crowd gathered around two good-looking gents. One bent over, pants down, shirt and coat pulled up, with his fine white ass pushed into the other gent's face. He gnawed on that thing and pushed his wide pink tongue way up there. The bent over man encouraged the crowd to slap his butt. Blue collar types with long hard dicks asked if they could `have a piece of that?' I got into it and ended up in a little daisy chain with the two gents that started it all. The third time everyone's eyes grew wide with disbelief and glazed with horniness. The group spilled onto the patio. Three leather men bent me over to suck their buddy's helmet head while they played with my ass. Later, I took someone I met there and the whole crowd peed on someone lying on the floor. I thought, `Not for me', when my new friend starts sucking on the other guy's wet pants!"

Everyone hoped we'd see that tonight. I held the floor while retelling my previous evening. When the topic moved on, the conversation returned to normal with the date's desperate smiles, Jack's and his buddy's tighter banter, and me barging into the conversation and joining the fun as they grew louder. But the beer took its toll and they got more sarcastic and their laughter harder.

I pulled Jack's best friend aside. "You and Jack remind me of me and my best friend. One time we took acquaintance fishing. I wasn't paying any attention to our new friend. We worked the boat and discussed where to fish, who would work the anchor line and just normal stuff. I finally asked our acquaintance what he thought. He said, `You two have diarrhea of the mouth.' We laughed. He was right. We just kept going on and on and never let him get a word in edgewise."

"So, you're saying Jack and I have diarrhea of the mouth?" he asked with a grin.

"I'm not trying to insult you," I apologized. "I'm just trying to tell you that you're not giving Jim's date a chance."

He smiled and nodded noncommittally and went back to eating peanuts.

"And with that I'm leaving."

"Where you going?"

"Neighbors."

"Maybe we'll see you at the Bond later?"

I shook hands with the date, awaiting Jack's return, and walked out the door.

As a matter of fact I did meet them there later. I'd been at the Bond a while by then. I made the circuit off the back patio, up the stairs, around the main bar, and right into Jack.

"Imagine meeting you here!" I called.

"Yeah!" he said with a grin.

"How's it going?"

"Great," he replied, but he wasn't doing great.

The light blue eyes in his rugged face looked puffy with emotion and not too far from wet or red. He stood with his solid chest thrown out and left hand pulled back in a fist. His right hand could barely lift his beer without trembling.

"What happened?"

"My date split."

I suggested lamely that maybe he was in the bathroom.

"For twenty minutes?" he scolded.

"Where's your best friend?"

"My friend with diarrhea of the mouth is trying to get laid," he said without anger. His chin pointed across the room, where his best friend stumbled drunkenly with the flow of traffic eyeing possible candidates.

"I didn't mean to piss you off. Just to warn you."

He spewed his frustration a little longer about the missing date. I tried to keep my mouth shut and just be sympathetic.

"Fuck it. Let's go check out the dance floor."

I followed. As we came down the steps onto the dance floor, I got to thinking of the last time I came here. Someone amazing had met me on the edge of the dance floor. He stood 6'5", 270 #, built like a football player. His small dark eyes had twinkled. His small lips showed pink beneath an angular nose. His dick was so big it took both his broad hands to pack it up my ass. When no room remained in my body cavity he had amazed and delighted me by pushing off the bed with his toes to get deeper into me.

The next morning he dropped me off at my hotel. As soon as I got out of the truck I regretted not saying something. His last relationship ended due to the scars that made his handsome face puffy. Had I hurt him by not being more affectionate after seeing him in the broad daylight? For me it had been love (err, lust) at first sight. We left within 5 minutes of meeting. We couldn't stop smiling at one another. We answered to the same first name, worked for the same company, and shared a love of tequila.

"Tequila?" Jack asked

My eyes bugged out as my mouth dropped open.

"It doesn't mean I'm going to fuck you. It's just a shot," he responded loudly with a grin.

Thoroughly confused, my eyes tried to bat back to normal shape. My mouth mumbled, "Tequila, yeah."

We downed the shot at the bar out back and returned to our stand up table by the dance floor. Jack started talking about his date again.

"You know, Jack, I listened to the bad thing that happened to you to night. It's your turn to listen to my bad thing:

When I left Sprags for Neighbors, my cowboy boots followed Madison to Broadway. There's a pancake house at the intersection. My stomach started grumbling. When I looked in, a big black man about my age sitting at a table looks

at me. My boots keep walking. When my eyes looked, again he's still looking. There's no way I can walk into an a pancake house and pick up a Nubian dream. On the other hand… I go in, telling the hostess, "I'm sitting with someone."

"Can I join you?" I say to him

He nods. We order. He's big, quiet, and serious looking. I toss out every double entendre and outrageous thing, until he smiles. It's one of those enormous laughing smiles, which he covers with his hand a la Whoopi Goldberg in "The Color Purple." Sweet talk flows all through dinner and into the parking lot after, with him saying yes or no. That's always a bad sign when I have to work so hard at it. We check out his new car. "Lean your seat back and undo your pants!" I tell him. After veiling the delight on his face with his big soft black hand, he complies. My right hand reached for his cock. My aching jaw dropped open. It was enormous! My hand barely reached around it. How would we get it in my ass later? My tongue barely got a lick or two before a car drove up. He freaked. We drove to my hotel and I sneaked him in the back door. I finished undressing as he announced, "I can't stay."

Jack called him a bastard and chattered supportively. I failed to mention the black security guard worked as an AIDS volunteer that he feared being recognized at my hotel because it was attached to Virginia Mason where he worked. Jack and I moved up the stairs to the less noisy "Leather Room". Jack went to the bathroom and left me in charge of the beers.

"You'll be here when I get back, won't you?" he grinned.

The crowd cruised by – muscle gods in tight shorts with wide well-defined chests; daddies with five o'clock shadows, tight blue jeans, and dress shirts open half way down their chests to show off the hair; tall straight looking college boys with bedroom eyes; and more. I talked with the leather men occasionally in their black leather pants, harness on their bare chests, leather police caps, smoking well-chewed cigars and their cool appraising stares. Jack's date appeared, wide eyed and out of breathe. The upper portion of his light blue shirt was dark from the rain.

"Where are they?"

"Who?"

"You know."

"Jack's in the bathroom. He'll be right back," I said indicating the bathroom behind us and around the corner. His date dashed that way. The parade of studs continuing to pass included a puffy skinned giant. My friend from six months before! My heart pounded. I didn't want to appear too desperate. I waited. Jack returned with his date in hand and big grin on his face. True love conquers all, I thought. "True love calls," I said instead.

My boots clucked down the stairs. I found him pretty much where he'd stood six months before. He kissed me softly in greeting. His large gentle hands touched me, but his massive muscular arms didn't reach for a hug.

"Before we say anything else, I need to tell you something. When you dropped me off, you said how much you enjoyed our night together."

"I did."

"So, did I. But I should've said, `How about we do it again?' This is crazy, me saying this and being married, but you can't imagine how much I think of you. You made me feel like no man ever has."

"Thank you," he interrupted.

My shoulders fell in relief to see his eyes did not water with hurt revisited, and disappointment to see they did not glaze with passion aroused.

"Whew! That's over!" I sighed and took a place beside him against the wall, "What's happening?"

"I'm moving back home. My boy friend is still back there."

My eyebrows arched in question. He told me about his dream of transferring back. But there'd been no boyfriend six months ago.

"It's my old boy friend. I know it didn't work last time. These gay things never work. But I've got to give it a try."

I didn't want to see the hurt in his dark little eyes. I wanted to remember them full of passion in the night. I suggested I should go. He said, "No" and asked about the wife and kids. We talked.

"Got to check in with my friends," I said before it got more awkward.

Jack and company were nowhere to be seen. I wandered around a bit more in the maze of man meat, eventually running into my gentle giant again. He introduced me to his friends.

Last stop – the Hawk. I circled the bar on the first floor and stopped at the bathroom to pee. They don't close the door there, so everyone can see. I went out back. No one was crowding behind the partition. Upstairs it wasn't hot enough for the bears to be shirtless. But the crowd stood thick against the railing upstairs and my crotch rubbed against lots of butts to get through. At the bottom of the stairs Jack stood flirting with the bouncer.

"What are you doing here?" I asked with a smile.

"I'm going home with the bouncer. My date and I fought during dinner."

"I'm sorry to hear that."

"He didn't care!"

"Yeah, he did. I heard the kiss when he greeted you. The way he massaged your shoulders. He tried really hard."

"I figured he wasn't even going to show up tonight. That's why I hit on you. In case he didn't show. So, if he cared, what the Hell happened?"

"You're really good looking." I began.

"I'm a bottom. I'm not going to fuck you."

"It's not flattery, it's fact. Shall we walk around and take a survey?"

Jack blushed rather than admit it.

"The point is you're good looking like my wife and people are willing to put up with a lot from good looking people, but you ignored him."

"You're too used to dealing with women. Guys aren't supposed to care."

I'd already told him he'd been wrong too many times tonight.

"This is such a bottom town," he shouted. "This is a one night stand to you and then you go back to your wife and kids. But this is my life!"

I couldn't respond.

"Let's see if anything's going on out back."

Nothing was. After making the circuit, we ran into a stocky red headed acquaintance. He admitted to recognizing me, but not remembering where we had met. I remembered. He'd changed his mind in my room long ago like the security guard did tonight. I didn't mention it. The three of us joked and gossiped for a while. After he'd wondered off, someone else I recognized cruised by.

I nudged Jack. "That's the one." I said nodding towards a farm boy type in a yellow hat. "The one everyone peed on last night."

"Oh, yellow." he whispered back. "That means water sports."

"I'll have to remember to never wear yellow in a gay bar!"

"Closing time!" Jack's bouncer called.

Jack wanted to give me his e-mail. A gay acquaintance once told me, "We exchange phone numbers and it doesn't mean anything." Jack walked me to the door. He went back to flirting with the bouncer, whom I handed my drink and slipped out the door. Lots of us left then, heading down Pike Street.

Someone behind me said, "Watch the whole crowd cut across the street to the Club A."

The Club A is a bathhouse. I hadn't been in one in 20 years. I thought "What the Hell?" I left my clothes in a locker and wrapped the towel around my waist. All types of men walked the carpeted halls and stairs peeking in the private rooms. A couple of bottoms lay in hammocks waiting for the right top to come along. Three large well- greased dildos lay next to one beckoning bubble butt. Other men lay wantonly on their bellies or sat up stroking their cocks, shaking their head to those that peeked in. In the "Porno Room", big buck naked boys watched a video trying to get hard, rarely helping one another.

Even at this desperate hour of the morning in the "Blowjob Room", few dropped to their knees or started making out. I'd seen more passion and action behind the partition at the Hawk the night before. Plus, as Jack said, Seattle is a bottom town. Particularly at 2 a.m. when all the tops became too drunk, too tired or too self-conscious to perform in public. But after a lot of groping in the dark, a short, thick, hard, hooked, black cock, appeared in the darkness that I could get stiff.

"Want to fuck?" I asked

"Yeah, but not here," Regan answered.

He took me to his room and turned up the lights. His similarity to the security guard earlier in the night struck me, including the beaming face. But, Regan was a little shorter and a lot prouder of his smile He suggested I get on my hands and knees on the bed. I braced my face in the pillow and waited while he got a big glob of lube on his right index finger. He slipped it in slow and smooth. Then started working his hand back and forth.

"Go for a second finger," I moaned

"No! We don't need that."

He slowly slipped his curved cock in where his finger had been. Then began a long slow fuck lasting 20 minutes before he came. It felt so good while we fucked that my back arched in delight. That made it even better for him. Still on knees and elbows my back arched again, this time my head lifting with an "Ah!"

My blue eyes stared into a mirror at the head of the bed. Over my shoulder my white cheeks spread apart every time his firms black belly plowed into them. His muscular thighs spread out on either side of my hips. His sleek, well-muscled chest leaned over me as his gripping arms pulled and pushed us apart. We both smiled.

A few hours later, my butt sat on the front steps of my hotel waiting for a taxi. My AIDS volunteer strolled by on his way to the clinic.

"How you doing?" he asked.

His face revealed neither concern nor apology. He wore the same non-committal expression from the night before.

"Fine," I said and told him about Club A.

He didn't know the place. I described it. His bulging belly hid any indication of the enormous cock in his trousers. A co-worker joined him. They continued on their way to the clinic. My taxi came. Like Jack said I would, I returned to my loving wife of many years, great kids, dream home and big black Labrador.

ANOTHER NIGHT IN SEATTLE

"That's him," I said to myself, as the light turned.

I gulped and started across the street. His tall frame swayed slightly in his white dress shirt and tight faded Levis. Wide spread fingers braced against the barn wood railing outside the Seattle Aquarium. I noticed the confessed graying hair and slight paunch.

I wore grey shorts and a white tank top, due to the summer heat, with a blue zippered hooded sweatshirt tossed on when the afternoon rains started.

He recognized me from that distance. I tugged at the sweatshirt and smiled his way. Bruno says my smile is a smirk, which people interpret as a snarl because I'm 6'2" and almost 300 pounds. So, I smiled again, better, I hoped. He smiled in return watching me cross the street. My smile widened when we got within handshake range. Then I realized I was smirking again and tried once more.

"You must be Larry!" he said heartily.

"Yeah, I am. That makes you, Bill."

His left hand touched my arm as our right hands shook.

"You were right. Lots of places to eat around here. The next one down looks nice and has a great deck over the ocean."

I said something lame like, "Great sunset, eh?"

"Yeah, hopefully it'll last through dinner." His blue eyes glanced my way. He took a breath as though to speak and then, apparently thinking better of it, smiled instead. No smirk, a very nice smile.

Once past the entrance of the aquarium, when the tourists thinned out a bit, he looked at me again. "I like your eyes," he said. They're green. We dodged some

street vendors, made comments about some "interesting" looking people along the way and discussed how to get over to the restaurant. The conversation lagged a little as we strode across the boardwalk. He glanced my way again. "Did I mention I like big guys?"

"Yes, you did Bill. Me, too!" I said eying his length from the tip of his full head of graying hair to the black riding heels of his brown cowboy boots. We took a table outside. I got comfortable; he seemed at ease all along.

Then I popped the big question. "Well, do I look like my picture?"

"Actually, you've got more hair on your head than I expected." I liked that response. Beneath the table my naked right knee pressed into the inside of his left thigh. His thigh pressed back.

"You always feel like you're putting yourself out there on the first meeting," I explained.

"Yeah, I guess it's different here. Back home in Southeast, when you place an ad all the boys in town respond, want to meet you, and want you to call next time you're in town."

We talked about all the usual junk you talk to a stranger about. Dinner was a while in coming. The slim, tall, hairy-chested waiter was cute and neither of us did a good job of keeping our eyes off him. Two guys about our ages (37 and 45) sat down at the table next to us. Rough trade types. I couldn't keep my eyes off of them and laughed when I caught Bill admiring the cute blonde girls who proved to be their dates. Off handedly I admitted the importance of family and friends.

"Who's your best friend?" he asked.

I must have smiled, "Bruno. He is so good looking. A real masculine bear; you'd never know he was gay. He's a top like me. Maybe you've seen his ad?"

Bill's eyes dwelt dreamily upon my face, as he shook his head. Then he squinted and stopped. "So, do you guys fool around?"

"Never, that can ruin a friendship."

"You're right there," Bill said and described what happened to his friendship with his best man after his "bachelor party".

"So, what's Bruno doing to night?"

I had wondered where this line of conversation was leading. We'd never screwed one another, but I was pretty sure we'd enjoy taking turns screwing Bill. My leg pressed up against his again. "He's got a date tonight, too."

I kept the pressure up on his inner thigh.

"Then you two should have a lot to gossip about tomorrow."

"Yes, we will," I promised, laughing, "because I'm good."

He laughed with me. I said I was done eating. We paid and left.

I was parked beneath the freeway, but there were too many people and too much light, until we got in the car. I pulled him up out of his seat to kiss him. He responded by trying to crawl on top of me. It was a warm, hot, wet kiss, with stubble of his chin on my cheek and his lips locked on mine. We kissed again once I got the car out of the spot. Then I got our arms untangled and invited him to grope my

crotch. He was playing with my balls for the longest time until his left hand strayed a little further to the left and he found my hard cock trapped down the leg of my shorts. "Wow!" he exclaimed, tracing its hard bulbous head with the middle finger of his left hand.

We found a place down the hill from his hotel, parked and headed up the steep sidewalk. I assured him I knew the drill and fell a few paces behind as we approached the lobby. Okay, actually, I'm not in that good a shape, I lagged behind. He kept up a nonchalant pace while going up the steep sidewalk, glancing about and smiling oblivious to me (and thank goodness to my condition.)

His ass, jacked up by the cowboy boots, bounced along ahead of me at eye level. Nice, firm, muscular haunches pulled the denim tight with each long stride. I kept up enough to maintain the arousing view. But, when he headed for the stairs to his room, I had to ask which floor.

"Third," he assured me and then went back to his I-don't-know-this guy routine.

By the time we made his floor, I was huffing and puffing. Once, in his hotel room, as he stripped off his shirt, I fell back on his bed exhausted. His mouth fell open in concern. I didn't know if he thought I was having a heart attack or was concerned that I wasn't going to be able to perform. Now, my heart was really pounding.

He knelt next to me on the bed in his Levis. He kissed my clammy brown hand and stroked the sweat-soaked tank top that stretched across my hairy belly and chest. He was gentle and assuring. When he suggested I get out of my sweatshirt; I let him help me up then rapidly stepped out of everything else.

My cock's about 7 inches long and 3 wide – more wide than thick. He must have liked what he saw pop straight out of my shorts, cause he beamed and then immediately leaned forward from where he sat on the bed and started sucking my sweaty slab of meat.

"Let me go over here," I said and stepped around him to lie on the bed.

My belly rolled back and his lips had a clear access to my cock. It stood straight up, the skin on my helmet head ached in anticipation of a tongue lashing. Bill went right to it, deep throating the head and licking the shaft.

The flickering pink thing attached to his mustached lips wiggled its way on to my balls. They had to be salty as much as I sweated coming up the hill and stairwell. He tried to lick his way down further, but I kept my heavy legs flat on the bed. I'm strictly a top.

"Come here." I lifted my white arms and puckered my lips as I said it. Bill looked up from my crotch in response. "It don't need to be any harder. Come `ere."

He stood, dropped his pants and crawled over my belly to kiss my face. With my bulk his legs were spread nice and wide. We kissed hotly again. My hairy hands pressed him close to me. His thighs rubbed his cock against my belly. Our

tongues dueled. His butt rose and fell with his mouth thrusts, just inches above my rod.

My hips started rising to meet his quickening down thrusts. My hands rode down his back to enwrap his buttocks. He was breathing heavily, his eyes glazed. My helmet head started knocking at his backdoor. He mumbled something about condoms and k-y in the bed stand.

I just kept jabbing at his ass. His right hand reached back and under to grab my dick and guide it into his hairy bung hole. He struggled, a little, to get it in. I spread his taut ass cheeks further apart, causing him to emit a quick, sharp breath into my mouth. When the head plopped inside, his body jumped upward, but I held his ass tight. He started taking little strokes downward to ease my monster in.

Every time, I thrust upward, even though I knew he wasn't ready yet. Eventually, I just arched my back pushing my pelvis and prick into the air so he had to slide all the way down. He finally got comfortable and started working his ass in a tight spiral around my throbbing man-meat. But I wanted deeper.

"I want you on top of me, Larry," Bill snarled, pulling his ass upward so that my cockhead popped out of his tightly stretched manhole.

I jumped up, dumping him unceremoniously onto the bed, rolled him on to his back, lifted his legs and took up a position on my knees behind his thighs. I hooked his ankles on my shoulders, held his ass with my left hand and aimed my meat for his ass with my right. It slipped it easy this time, aided by the accumulation of my slippery precum.

I took a few strokes and knew I was going to get in deep now. I leaned forward, my weight pinning him to the mattress.

"You like it hard, Bill?" I grunted into his sweat-covered face.

"Give it to me, Larry. Give it to me hard," he responded, sliding his pulsing ass ring further down my slimy pole.

I pulled out slowly, almost all the way, his velvety channel clinging to my sensitized glans. When the rim of my cockhead met the muscle of his ass ring, I slammed my balls to the bone.

"Like that?"

He nodded yes, while biting his lower lip. I pulled out slow and slammed hard again. He forced a smile. His long fingers went to my hips, so they could help me slam harder! I kept slamming and slamming. I kept slamming for a good long time.

"I told you I was good," I reminded him as I slowly pulled almost out again.

"You are good," he agreed as he wriggled his white ass teasingly around my imprisoned dickhead.

I slammed him a few more times and then he wanted to see me come. I warned him that the show would be over if I did. I'm a one shot kind of guy. Hearing no protest, I started grinding away on his bottom, feeling my orgasm gathering in my balls as they swirled in the sticky hairiness of his ass crack.

With a flurry of puffing, huffing and sweating, I filled him up with my load of jizm. He gripped me tight in his arms and thrust his slender hard prick against the brushy folds of my lower belly.

"Oh, oh, yes, Larry…ugh, cumming, too," he rasped. I felt his dick twitch wetly between us.

I fell on the bed beside him. He got a towel and cleaned us up. I pulled him to my shoulder and we cuddled as I regained my strength.

"You were right," I admitted, sliding my dark hand down his plump white belly to tickle his pubic bush. "I'll have a lot to tell Bruno. I should call him tonight."

"What's his number?" Bill asked, rolling over to the phone. I told him. He dialed and handed me the phone.

I laughed as I listened to Bruno's message, then handed Bill the phone back. "He's good!" Bill exclaimed into the mouthpiece. He lay back in my arms. I howled. He handed me the phone back.

"This is Larry. Boy, have I got stuff to tell you."

Bill and I laughed and talked some more. As I dressed I said, "I really enjoyed myself this evening."

"Me, too," Bill grinned.

"I hope you'll call next time you are in town."

"You bet, I will."

"Maybe," I fiddled with my sock for a moment and mumbled something about Bruno joining us next time.

To my surprise and delight, Bill answered, "I think, I'd enjoy that, too."

COMING TO GRIEF

Did I ever tell you of my "Tijuana" fantasy-come-true from when I worked there years ago?

Still in my early thirties, still tan from summers in the Southwest and sinewy from swinging a Pulaski on the fireline. Oh, and I was still carried just 185 pounds on my 6'1" frame. Grey strands graced my brown hair but just enough to be distinguished.

On my weekend, they flew me to the "Tijuana of Southeast" from Prince of Wales Island. We call it "The Tijuana of Southeast" because it's the closest port for all cruise ships coming from Seattle. It gives the town the tacky, tinny appearance (and smell) of a border town. Fortunately, we live in a temperate rain forest so at least we don't have to put up with the smell of tourists. Company put me up in the Super 8. Didn't know a soul, so I didn't care much what anyone around there thought. I dragged a chair from my room. Wearing nothing but a pair of tan velour shorts and carrying a bottle of tequila, I intended to sit out back by the channel and enjoy the sunshine.

I took along a paper, and between fanning myself, I studied it for action that weekend. "Not much to do here." I surmised, and started getting bored quickly.

I guess the flapping of someone else's paper is what finally got my attention. The guy was mid-forties, buzz cut, stocky and pot bellied, but he was big. And I like 'em big. I thought he'd been looking my way before, but wasn't paying attention. In retrospect I think he was probably looking at my crotch. The shorts were baggy and clingy. The only way to keep my crotch cool was to shake my shorts enough to shake out my bag and cock. My jewels could catch the breeze

and may have been fully exposed to the air more than once. Like I said, I didn't know anyone there so I didn't care.

"Need help reading that?" I said, indicating the unfolded map he was holding. "I'm a professional navigator." I strolled over, naked chest puffed out.

"Nah, I'm studying for my pilot's license tomorrow," he responded, a pleasant smile on his craggy face.

The Coast Guard requires a local skipper to pilot the big ships into harbor. He told me all about it. He seemed a little hesitant to expound upon the subject until his brown eyes fell upon my tanning torso and seemed to linger there unnecessarily long. He took a deep breath and suddenly warmed to his subject.

He stood closer as he spoke than men usually do for a casual chat. He had the smell of cigar smoke to him. When he opened his chart to show off his knowledge, the blond hair of his upper arm rubbed against my belly.

We ended up having beers and dinner at the neighboring bowling alley. As supper wound down, I tried to figure out what to say next that would get us naked rubbing nasties. I was new to the sport of picking up big boys on the street. (Yes, there's a story there but never mind.)

While I hummed and hawed, he drunkenly complained, "That test I got to take tomorrow is so stupid. You can't believe the stupid questions they ask. Do you know where Grief Island is? Why should anyone know that?"

His question was rhetorical. But the look of wonderment on my face must of given me away. His tirade rolled to a stop. "You know?"

"It's the south end of Duncan Canal. You use it as a landmark, so as not to confuse the mouth of the canal with Keku Straits."

The look on his face! The sudden pallor followed by if the embarrassed flush on his cheeks. The cocky twist of his lips fallen into a mute open mouth. The sudden emotion in his drunken blood shot eyes. That killed the mood and we staggered down the hall to our coincidentally adjoining hotel rooms.

I did chores, made calls, wrote in my journal and then crawled into bed with a good book. The phone rang.

"This is Ed," he said. "So, I got myself a bottle of whiskey and some of them 'good' videos. You like them, hmm, 'good' videos, Bill?"

"I'll say I do."

"Well, come on over."

"Okay. It'll take me a minute to get dressed I'm in bed."

"Don't bother; I ain't wearing nothing but easy access boxers."

"But, I gotta go out in the hall."

"Nah."

I heard a thump against the wall between our rooms and the rattling of a doorknob. What I thought was a closet was a couple of dual doors between our rooms. When I unlocked mine he stood before me bottle in one hand, videos in the other, his cream colored boxers pushed low enough under his belly to reveal dark pubic hairs.

As we'd spoken, my six incher had started swelling. It wasn't hard, but about as thick and long as it would get. A brief glance revealed that Ed's pole was just starting to tent his saggy baggies.

He indicated I should sit on the bed then scooted me on across, turned on the VCR and then sat next to me, both of us leaning back against the wall. He handed me the bottle. I sat with my legs in front of me with my ankles crossed. As I went to sip the booze, his left hand pressed up against my lose balls.

"Nice sack," he said while taking the bottle from me.

"Thanks," I said looking at his crotch with a questioning look.

He whipped out the whole package with his left hand.

"Nice." I assured him likewise.

"Looks a little bigger than yours," he grinned. Then he looked in my eye instead of my snake eye, and continued: "But it ain't big enough to hurt anyone."

He kept stroking it with his left hand, while he watched the movie. I started rubbing my sparsely haired balls and dick.

"Like this part?" he asked

I did – two guys and a girl in a very hot three-way.

"Here," he started reaching his right hand over to me. "I'll do you, you do me."

He wrapped his big paw around my now solid member and began stroking before I could reply. I had to reach under his arm to return the favor. His dick was hard as a rock and rigid to the touch. Its thick veiny shaft rose to a large mushroom-shaped head, which was dark purple and glistening in the room's dim light.

He ended up twisting my shoulders and turning me so he could suck my sensitized organ, already oozing a good bit of precum. I was glad to return the favor. His soapy dry cock soon lubed up under my drooling tongue. Did I mention he was bigger than I was?

He pushed himself off the mattress and turned me again. This time away from him. Then wrapped his hairy right forearm around my belly and pulled my ass up off the bed, as he grabbed my left ankle and pulled me on to all fours. As he wedged his cock head against my brown bunghole, I heard him say, "I'll show you where Grief is."

I looked over my shoulder. He was smiling. So was I. "Lead the way, skipper," I said.

And he began working his plump cock in with short strokes, grabbing my shoulders for better leverage. A few globs of spit and the sweat dripping from his balls and my crack provided a slick entrance. Once his larger head was past my sphincter with amazingly little pain, the shaft slid smoothly through the passageway. "Ugh, damn, feels good," he grunted. He was soon pounding desperately at my ass while holding my hips in his strong hands. I was dripping precum like a lawn sprinkler as his rigid cock knob massaged my prostate. "Oh, man, that's it. Yeah, right there…man." He managed to pull out before he came, and sprayed his milky love juice up over my balls and cock to mingle with my own orgasmic flood.

He slept soundly, but I always wondered how he did on his pilot test. Did everything come to grief?

DEFINITELY NOT A VIRGIN ANYMORE

Bill and Chubby-Ray didn't sit together on the jet to the state capitol, but they got off together. Bill, the taller, full of smiles led the way to the luggage. He positively jittered as they awaited their bags and even more so as they awaited the courtesy van. He keeps looking down at the older man with a shit-eating grin. Ray's only response each time Bill caught his eye was a delighted smirk and then to talk about the weather.

By, the time they got to the elevator, Bill could no longer restrain himself. Once the doors close he bends over Ray. Their lips meet, their tongues wrestle, moustaches mingle and Ray's graying goatee cuddles the younger man's naked chin.

They break before the door opens and head down the appropriate hallway. Ray comes to a dead stop. Their rooms are side by side. "Connecting door," he says knowledgeably with a quick nod of his head. "We'll have fun tonight."

He grins more to himself than at Bill. He opens his room as Bill opens his, and closes the door behind him. He doesn't hear Bill's luggage land on the floor, but he hears the other side of the connecting door swing open.

"Oh!" Rays whispers to himself with an arch of his brows while he fumbles with the lock on his side. When the door swings wide, Bill's butt naked in the doorway.

"Oh, friend!" Chubby-Ray stutters as though surprised.

Bill's right hand is pulling on the sticky head of his dick, his belly is flatter than last Chubby-Ray saw it and either he'd been hitting the tanning booth or he'd been someplace warm and sunny. Bill's left hand lands firmly on the other's broad

thick right shoulder. As he urges the cum-monger to his knees, Chubby-Ray gets flustered again. Something about going to dinner with a surveyor friend: "George, you remember him. Really wish we could do this right now, but…"

"Cool. It's cool, Ray. When you get back, I'll be ready."

Ray returns from dinner with his professional acquaintance later than he'd expected. A piece of paper lies on the floor obvious slipped through their shared door. "Ray" it says on top. When Chubby-Ray unfolds the paper, the bottom half says, "Cum – on over. Watch a movie with me."

Ray can already hear lame music and appreciative groans coming through the joint wall – just the sort of "movie" he and Bill enjoy watching together. He pops the door open. Bill is still naked. His lanky frame lies atop the bedspread on the far side of the bed. His solid six incher points towards the ceiling and the thumb and index finger of his right hand play with the precum forming there.

"Come on in." Bill's left hand pats the empty side of the bed. Ray quietly approaches stops when he is far enough into the room to see the television screen. He gives the beauty taking it up the butt an appreciative nod and continues to the bedside.

"Did you save some for me?" he asks as he undresses.

"I saved it all for you."

"Well, shall we continue where we left off?" Chubby-Ray suggests dropping to his knees. Bill scoots across the bed and throws his long legs over the edge. Sitting there, he lets Chubby-Ray go down on a dick well lubed by precum and red with excitement. Chubby-Ray deep throats the thing right off the get go and gets a nice little bopping rhythm going. Ray's right hand is working his thick little knob while the middle finger of his left hand is working his hole. Bill is back to smiling, and quickly rises to his feet so that he can drill down into Ray's face.

"Like that?"

"What?" Chubby-Ray responds after grabbing the shaft and spitting the head out.

"Like that?" Bill asks again while tousling Ray's hair.

"Yes," Chubby-Ray says, eyes ablaze looking up into the taller man's eyes, drool and love juice dribbling from his lips.

"Then you'll love this, too. Time to pop your cherry," Bill says, tearing open a condom.

Ray spins his stocky frame around on the floor and assumes the position – that is, hands and knees on the carpet – while Bill lubes up his sheathed shaft.

"This is going to hurt at first," Bill warns as he begins sliding his cock through the crack of Ray's ass.

Obligingly, Ray's stubby hairy fingers reach back and pry his muscular hairy cheeks apart for easier access. Using his thumb, Bill pushes the head of his rod into Ray's behind. "Truth be told, it doesn't hurt all that much," Chubby-Ray considers to himself. "Bill isn't that big."

But Chubby-Ray loves every minute of his butt banging. He's eyes tear up with each thrust. He alternately holds his breathe against the pain or gasps in delight. His whole face and upper torso grow flush and red. Perspiration forms on his broad back and in the hollow of his semi-hairy chest. His own dick aches for relief, but Chubby-Ray is here to give, not get.

He doesn't have to wait long. Bill's panting grows more rapid and his hips lose their rhythm.

"I'm going to cum. I'm going to cum." Chubby-Ray spins around. Bill waits until he is in position to unwrap the protective sheath from his joystick and stuff his throbbing cock deep into the bottom's throat. Bill clamps the cum-monger's head to his pubes and waits for the three thigh knocking jolts that unload him into Ray.

"Thanks buddy."

"Thank you!" Chubby-Ray replies as they crawl into bed and go back to watching the movie.

"How was dinner with George?" Bill asks as they settle up against the headboard and begin watching the movie.

"Personal," Chubby-Ray responds.

"Wasn't he the one on the North Slope with the boss into watching butt-fucking movies at breakfast?"

"Yeah! He brought that up again at dinner."

"It's something you two have in common."

"I kind of wonder."

"Ever try hitting up on him?"

"You know me. Besides, he works out all the time. He could beat me to a pulp. Solid muscle. Yes, buddy, George could pound your ass to a pulp too!"

Bill continues absently, his last words interrupted by a hard knock at the door to Bill's room.

Ray starts up in a panic.

"Relax. Someone's got the wrong room. I'll send them away," Bill says.

Ray watches Bill crawl out of bed and stride across the room. He takes a quick look out the peep hole, smiles, steps back and swings the door open. George steps in. He and Bill laugh at the look on Ray's face. George is a little tanner than the older men and about midway between them in height. But George works out. He has muscles everywhere, including his thick neck. Chubby-Ray was about to find out that his neck wasn't George's only thick part.

"So, looks like you were right. Chubby-Ray would like to play," George said as Bill threw an arm across his shoulders.

He laughs, glancing away from the stunned Ray. In the process, he notices Bill's limp dick, all wet and sticky.

"Guess you already got yours, Bill. My turn?"

George and Bill both look at Chubby-Ray and laugh again at the bottom's beet red face. "I'll take your half open mouth as a yes," George said pulling off his shirts as he heads for the bed.

He was stepping out of his oversize Carhart pants as Chubby-Ray finally mumbles a smiling permission with a nod of his head. He then falls silent again at the sight of George's cock, a massive piece of flesh even in its flaccid state. Chubby-Ray doesn't need to suck long to get it hard. It is curved, maybe 8 inches long with an impossible wide base and good sized head. George bends back Ray's head and guides the purplish head into the gaping mouth.

Ray goes to work. He tries to swallow the whole thing, but gives up and reaches up to massage the massive base of the shaft. George's quick hands catch Ray's chubby wrists. George is going to stay in control. He plops both of Ray's hands on the older man's head and keeps them there with pressure from his right hand. His muscular left arm pulls Bill in closer. His hand slides down the taller man's back, land on his ass and shove him closer to the action. A few more strokes of his rock hard rod into Ray's willing lips and then George turns Ray's head so he can start sucking on Bill.

Ray laps at Bill's spent cock, happy for the relief from George's huge prick. He rolls the head around in his mouth; a technique he knows really works for Bill.

"Okay. I'm ready," George announces. He'd rolled on a condom and now stood before Ray, lubing up.

"On your back, bitch!" he jokes. He lifts Ray's short legs and braces them against his pecs. "Your ass lubed up?"

Bill has already moved to the other side of the bed and is getting ready to mount up on the bottom's face. "I took care of that already."

George lifts a leg a little higher exposing Ray's hole. Bill shoves his hardening cock into Ray's mouth. George drives his thick rod straight into Ray's wiggling ass, wet and yielding from the earlier invasion of his tight shaft.

Bill begins to face fuck him, setting up a rhythm with his ass-prodding buddy and Chubby-Ray seems to love it.

George keeps the pressure on, but doesn't force his cock too far into Ray's relatively virgin hole.

"Yeah, oh yeah, Ray, that' good," George repeats as Chubby-Ray tries to impale himself on that pyramid from George's pants. "Damn. I'm not going to last long… the first time. Chubby-Ray had me so horned up at dinner. He ain't good at getting the subtle hint." George starts pushing and pulling out of Chubby-Ray ass.

"Yeah, he could have joined us twenty years ago!" Bill grunts between pants. He is hard again what with the fine blow job and getting to watch some fine butt fucking.

"I'm gonna cum. I'm gonna… Grab his ankles, Bill. I want to shoot all over his ass."

Bill obliges. He pulls on Ray's ankles until his big white ass in pointed to the sky. George whips off the condom, jumps to his feet and shoots all over the bottom's exposed hairy bottom. Globs land on both cheeks, but he aims most of his jizm for the crack. The sight of George's climax is too much for Bill. His thighs grasp the bottoms head and he unloads deep in Ray's throat.

"The only thing better than fucking ass," George declares, "is eating ass."

George's gnarled hands, fingers spread, slap down on the upturned bottom and he spreads the cheeks even further apart. Cum is pooled over the bung hole. George's grizzled chin and pink tongue dive right in. That's too much for Chubby-Ray who shoots all over his own face and goatee until Bill's tongue intercedes.

Ray definitely isn't a virgin any more.

ER, GREG

"Okay, I'm here. I'm out back on the veranda. I'm wearing a red shirt."

My e-date's name was, er, Greg. Greg said all the right things over the phone about living close and being there soon. He seemed excited too.

Did I mention I wore a short sleeve red shirt? It felt kind of cool on this part of the deck in Seattle in May. (I was just passing through on business.) At the far end in a large sunny spot stood a big guy in work clothes – blondish, stern and beefy. Did I mention I like `em big?

At 6'1", you've got to be really big to impress me. So, I strolled along the deck, skipped up the step, asked if he minded sharing the sunshine and sat down. From this angle, his highlight faded to brunette, the stern frown to a constant and friendly smile and he lost about 6 inches in height. (I'd had to step up to his part of the deck.)

But he was chatty and fun. We were gabbing away when a man mountain sat down with us. The guy stood 6'7" dressed in layers and wearing a Carhart jacket. He sported a curly black beard and fine head of black wavy hair, with just enough gray in each temple to give his hair a grizzled look – odd for a guy in his 30's. (He also possessed a small forest of graying curls on his chest. I checked early on.)

"Cutter" and I introduced ourselves. "Greg," he answered to our names and hands.

He must be my date. He was tan, with broad shoulders and a lot less weight than he'd admitted to in his profile. Maybe he just carried it better than most guys. I enjoyed talking to him for half an hour or so. We discussed his "partnered" lifestyle and my "married" lifestyle. Then his cell rang, then mine, then the obligatory calls

we just had to take, introductions to his friends, the arrival of his boyfriend, and finally the Friday night crowd getting thicker and louder.

Forty-five minutes later I found myself sitting on the outside of his circle of friends thinking we might have lost that start of a relationship, the rapport we had known before the phones went off.

But when Greg returned to his seat, he centered his attention on me. His friends made me comfortable and included me in the conversation, but I hungered. In retrospect, I wonder what I hungered for specifically. Anyway, Greg knew a Mexican place and we went. The conversation followed easy and frolicking.

"Now what do you want to do?" he asked.

"What do you want to do?" I replied.

"Well, we could go some other place, or to your place or back to the bar?"

"Well, we could go dancing, or back to my place. We've been to that bar."

"Let's go to your place."

Once in the door, I fell into his arms. With a gruff burst of laughter, his massive body engulfed mine. His lips were soft. His breath and mouth were clean tasting, or maybe the salsa at dinner burned out our taste buds. Regardless Greg made me hot. He nuzzled into the small of my neck and began growling. I returned the favor with a snort, then pulled myself up to suck on his earlobe.

He laughed again. I took him by the hand and led him to the bedroom. We kissed again at the foot of the bed. My hands played across his broad back and felt up his hard small ass. We kept at the dry mouth kissing until I realized his stubby fingertips struggled at unbuttoning my shirt. I returned the favor on his belt. It didn't go well and we decided to undress ourselves.

"Gotta use the bathroom," he interrupted. He found me naked and stretched out face up atop the bed spread when he returned. Greg growled with a smile, bent to kiss me lightly and then his lips worked their way quickly to my twitching six-inch rod and engulfed it.

"Oh, yeah," I moaned as I tussled his brunette curls.

He twisted my nipples. I managed to roll away from his hand.

"That doesn't do it for you?" he asked.

"Sorry."

"Gee, you aren't gay."

However, what he did with his dry thin lips was doing it for me, but it also reminded me that I needed to use the bathroom.

"My turn," I said.

I found Greg naked and stretched out, face-up atop the bedspread when I returned.

Even naked he didn't look particularly overweight. His chest hair spread south to about mid chest. His cock, though not much larger than mine, was hard! I

straddled his thighs and we went back to kissing and growling. The latter a recent trick just taught to him, he informed me later. It worked for me.

With a little help from my bud, I managed to roll us over and get him stretched out on top. Our long frames pressed one another. Our hips stroked our cocks into one another's crotches.

Greg's long arms pushed off the mattress so he could see my face and bend to kiss me. Meanwhile, I got to play with his hairy chest and gaze into his eyes. His slow rhythm thrusts got heavier and we bounced more atop the bedspread. I couldn't resist any longer. When his body lifted off me with the next bounce, I pulled my legs out from under him, lifted my knees towards heaven and rolled my ass into the path of his down rushing cock. He kept it there.

The brown head of his cock pressed against the entrance of my body, each slow stroke testing the resistance of my body and the craving in my ass.

"Got lube?"

I pulled some out of the bed stand and we greased him up.

"A little soft," he said. So he went back to rubbing it against my quivering body. His cock stood ready again in seconds. "There?" he asked, prodding forward.

"A little lower."

A stroke or two, "There?"

"Yeah."

And he pushed, pushed just the head in, and kept swaying above me. Just a touch of pain, then he pushed all the way in and kept stroking. I assured him it felt good as soon as I could. And it did!

Greg was a slow solid fuck like the waves working the shoreline. Slow and steady. It had been six months since I had a good fuck and Greg broke my ass in right. The juices started to flow. I lusted for this mountain of a man towering over me, the forest on his chest and the lightning bolt he used on my body. His brown eyes were glazed with lust.

"Sorry, it takes me a long time to cum."

"Not a problem," I assured him with a smile. First spreading my ass cheeks wider to give him greater access. Then playing with his nipples, brushing his hairy chest in delight. I could feel my pre-cum pooling on my belly. And kissing, kissing, kissing, until the saliva ran between us like a silver cord connecting our souls.

Greg's hips began to gyrate faster, the occasional growl became a loud panting, his shoulders pinned mine to the mattress as he drove away at my sloppy ass. He grunted, grunted and grunted. His orgasm was announced with a long, low growl. Then he collapsed upon me.

"Thank you, thank you, thank you. That was so good Bill," he whispered amid heavy breathing.

I assured him it was my pleasure. We headed to the shower to clean up. His partner expected him at home.

I laid in my bed and replayed our adventures in my head. I made myself come twice that night. I hope we can get together in August!

THE GRAND SLAM

My soon-to-be wife was coming back to town to live with me. A gay friend had accepted a job somewhere else. (Coincidence?) "Salt", that was his nickname, had hit on me forever. I'd hinted that it might happen someday, but never committed. It wasn't that the idea didn't turn me on, but Salt positively swished when he walked. He was a stereotypic twink – too skinny, balding, a moustache. He thought the only reason for going outside was in case the building was on fire. He just wasn't my type.

But, it was sort of a going away present for him. So, I told him if he had enough shots of tequila, I'd watch one of his videos. I got there early and started slamming shots as he, full of hope and giggles, loaded the video.(I'd watched it before while house sitting for him, but never told him.)

Four shots and twenty minutes later, I stood up, dropped my pants and pulled off my shirts. "So, we going to do something or what?" I grinned, a little drunkenly. He took me immediately to bed. As soon as we lay down, the room started whirling and he yanked me out of bed and over to the sink. The last thing I recall was him holding me over the sink, one arm wrapped around my chest, the other cupping my groin. I felt his smooth small chest against my back and his large hard cock lying against my butt.

I awoke in a darkened room lying up against my buddy with my left hand on his swollen member. By the size of the cock, I assumed I was in bed with my buddy Drew (see below) but when my hand glided up his chest there was no forest of fuzzy red hair to greet me. "Salt!" I remembered.

He said nothing as I rubbed my hand over his body, rolled him on his back and straddled him. My eyes fell on the KY on the headboard and I lubed up his very stiff cock, gradually sliding its full length into my hot tight asshole. I rose up and down slowly before going for it.

"You've done this before?" he asked. "Uh huh!" I moaned. "Why didn't you ever say anything?" he puzzled. "I didn't want to confuse why we are friends."

I quickened my pace on his seven inches of somewhat slender cock meat, feeling his ample pubic bush tickle against the fuzziness of my balls and ass cheeks. He reached for my semi-erect cock and began to stroke it vigorously as I wagged my ass back and forth in frenzied lust. "Oh, oh, God, Billy, I'm ready to–" He began thrusting his cock into me in alternate rhythm with my pumping backside. His fist fairly flew up and down my now super hard, precum-drooling prick. "Ah, oh, I'm cumming, I'm cum–ming," he grunted, keeping his one hand moving on my man meat while the other began fondling my tightening ball sack. "Uh, oh, me, too," I responded, "yeah, here's my load! Yeah!" The sensation of his long peter twitching and spurting inside me sent we over the edge and I shot three or four good jets of cum on his slim smooth chest. He didn't hesitate – scooping all he could of my load into his hand and transferring it to his mouth. I eased down from my orgasm and his softening cock slid out of my well-fucked ass with a sloppy popping sound. I kissed him on the cheek, bid him farewell, cleaned up, dressed and headed home.

Salt and I played around a few more times before he left town, but too quickly that morning he had to get me home. Tall gangly Drew usually came for coffee on Saturday mornings. He didn't know about Salt, nor Salt about Drew and me. Drew usually stopped by early tossed a few pieces of firewood on the front deck and then came in the back door. I would rise to greet him from my bed, nude. He would greet me as he routinely did with a big bear hug and a wet kiss. Sometime, not always, one of his rough work-scarred fingers would work its way up my asshole and the action would start right away. Usually he'd make coffee as I dressed.

Drew's as tall as I am (about six feet), thin, but muscular from hard physical labor. His face is surrounded by a shock of red straw like hair and a positively patriarchal beard. His whole body is covered with a forest of copper-colored hairs that show up nicely against his white skin. White as the underbelly of a halibut, only as white as a Southeasterner can be.

We drank Kahlua laced coffee, bullshitted with ease, talked about women with big titts, talked about my soon-to-be wife and before you know it, he had to leave. I didn't rise to hug and kiss him goodbye like normal. He left the doorway and returned to where I was sitting, a look of puzzlement on his bushy face.

"My girlfriend's coming tonight," I said. "This might be last time we have Saturday mornings together. You want a blowjob?" Drew thought a moment. Just a moment. Unbuttoned his levis, pulled down his pee-stained shorts and pulled out "Moby Dick" – a nice hunk of uncut man meat, which grew to almost eight inches when it was at full erection. It was already getting hard. (He never took that much

convincing.) He started stroking in and out of my face, briskly as usual. (When he fucked my hot ass he always slammed it in to the hilt without giving my butt a moment to adjust or for me to catch my breath.) Real quick, he was warning me it was cumming. I locked my lips on his thick pink penis head and sucked every drop out. I stood as he buckled up his pants. We hugged goodbye and his thick wet tongue explored every inch of my mouth in search of a taste of himself.

When my girlfriend arrived that night, I paid close attention to her. She was tired and trying to put the best foot forward. So, I suggested we go to bed. She's tall, blonde, with enormous tits and skin as white as Drew's. She likes her left nipple sucked on. I went at it pretending it was a real small dick as my right hand loosened her pussy like it would if I intend to invade someone's butt.

She stroked tentatively at my cock, until she couldn't stand it anymore and wanted me to "put it in her." I flipped her over on her hands and knees and slipped my very stiff six-inch white cock between her pussy lips. She had to wedge the pillow between her head and the wall because I was banging her so hard. What was really turning me on was the smell of her unwashed all-traveling butt crack wafting up to my nostrils mixed with the smell of pussy juice. I came! I came a lot! She seemed very satisfied and we drifted off to sleep in each other's arms.

So that's my grand slam – homosexual for breakfast, bisexual at lunch, heterosexual for dessert! That's also my record for lovers in one day. But even now I wouldn't mind repeating that performance.

HI, LAX

"That was good!" I assured my first e-date at Los Angeles International Airport (LAX)

I knew it was going to be good as soon as our lips met. Chuck tasted sweet like the fresh-faced co-eds I use to fuck in college and he kissed like my best man – deep, wet, and wild. He was a big man trapped in a small man's body: big behind, big belly hanging over his belt, broad shoulders, and large upper arms dwindling to thin wrists and tiny little fingers. He had a handsome face with manly features, short black hair and goatee with a touch of gray, thick lips and a mottled complexion. Aside from a small patch of bristle on his chest, his body was as smooth and dark as chocolate. His small cock, sliding in and out of my hand, leaked precum constantly. His balls were small and rough.

"Why don't you roll over on your belly, Bill?"

Oh, and me: I'm 6'1", 190#, blue eyes, brown hair, bi, married, and a bottom. I'd just arrived in LAX on business for two weeks.

"We don't need a pillow under you. Just lay flat. I'll climb on top." Chuck further assured me he'd just slid his dick up my hairless crack to get it hard rather than push it into my hole.

He stroked for a just a few seconds, rolled on the condom and pushed the head in me. Kneeling astride my thighs, Chuck rocked his very stiff rod in and out of me.

"Yeah, Bill, I like your manhole. I went in easy."

I failed to mention I'd spent the weekend with a former, still frisky boyfriend who is hung like a horse.

"Yeah, yeah, Chuck, fuck my hole."

He kept rocking in and out of my ass shaking the whole bed and massaging my whole pale frame. When I looked back over my shoulder to admire the view, he was twisting his nipples and gazing up at the ceiling. When he glanced down, he leaned forward until his tongue met mine. Then he found my ear, kissed my neck and forced my head down as he fell to all fours and started thrusting more insistently. Only the shears were drawn against the airport lights and I could see the shadow of his shoulders, head, back and ass fucking my darkened figure on the wall beside us. He was sweating profusely and panting in my ear with ever increasing breath.

"Want me to get on top and do some of the work?" I asked.

"Yeah," he gasped.

He rolled onto his back. I straddled his thighs and settled down on his short rod. I started dry humping his big black belly with my little white dick, while my ass held tight to his manhood.

"Like that?"

"Oh, yeah," he said as he began to stroke up into me and I began to bounce up and down.

We worked it like that for a while until he pushed my shoulders back to improve his angle of attack. And we discovered that by interlocking our fingers he could pull me and push me on and off of his rod. Until I wore him out again.

"Better suck on that thing again, Bill."

When I rolled off the latex and went down on his veiny cock, I tasted Chuck juice rather than latex.

"You come?" I asked, pausing in my oral activities.

"No, not yet. I gush pre-cum. Did you notice the cooks at the restaurant tonight?" I mumbled that I had. One was a cute Mexican guy about our age. But my lips kept around his dick.

"I got to hit on the older one. I got a sure fire technique." I hummed encouragingly. "

You ask 'em if they got a wife and kids back home. They say yes and show you pictures. You ask if they have a girlfriend. They say yes and show you her picture. You ask if they like porn. They say yes and you take home and show 'em, some. After a few beers you say, I'll bet yours is bigger than his. As soon as they show you their dick, it's guaranteed you'll be on your back getting fucked in the ass. Works every time."

His story seems to work because with a few deep-throats and licks of the shaft, Chuck was ready to go again.

"Guess, I'd better fuck you some more." He climbed on and began banging away, much to my encouragement. "Oh, if you like this, this is nothing compared to what Mark is going to do to you. He's got two inches on me and can fuck for an hour straight."

"Who's Mark? "

"A buddy of mine. I'll introduce you."

He stayed in the saddle a respectable amount of time and finally confessed that he hadn't been going to the gym much and his legs were killing him. We cuddled instead and stroked. When I kissed him all over his face, his passion knew no bounds and large white gobs of cum shot all over his dark inner thighs and belly. He held me tight and made me do the same thing. We napped for a while before sending him off to work.

"Well, welcome to LAX. I'm sure you'll have a great time." He stopped in mid waddle towards the door. "Shall I mention you to Mark?"

"That would be great. You two talk it over and give me a call."

He hesitated just moment. "Maybe we'd tag team you. Would you like that?"

I assured him I would and he was gone.

The next night I was at the hotel bar waiting for "Ramon". I'd assumed he was Hispanic, this being LA, but had been surprised when I called his machine that day. His accent wasn't Mexican nor the melodious accents I grew up with in the desert Southwest. Ends up Ramon was Spanish, raised in Europe. A Hispanic man in gym clothes walked by the bar, younger than I expected Ramon to be. His glance seemed to rest longer on me than on anyone else in the bar. He was stocky and smiling. A few minutes later Ramon walked in, tall and dark with short-combed hair, well-trimmed moustache and a light black leather coat. He had a ready smile and a high sweet voice. We left for dinner shortly after. He opened the car door for me, everywhere we went. His hairy hand constantly on my ass and his Castilian lisp constantly complimenting it.

He took me to Pistons to romance me around the campfire and then on to the Crest to gaze into the rose light waterfall flickering in the garden. His voice was pure poetry, weaving in and out of a dozen languages (including Japanese), stringing words together in ways I had never heard before. It was the phrase he used to describe an elderly friend "He perspires stamina and sexuality" – that convinced me to take him back to the hotel, now!

His arms and legs were seriously hairy. He skin nice and brown. He pulled me down on the bed beside him and began kissing me softly, cuddling, rolling us around, saying the sweetest things, his hand finally finding its way to my crack and began loosening up my butt hole. My right hand had been pulling at his thick six-inch cock for a while when he said, "It's time."

Ramon leaped from the bed and with his back to me rolled on a condom. Then he returned to me with a big bottle of lube in hand.

"Roll over on your back, baby."

He poured loads of lube on his rigid member and spread my legs in a "v". He tried to push into me, but went high, then low, then his rod stroked mine again, and then way down my crack, then: "Baby, stick it in yourself"

I complied and he pushed almost all the way it. It felt good. He began to push in and out, which raised the ache and pain in my butt. Only one thing left to

do, I wrapped my hands around his hairy butt and pulled him all the way into me. He kept my ankles far apart and legs straight, which opened my ass wide for his attack. He pulled my thighs to his belly and ankles to his ears. And this handsome hairy stud began pounding away frantically.

"After this, Bill" – he said it like "Beal" – "I want you doggie style."

When that time came, I pointed out our shadows on the wall. Ramon stood tall behind me, throwing his strong shadow on the wall. It was too much for me. I dropped my shoulders to the sheet, reached for my own cock and started jerking off. Ramon was panting away behind me and whispering enthusiastically in Spanish or French. Or both.

"Hold on, Ramon! I'm going to cuh-cuh-cum!"

As I splattered a couple of loads onto the linen, my ass clamped down on his rod, sending him over the edge. He rushed to orgasm with grunts and whimpers and a copious, dripping deposit in my twitching ass. Later he offered to take me anywhere while I was in LA. He certainly took me somewhere this night.

Next night I was waiting for Mickey at the hotel bar. He was a red head, just like my best man. I've always had a thing for them. He walks in grinning sheepishly. Short red hair, fair easily blushing skin, slight of build, a little shorter than I, coppery curls peeking out of his collar.

"Hi," he says and snuggles onto the bar stool next to me.

We were off to dinner, a tour of Hollywood and then "Underwear" Night at the Quake. It was pretty wild, although all those guys in camouflage jock straps at the Quake is pretty wild, too. So was the video on the monitors and the action in the corner of the darkened dance floor. I was enjoying the shows and wondered why Mickey went out to the patio.

"I decided to check my pants at the door," he explained.

I guess my hands got too wild after that cause Mike suggested soon afterwards we head for my hotel. His chest was hairy and graying with a treasure trail leading to thick curly pubes that were almost maroon in their dark, heavy profusion. I was on his cock and nestling into his crotch in a second.

"Yeah, yeah, Bill," he grunted.

His white cock was a seven-plus incher and it didn't take long until he was ready.

"Yeah, yeah, want to climb on top?" he queried, waving that long thin pole lasciviously.

I settled comfortably astride, but once it was in, "Can I get on top, now?" he asked.

Mickey mounted up and began seriously pounding my behind. He had me curled up and with a grimace on his ruddy face kept fucking me vehemently, almost shouting his pleasure.

"Yeah, yeah," he panted.

His six-pack abdomen slapped so hard and so repeatedly into my crotch, I thought my balls would turn blue. I pulled them up out of the way.

"Just breathe. Just breathe." And he pushed my shoulders into the mattress and forced me to relax.

He kept hammering away; serious and intense. "Yeah, fuck, yeah," he grunted.

Eventually, it must have been clear I was getting cramped up. "Need a break?" he muttered breathlessly.

When I returned from the bathroom, the one with the green harp on his shoulder was laying up against the headboard his hardon pointing straight up. I mounted up.

"Bill, I want you to stroke it."

I was glad to oblige, cupped my hand and started stroke my soft six-incher.

"Yeah, yeah," Mickey whispered encouragingly.

I was getting close and put my left hand up to the wall. Mike took over, slapping his thighs hard up against my behind. "Yeah, yeah, oh," he whispered as I was starting to lose it. With a hand full of man-juice, I collapsed beside my red head. I had a good time. I guess I should call him about going out St. Patrick's Day.

Friday night; I was back to the Quake after walking to the corner, taking the Culvert City bus to the "Green Line" monorail, transferring to the "Blue Line" train, switching to the "Red Line" subway and walking two blocks. The place was crowded and the boys just as nasty in the far corner. I talked with an ex-marine recovering from surgery, a (damn) fellow bottom and a thin fun-looking bearded guy that my previous companion might have liked. I was back checking out the action on the dance floor. (Some small black guy with an enormous dick was trying to penetrate a willing versatile couple going at it. Several of us added our saliva to his enormous wang, but no luck.)

As I headed to the patio, a big bear said, "Hello"

"Hello."

"How's it going?" I ask.

"Good."

We kissed shortly thereafter and left not too long afterwards, in such a hurry he forgot to say goodbye to his buddy. We chatted one another up waiting for our taxi. We almost missed it. Our driver missed three red lights and directions to the airport. Garland was beefy, big, and hairy in the perfect chest formation. His eyelids lounged lazily upon his cheeks and I worried he'd fall asleep, but he was wide awake. He was hard when we undressed at two in the morning, showing seven inches of dark thick meat. I rolled on the condom and climbed on. I rode him up and down. Garland liked it slow. I rubbed my hand across his furry chest and played with his soft nipples. He liked to suck on mine. I rolled off the condom, so I could suck on his cock some more.

"Scoot down here, buddy," he lisped pulling my hips towards his mouth. He jerked himself with his left hand to give my mouth access to his thick brown head. Meanwhile he licked my dick and moaned encouragingly. I awoke two hours later to find us atop the sheets still in the "69" position. We had to leave too early the next day. Damn, I would have liked seconds of that.

Next time I could go out it was a St. Patrick's date. So naturally I asked the red head for a second date. (Okay, I asked him out again, because he had the biggest dick.) Mickey showed up right after work, changed clothes in my room and we were headed out on the town. We hit one of those hotspots on Hollywood Boulevard with valet parking and a line to get it. It wasn't the "Northern New Mexican Cuisine" I grew up on, but it was fun, and Mickey seemed to know everyone in the place and all its history. Then we were off to the gay district in Long Beach, which was surprisingly quiet for St. Patty's but it was mid-week.

Finally, back to my room! We took turns using the bathroom, each exiting in the nude. When I joined him in bed, he was laying bellying down in anticipation of a promised back rub. I started lightly massaging his back, looking for a knot to attack, while my 6 incher settled into the crack of his ass. I started rubbing his shoulders, leaning into the work, letting my cock ride up and down his behind as I worked. He moaned encouragingly. He was enjoying the rub down, as was my hardening dick. Soon, enough, I was ready to massage something else, and I rolled him over on his back his lithe naked form was stretched out atop the sheets, propped up against two pillows. I straddled his hips and bent to kiss his blushed face. Not a great kisser nor overly affectionate in public, but I knew what he was good at. While I kissed him, I rubbed my hard cock against his longer, thicker beast and was rewarded with a returning jab to my abdomen. My lips worked their way down his frame until I was slurping at his thick bitter white cock and long hairless balls.

"Yeah, yeah, that's good," he mumbled.

I rolled his rod back and forth across his belly with my tongue, then slurped it into my mouth again. With constant stroking by the pink inside of my mouth and with encouraging words from Mickey, it started getting harder. Eventually, it was standing straight up, my hearty redhead was leaning back on the pillows moaning "yeah, yeah" and I was bobbing for his apples like it was going out of style.

"Want to roll a condom on it and mount up on that thing?"

I reached for the supplies in the bed stand, opened a condom. He moaned as I rolled it on. A little lube and I was settling on his shaft. It was a slow slide, I guess I should have lubed up more, but eventually my butt settled into his lap, then I leaned back for that little bit more of penetration.

"Oh, God, yeah, that's good."

I started sliding up and down his cock while Mickey continued to moan and pinch his little brown nipples. I kept rising and falling, giving him a slow full fuck, but figured he'd want something a little more active. Settling my ass down as

far as I could, I clamped onto his shaft and started rapidly grinding my ass into him, while my lubed up cock humped fervently into his furry flat belly.

"Oh, oh, sorry, too much green beer. Go back to doing it slow."

I complied until he was ready to take over, then I rolled back while holding his shoulders, unfurled my long legs, grabbed his hips and held him tight as he pushed off the mattress atop me. I knew his style this time and pull my balls up out of the way before they got bruised in his furious pummeling of my hole.

"Yeah, yeah." He recited the words like a mantra, barely able to keep his eyes open as the passion overwhelmed him.

He straightened his back for a moment and pulled my ass up on his knees. This left my feet dangling in the air and his hands free to twist his nipples and he wiggled the sheathed head of his cock in my love canal. I could tell by his "yeah-yeah's" that he was loving it. Then he reached under my arms to get a firmer grip on my shoulders, so as to get even further into my ass.

"Just breathe, Bill. I'll make it easier."

I took his advice, giving my ass over to his assault, watched his eyes glaze and heard his breath turn to pants.

"Yeah, yeah."

But the green beer and late hour was taking its toll and after a half hour of that Mickey said, "I gotta take a break."

As he fell back on the pillows, he called for me to join him. I crawled up to him, his right arm came up under my shoulder and his hand grabbed the back of my head. I figured he was pulling my mouth to the enraged head of the cock his was furiously jerking. Instead he pulled my face to his chest.

"Suck on my nipple," he begged. "Yeah, yeah"

His fist flew back and forth, he writhed in my arms. I sucked, I mouthed, I lightly bit his tit.

"Tell me your fantasy," he urged.

"I wish there was two of you, so I could do two guys at once. One in my mouth and one in my ass. I'd be on all fours so they could get in deeper. I'd be theirs to fuck anyway they wanted. When the guy in my ass came, he just come around to my face and I'd start sucking him hard again while the other guy started fucking me. That way we could do it all night long."

Mickey was heaving off the mattress by now, yelling, "Yeah, yeah." He came in convulsions and spasms, then promptly fell asleep in my arms.

So that was Los Angeles International Airport: an Afro-American with a fondness for Mexicans, a Spaniard fluent in 10 languages, a big-dicked Irishman on St Patty's day and an all-American bear. I guess it really is an international airport.

CARLOS:
HOT TUB TO SHOWER

A straight buddy visited me here in Fairbanks during Christmas. He has brown hair, blue eyes, a wicked smile, a slightly graying goatee, long legs and an ass just made for pounding. And I wasn't getting a single vibe he was interested in getting pinned under my hairy brown body. After days of over eating Christmas goodies during the day and drinking too much beer with me during the evenings, he'd gotten in the habit of taking a nap in the afternoon.

I got in the habit of jacking off in the Jacuzzi for a couple of hours while Bill slept. I love to run the jets on my asshole for a while before jacking off. It feels so good. Then I take the hand held water spray and run it on my balls and up my eight-inch dick. I can lift my legs up on each side of the hot tub and get right in there with the water spray. It drives me wild.

At times I can bring myself off just from the intense feel of the water on my balls and then up my dick. A couple of the nozzles just hit the rim of my cockhead, which takes me over the edge.

So once in the Jacuzzi I start thinking about Bill sitting on top of my dick when I cum. My buddy Mike calls it my Chinese water torture. I put him in the tub one day and ran the spray over his balls.

Strange since my sinus surgery my sense of smell has become more acute. I can sit here and smell pre-cum oozing from my cock where I didn't used to be able to smell it until I had sprayed it all over the place when I came. It was sort of stimulating sitting there in the Jacuzzi seeping in raw sex. I would make it more fun when I go upstairs for some lube to jack myself off before heading out for our big

New Years Eve. I figured I would lay back on the bed and stroke with visions of Bill settling on my (not so) little head.

Unbeknownst to me, long legged Bill's usual form of relief is in the shower. He lathers up his head while the hot spray is loosening up his back and thighs. He keeps rubbing his scalp until soap starts to flow down the crack of his hairless white ass. Then his left hand carries a big load of suds down there, gives his ass a "Vulcan salute" and the middle finger grabs the opportunity to attack his asshole. Soap makes a good lube for a while and then he has to grab another handful off his face. Once the middle finger and a buddy or two are settled comfortably inside his tight sphincter, his soaped-up right hand settles on his balls and six-inch cock.

He loves the feel of his fingertips cupping and lifting his egg sack as the palm of his hand pins his struggling cock against his flat white belly. His left hand will start fucking his ass, which makes his cock squirm even more under the palm, but the palm over powers it and keep it pinned there, having its way. They take turns. As left slides into him, his cock rises up against its master, who then slides down to double the friction as the left slips out to gather momentum for the next thrust.

I open the door to the bathroom to get some lube for a jerk off session. As I walk in I can hear him groaning in the shower. I begin to think about joining him but no, he's married; he probably would get pissed if I opened the curtain. I can see his outline bent over next to the wall with his fingers up his ass, so I figure what the hell, I'll try. I drop my towel. My dick is already rock hard. I reach for the curtain. Bill gasps as I open it, then looks down at my hard on and snickers a little bit.

"Carlos, what are you thinking about doing with those balls of yours and that ram rod?" he says. "Can't a guy jack off in private?"

He continues to stroke his cock, so I run my fingertips over the head of mine and smile.

He says, "You can watch me but don't touch me. I don't have sex with gay guys"

That was all I needed to step right into the shower, shoving my rock hard dick onto his slippery backside. I begin to move it up and down his back. He struggles a little bit.

"What are you doing?" he says.

I grab his arms and hold them above his head, bending him over as I do. I can feel the head of my dick slide up until its nestled right against his asshole.

"So you don't like men, huh? What were you thinking about when your fingers were shoved up your ass? Admit it – you'd rather have a cock up there."

I start to press on his asshole with the head of my dick.

"No," he says. "I'm not a faggot cock sucker. I don't like men."

That does it. I shove my dick in as fast, hard, and as deep as I can get it.

"How do you like this?" I say as I hear him start to moan.

"It hurts, damn it! You shoved it in too fast."

"Just relax. It will loosen up," I say.

I start to slowly move my now-throbbing prick back out some, then slowly move back in a few times. When he starts to groan again, I can feel his ass loosen and open up for me. He tries to pull his hands away from my grip but I continue to hold him down and against the shower wall. I start to pick up the tempo slamming hard into his ass. I can feel the warmth of his slippery ass cheeks as my balls slide into them. I reach under his belly and stroke his cock a few times. He moans again. This time I grab his shoulders and pull his ass back down as hard as I can get it onto my dick. He starts to spray cum all over his stomach and legs.

"Fuck me more," he begs, almost whining.

I'm about to cum so I stop and just sit still feeling the heat of his body wrapped around my dick as we rest. It starts to soften a little inside him so I start sliding it out and back into his ass slowly so it won't bend over from being too soft. It quickly gets rock hard again and I start to slam into his ass as hard as I can again. This time my desire for relief overcomes my ability to keep fucking him and I spray my cream deep inside as I continue to slide into his warm moist asshole. I can feel the cum dripping out of his asshole down on my balls as I continue to fuck him.

He looks up and says, "You know, if you were a real man you'd be able to keep fucking me."

That was it! My dick was still inside of him. I grabbed his hands shoved them back against the wall and began to shove my ever growing dick back into his ass. He starts groaning again and I stop.

"What are you doing?" he says. "Fuck me more!"

I pull out of his ass and turn him around. I say, "Take that bar of soap and get my dick real soapy, then run that bar of soap into my ass get it real clean, rinse it out then show me with your tongue how bad you want me to fuck you."

He soaps up my reviving prick and aching ball sac. The dwindling bar of soap almost disappears up my ass as he scrubs it clean. After rinsing in the streaming hot water, I bend over and he runs his tongue over my hanging nuts and the base of my balls.

"Now take your tongue into my crack and start teasing my asshole until I begin to moan."

"Please fuck me again," he say as he buries his tongue into my ass. He's got me moaning in no time. The sensation is wild. My balls swell up and suck up against my body until they are hard and trying to crawl into the base of my dick. I raise up and turn around.

"Now show me how a straight guy sucks cock."

He runs his mouth over my dick a few times. Straight guys are not good cocksuckers. Then I raise him up and bend him over against the shower wall. My dick slides up in between his legs and moves into the warmth of his ass cheeks until it sits waiting on the moist opening of his asshole.

"Now, what do you want?" I say.

He says, "Please shove it into my ass as far as it will go." As I do so, he adds, "Oh yeah, and daddy, fuck me some more. I like it."

His insolence once more ignites my Latin temper so I ram it in as hard as I can. He jerks in pain and squirms beneath me, but I keep at it fast and hard. After a while I slow down, move it in slow and lay still letting it soften for a bit and then ram it in hard and fast again until my cum is dripping out of his ass down onto his balls. His knees are shaking and his cock has risen to almost full erection again. A few strokes and he spurts the little jizm remaining in his drained balls onto my leg.

As he gets onto the airplane leaving for home, he smiles and says, "Nice trip. I particularly liked the New Years Eve present you gave me this time."

I smile and say "See you next time".

I DON'T THINK SO

Bill checked out several gay bars on his way to "Sprags". The "Manray" was an art deco emporium that played "dance music" way too loud. He'd followed a group of older men to "Hour Place". He felt comfortable at "Hour Place" – three floors of wood and glass with a mixed crowd of mostly gay men of undoubtedly legal age. But he wanted to get to "Sprags" for a particular reason. It was the monthly gathering of the Northwest Bears.

He walked in about 8:30, finding it busier since the bears moved in. Bill found a beer, a place to hang his leather jacket under the bar and a wall to lean against. He'd been well fucked twice the week before in the state capitol on business and had met a handsome, happy, quiet, bottom bear upon entering "The Bond" last night. He felt satisfied and wondered what he was doing there. On the other hand he looked forward to seeing "PDA's", the public displays of affection, that bears are notorious for.

At 6'1", 180 pounds and 44 years he didn't stick out in the crowd too much, even as hairless as he was.

"Hello," Ricky said.

Bill glanced over and then glanced again. "Hi," he said to the small bear in a blue dress shirt standing next to him. A small tuft of black chest hair displayed at his collar. He kept his hair cut short and sported a small moustache. Bill looked again at Ricky. This time into those dark tinkling mischievous eyes under arching eyebrows that offered fun, lots of fun.

As they spoke, a wild eyed friend of Ricky's greeted him with a kiss. Ricky introduced Bill to the T-shirt and shorts with a baseball cap and longish hair. Doug, aged about 35, was a hoot as far as Bill could tell over the loud music.

"You should see what my partner is into on the `back veranda'!" Doug shouted above the music.

"Back veranda" proved to be a popular local euphemism for the outside porch following recent events at "The Hawk".

"Hi." came a hesitant voice at Ricky's side. Ricky introduced Chuck to Bill and Doug.

Chuck looked thin beneath his bulky T-shirt and coat. But solid hairy legs snuck out of his soft shorts and heavy boots. He was a blond with straight hair, brushed straight back, a bristly blonde beard and a constant line of chatter. He was also tall, much to Bill's delight.

"Doug was just telling us about his partner," Ricky explained.

"What's going on?" Bill asked.

He's sort of in the middle of a three way. It's hot!"

Ricky and Bill asked for details and pressed for directions.

"This is too. I need a beer or two," Chuck joked as he headed for the bar. Bill proceeded toward the bathroom and the other two to the back veranda.

When Bill returned from the bathroom only Doug was recognizable among the twenty or so friendly bears on the mostly enclosed back porch. Doug introduced his partner, whom Bill gave grief about ending the show before he'd gotten there.

Doug's partner seemed more embarrassed than amused. He was another short bear like Ricky with a rosy complexion and nice smile. Ricky joins the circle on the crowded narrow back porch just as a skinny dark man in a leather jacket approached Doug's partner.

The stranger greeted him with a kiss, played with his chest and then lifted his shirt to admire the short bear's hairy chest. With a few strokes of the fur, the skinny stranger went to his knees, undid Partner's pants and started sucking his small cock. Ricky scooted in closer to Bill in order to see and put his arm around the taller man's waist in the process. Doug whooped and hollered. After watching his partner get sucked for a few seconds, Doug undid his own pants and pulled out a moderately thick eight-inch anteater. The pink head was totally hidden by the foreskin until he pulled it pack. He guided his rising member to the stranger's mouth. After an "un-suck-sessful" attempt to engulf both cocks at once, he simply started alternating. When he finishes a little of that, the two suckees pulled the jacketed stranger to his feet. Doug spun his ball cap backwards and dropped to the ground to return the favor. Shortly everyone thanked the other and departed, leaving Doug's partner, Bill and Ricky to "guard the beers".

"What's happening?" inquired a familiar voice behind Ricky and Bill.

It was Chuck. They tried to explain that the threesome had just happened again, but with the music and burly bears pushing through the writhing crowd, Chuck didn't understand. Doug returned to their little circle.

"You been sucking cock?" Chuck joked.

Everyone turned to look at him. "He's got his cap on Backwards," Chuck grinned knowingly.

"We were just telling you that," Ricky replied quietly.

"Weird," Chuck joked. Ricky reached up Chuck's shorts to fondle his cock, pulling him closer. Now massaging Bill's ass he looked up into the taller man's eyes. Bill unable to resist, bent down and kissed his little lips and soft thin black moustache. Ricky broke from the kiss to lean over and kiss Chuck, then pulled back and with a hand in Bill's guided his lips to Chuck's. They repeated the sequence again. Until Chuck, apparently jealous of Bill getting longer kisses began to gnaw on his leather jacket. Bill broke from his embrace with Ricky. He lifted Chuck's bearded jaw off his shoulder with the thumb and forefinger of his right hand.

"I don't think so. It would be awfully hard to explain teeth marks in the jacket she bought me to my wife," Bill warned.

"Just being weird," Chuck joked.

No one is ever a hundred percent kidding, Bill thought.

Meanwhile Ricky released Chuck's cock and worked his hand into Bills shorts. Chuck pulled out Ricky's hard dick and Bill's hand snuck up the jokester's shorts, moist with precum, to fondle his Moderate-sized cock. When it was Bill's turn to fondle Ricky's cock he found a hard curved cock ready for action. It swelled when Chuck jokingly spanked Ricky on the butt.

Bill pulled his sticky hand from out of Ricky's pants and suggested Chuck lick his palm. The crowd cheered when it happened. A parade of three large bears forced their way through, splitting Chuck off from the other two.

"Can I ask you a personal question?" Bill asked in the relative privacy. "I'm a bottom. Are you a top?"

Ricky nodded and smiled silently.

When the wake of the passing grizzly bears subsided, Chuck rejoined them. He and Bill sandwiched the smaller man. Leaning over Ricky's head, Bill asked "Are you a top or bottom?"

"I can do whatever needs done. I think I'm sort of closet heterosexual, actually," he joked.

Bill smiled at Chuck and nodded towards the door. He grabbed Ricky by the hand and started dragging him that way.

"Where we going?" Chuck shouted, preparing to down his beer.

"We're leaving," Bill called as he started pulling harder on Ricky's furry hand.

"Oh!" exclaimed the enthusiastic bear as he threw down the bottle and started pushing Ricky ahead of him.

Outside Chuck said, "How we going to do this?"

"Well, I walked so I don't have a car," Bill pointed out.

"I do," Chuck rejoined.

"That's taken care of. I've got a hotel room, what about you guys?"

"I can't do this," Ricky confessed.

"Too bad," Chuck joked.

"I'm sorry. I've been seeing someone for 8 months," the short bear confessed.

B & C hooted and derided him. "I don't see no ring on that finger," Bill pointed out.

"I usually don't do things like this. I'm shy."

More hoots from B&C.

"What if we forced you. What if we like, raped you? Would that make it okay?" Chuck joked. "You can be my "Junior"."

"Nah, he's a top. If he isn't comfortable he won't perform well. Let's let him go."

"You two have fun," Ricky wished.

"Okay," B&C responded in unison.

Chuck led Bill through the darkened house. They stepped around table saws and stacks of rough cut lumber on their way to the back of Chuck's two-bedroom house. Chuck stopped in the kitchen to show off the backsplash he'd finished that day, the cherry wood trim and casements, the new windows and astonishing deck out back.

Next Chuck led him to the bedroom and had him wait in the doorway while he tidied the bed. It was a queen bed with a cherry wood frame and a curved head board and foot board. A matching wardrobe and bed stand completed the room Bill looked down the hallway and saw the same style and quality in the second bedroom.

"Well," Chuck joked as he went to embrace Bill, "bend over the bed, boy!"

Lifting the smooth-chested bear trapper in his arms, Chuck tossed him face first into the bed. Chuck's furry hands slid down the small of Bill's back. As he pushed his shoulders further and further into the bed, Bill's ass rose in the air where Chuck ground the damp crotch of his shorts into the denim on Bills butt. Further and further his hands slid and harder and harder his thighs jarred Bill's body.

"Crunch!" snapped a couple of vertebrae.

"Are you all right?" Chuck joked, leaping back from the bed.

"I'm fine. That felt good actually. Guess I needed a little man handling. But we are going to have an accident if you don't let me go to the bathroom."

Chuck nodded as Bill leapt from the bed, kicked off his boots and doffed his coat in route to the bathroom. He unbuckled his pants. His heavy leather and Concho belt dragged his levis straight to the floor around his long legs. He dropped his naked hairless ass to the toilet and began to relieve his bladder of a large quantity of rented beer.

Totally naked Chuck the bear padded into the bathroom, with a semi-hard 7-inch cock in his right hand. Since Chuck was fully naked, Bill could see he was stockier and more muscular than he'd expected.

"I got to pee, too."

Chuck joked circling his dick in the direction of Bill's mouth.

"I don't think so. Not in my mouth."

"Actually," Chuck joked, "I was thinking about putting you in the tub later and peeing on your chest. I just can't get the idea out of my head. But that would be later."

He moved his white hardening hunk of man meat into Bill's willing mouth and started fucking his face. He was hard in minutes and he demanded Bill get off the stool.

"I'm going to bend you over the tub, boy. I'm going to slam it to you and fuck you hard."

Bill smiled knowingly. Chuck dressed and lubed his seven-inch hardon. Bill folded a towel across the edge of the tub, got on to his knees and bent over. Chuck knelt behind him doggie style. True to his word, Chuck slammed his cock up Bill's crack with such impact it knocked him head first into the tub.

"Like getting fucked hard, boy? You like it?"

Bill didn't reply, knowing the initial pain would subside.

"I'm going to get deeper into you, boy," Chuck jeered getting off his knees and crawling onto Bill's back. He supported his weight with his hand braced on the far side of the tub and continued the butt banging with even deeper harder thrusts.

"Now that's good, stud. That's good fucking," Bill shouted.

"I'll give you more than that, boy."

Chuck braced his paws against the far wall, pushed off the floor with his toes and now slammed his whole body into the willing bottom crumbled in the tub. Bill braced his thighs against the outside Of tub and smiled with the increased force inside him.

"I got to pee too bad to cum," Chuck snickered. "Get in the tub, boy. I got to pee."

Bill crawled into the tub standing on his knees so as to not have to take the spray in his face. Chuck stood in front of him stroking his muscular sandy haired body and mumbling about the boy wanting it as he relaxed enough to pee. A warm good-feeling stream of liquid finally came out the heart-shaped head of his dick. Bill smiled with the warmth. Not satisfied, Chuck climbed on the edge of the tub, maybe in order to wet Bill's face. But the stream dwindled.

"Pig! You're disgusting! You need a shower!"

"I need a shower?" Bill responded then scrambled up on his feet and pulled the bear to himself before Chuck could climb off the edge of the tub.

They soaped one another up. Chuck used his whole hairy body as Bill's personal scrub brush. As they dried off, Chuck jokingly called Bill a pig.

"Pig fucker," Bill rejoined.

Back in bed Chuck contorted Bill's and his bodies into various versions of face fucking one another and sixty-nining before confessing that he'd only be able to finish fucking Bill is they worked "Junior", a monstrous dildo, up his ass. Chuck

assumed a fetal position on the bed. Bill spread Chuck's very hairy cheeks apart and worked the flesh colored eight-inch long and very thick dildo up the top's ass, making him beg for more and swear how good it felt.

"On the bed, pig," Chuck exclaimed when he grew hard again.

Bill fell face forward spread eagle on the queen size bed.

"No, pig, put your butt on the edge so I can stand and fuck you."

Bill complied and Chuck spread the Bill's muscular dangling thighs apart to the point of pain before driving his dick into his juicy ass again.

"Like that, pig?' he joked, jerking Bill's torso back and forth on the bed.

Eventually in his frenzy it was too difficult for Chuck to handle Bill's butt and the dildo up his ass. He solved the problem by holding onto the back of Bill's head with a hand full of hair while stroking his ass with the dildo.

"I'm going to cum. Pig, roll over."

Bill did as told and Chuck squatted on his chest driving Junior further up his butt as he stroked his cock and leaned his hard-muscled frame backward, further moving Junior up his asshole. He came in globs making sure to get some in Bill's moustache and then kissing him and licking it off.

They woke early in the morning and began to sixty-nine. Chuck's cock began to grow rapidly inside Bill's throat. The bear trapper began to gasp and gurgle with every thrust. He pushed Chuck's thighs off his face.

"If you are going to stick that thing that deeply into me, why don't you do it in my butt?" Bill grinned.

"Too bad, pig. It ain't hard enough and I'm about to cum."

"I don't think so," Bill replied heaving him across the bed and then crawling onto Chuck to finish off the blowjob session. They drifted back to sleep.

Bill needed a ride back to his hotel early and rolled Chuck out of bed to wake him on time. Bill yanked on his clothes and stood silently watching Chuck. Chuck dressed slowly and put away his toys in the bed stand. As the cherry wood cabinet door swung shut, Bill glimpsed something next to the lubricant and "Junior". He saw several length of ropes and a foot-long paddle with electrical tape wrapped around the handle. The paddle was made of rough cut one-by-four lumber.

"Call me sometime, pig," Chuck joked as he dropped Bill off. They'd never exchanged phone numbers.

As the car drove away Bill laughed to himself, "I don't think so."

TESTOSTERONE TRIO;
MOUNTAIN MAN

Hi. My name's Steve. I work for a tree-trimming company in Ohio and have a mountain home in nearby West Virginia. It's a cozy little cabin far up on a hilltop about a half-mile from my next neighbor. I'm 48, divorced and live by myself, although I have people in here to see me pretty often. Sometimes it's a woman. Sometimes it's a man. I'm a hairy, horny bastard and I really don't care where the sex comes from as long as I get some. My job keeps me in fair shape. Lately, I've been having a good time with a older man I've known for years. He's a married guy from a town close by where he's something of a big dog. He's a writer and used to be something in book publishing before he retired last year at age 57. What the locals don't know that I do, is that he likes to suck cock, rim ass and fuck butt. He also has a nice-sized 7.5-inch man sticker and he pretty much knows how to use it.

We've had some fine three-ways with a lady friend of mine who lives up Piney Creek Hollow. I've also learned to like sucking on that fat-headed fuck pole, but I think my biggest shock came when I found out how good it feels when he plows my ass, something that really hurt at first. Now Jake knows to loosen me up with a few fingers first, get me good and hot and lay on the lube. One of the best times we had was when he face-fucked me and shot a hell of a load into my moustache. As a matter of fact, we get together about twice a month for a really hot session of man-to-man sex. Just last week he came by with a nice surprise – a bunch of toys he'd ordered on the Internet. One was a regular plastic-like vibrator like you see advertised for women, one was a slender candy-colored thing, then a

funny-shaped butt plug and a realistic looking seven-inch fake dick with rubber balls attached.

We both got naked. Jake, for that's his name, looks pretty good for his age, kind of skinny in the arms but a broad chest covered with graying curly hair, a small belly and that nice fat cut prick and low-hanging balls surrounded by a salt-and-pepper bush of thick hair. I'm more muscular, hairier and younger, but not a damned bit hornier than this hot fucker. When we get together, he likes to start out by sucking my seven-incher, which always gets instantly hard when he comes in the door! This night, he's down on his knees in no time, swirling his tongue around my rock-solid cock shaft and slurping at my precum-dripping mushroom.

"Mmm," he says. "Your cock tastes better than usual. You must be drinking a new kind of beer!"

"Nope," I tell him, "still swilling that Bud. But I was stroking my dick with this new flavored lube before you got here." I show him the tube – Slick Peach, it's called.

He dives down on my cock like it's the best piece of meat he's ever had between his lips. I move my hips in slow strokes, mouth fucking him while he groans and stares up into my eyes with that moony look he gets when he's dick-licking.

"Ah, yeah, Jake, suck that fat prick! Take the whole thing, you cock sucking bitch!" I grunt at him as I shove home.

Just before I get into high gear to feed him my cum shot, he backs off, trailing spit and precum down across his stumbled chin.

"Hold off, Steve. We wanna play a while, don't we?" he says huffing and puffing, moving his wet, warm mouth down to my low-hung nut sack.

He licks first one, then the other of my balls and starts fingering my hairy ass crack, sliding some of the love juice flowing from his mouth right up into my puckering hole. As he sucks my balls and slides one of his skinny fingers into my butt, he picks up the vibrator, turns it on and applies it gently to my throbbing spit-slick bone.

"Uh, oh, yeah, Jake, that's good. You're getting there now," I inform him, grabbing his slightly thinning gray hair and shoving his face further into my crotch.

He pulls away from me and sucks in a breath of air. "Now, to get your ass ready for the big one," Jake grins up at me, laying aside the vibrator and picking up the slender jelly-colored thingamabob. While he lightly nibbles at my hard prick, he begins to slide the thing up my ass, pushing it in an inch, then pulling it out. Then pushing it two inches, until after several minutes he has the whole six inches or so of the thing up my butt. The precum is flooding from my piss slit. He twirls the butt probe around inside me and I feel myself loosening up. Jake can feel it too. He slides the thing out of me and reaches for the seven-inch fake dick. He stands up and shows me that the dildo is about a half-inch shorter and somewhat thinner than the fat hard prong protruding from between his legs.

"Turn around and bend over," he directs me.

I do it. I feel the rubbery tip of the fake dick pressing against my ass pucker, which is now doing a sort of before-the-cum-shot spasm. He eases the head of the thing into me and I snort at the initial pain. But slimed up by his spit and the peachy, creamy lube I shoved up there earlier, it soon starts to feel comfortable, even pleasurable.

He slides the rubber cock all the way into my ass and reaches around with the other hand to start fondling my peter, which has somewhat softened up in the process. Soon he has it hard as a rock again as the fake dick prods spots up inside me I didn't even know I had. I back up into that thing and wish for more. And soon I've got my wish! Jake pops the rubber dong out of my ass and I feel the hot wet tip of his big-headed man fucker delving at my wide-open asshole. He shoves the fat sausage in with one swift movement of his hips.

"Yeah! Whoa! Easy, Jake, that hurts…" I tell him hoarsely.

He ignores me. Grabbing my cock in one hand and my balls in the other, he starts to ride me like a bronco. Soon, we have a rhythm going as our sweaty bodies thrash together. I can feel his balls hit just below my asshole with each rapid forward thrust.

"Uh, uh, uh, here it comes, Steve, I'm ready. Cum with me, baby!" Jake growls at me, raking his fat cockhead across my throbbing prostate and setting me off like a Fourth of July fireworks show.

"Ah, yeah, I'm cumming! Give me the whole cock, now!"

I feel him ram the full length of his veiny rod into my insides and the twitching of it as it begins to unload a week's worth of stored-up cum.

"Ah, oh, yeah!" he grunts, gripping my balls tightly and pumping my load from my pulsating pecker. We collapse onto the bed, both out of breath and both fully satisfied.

"Damn, that was good," he says, kissing the sweaty center of my back. "Very good."

We lie sticking together for a few moments before heading to the bathroom to wash up. We have to scrub the toys good, too, and it gives us both a laugh.

TESTOSTERONE TRIO; NORTHWEST PASSAGE

Hello, there. I'm Bill. Happily married, beautiful wife, a couple of great kids. And a life-long hankering for big, hairy, hunky men that I just can't deny. I live in Southeast where I work as a computer consultant and enjoy the great outdoors. A little over a year ago, I read a bisexual erotic story online and sent a note to the writer. We struck up an online friendship and we developed a genuine comradeship based on shared interests – mythology, literature, the arts and, well, big, hairy, hunky men. This guy's name is Jake and he's a retired publisher and writer living in West (By God) Virginia. We share stories about our erotic adventures. Since we lived so far apart, neither of us ever expected to get together. But a rare and happy set of circumstances caught us both by surprise. My company had a "camp" in West Virginia. Last fall, my supervisor asked if I'd like to go there for a two-week training session. I jumped at the chance and contacted Jake, my e-mail friend, to see if we might be able to meet somewhere while I was in the East.

He wrote right back, sounding excited as hell. He said the camp is only 40 miles from where a friend of his lives in a rustic mountain cabin. He offered to come pick me up for a weekend of "recreation" that would include the three of us after my first week of lessons. All I could think about for the next two weeks was getting sandwiched between those two hairy hunks of men. I ached to have my ass filled.

At last, I was on my way to "Wild, Wonderful West Virginia." The flight was pleasant enough and the trip through the countryside into the scenic mountains was spectacular. I rode in a company van with several other guys from the Northwest and from California. At site, I passed a pretty boring week of classes, outdoor

training and bunking in with employees from all over the U.S. The only excitement came at shower time in the evenings when I got to eye some of the hunky – and not so hunky –men in the shower room. It was all I could do by week's end to keep my rod from getting hard while I soaped up. A few times I had to face the wall and think about the day's mundane activities to forestall a raging boner.

Thus, when Friday evening came I was genuinely happy to see Jake's smiling face when he arrived in a brand-new pickup to rescue me. We shook hands and greeted each other like long-lost brothers. As we drove to his buddy's cabin, Jake told me a bit more about his relationship with Steve. Damn, this pair knew something about men having fun together.

I noticed an increasing bulge in Jake's snug khakis as he told of some of the pair's adventures.

"Hey, Jake, is that a Swiss army knife in your pocket or are you just happy to see me?" I grinned, sliding my hand onto his leg.

"Why don't you just check and find out," Jake said, grinning back.

I placed my fingers over the stretched fabric and found his long cock hard as a rock. I traced its shape with my left index finger and found a damp spot where his precum had leaked from his well-shaped cockhead. He slid down slightly under the wheel and I unzipped his fly. With some trouble, I finally fished his dripping, swollen peter from his pants.

"Oh, watch out, Bill. I've got to drive this truck, you know?" Jake laughed. "But, I'm pretty familiar with the road if you want to have a little some before we get to the good stuff."

I didn't hesitate, sliding my head down to his lap and licking at his piss slit. His precum was unusually sweet and the smell of his crotch was sweaty but clean, a hint of Irish Spring. I took his cockhead into my lips and swirled my tongue around the flared corona.

"Oh, that's good. Suck my rod, Bill!" Jake moaned, pressing the back of my head gently downward.

My mouth filled with saliva mixing with his oozing man juice and I slid more than half of it into my suctioning mouth. Just then Jake gently patted my head.

"Damn, Bill, we're almost there. Can we save this for later?"

I lifted up, trailing a string of spit and precum from my lips. "Oh, yeah, we've got plenty of time," I agreed. "The whole weekend."

As Jake shoved his wet dick back into his shorts and zipped up, my dick was still nearly ripping through my jeans. A wide wet spot was visible where I had leaked a goodly dollop of precum. I could see that Jake was just as excited as I was. The bulge in his khakis remained enormous and a dark stain spread outward from where a glance could easily detect the shape of his flared cockhead.

Steve was waiting for us, beer in hand. He offered us refreshments and as he turned I had a chance to survey his broad muscular back covered by a light t-shirt, a fabulous tight ass in well-worn jeans shorts and hairy, thickly-muscled

legs. He wore no shoes. We sipped our beers, chatted about the mundane for a while and nervously checked each other out. My cock had softened up some, but I could see Jake was still sporting a fat erection which he reached down and adjusted from time to time with no sign of embarrassment.

"What the hell's the matter with you, Jake?" Steve laughed. "You keep on playing with that thing between your legs like it's hurtin' ya."

Jake laughed. "Well, you know, my cock could do with a little air. Do you guys mind?" He stood up and started undressing.

Steve looked at me and grinned. "Shit, Bill, it looks like it's time for all of us to get comfortable," he said, as he pulled his t-shirt over his head.

His bright pink nipples poked out from the thick coat of black hair covering his chest. I sat mesmerized for a moment as he pulled down his shorts and his thick seven-inch hardon popped out. I glanced over at Jake who was now fully nude and sliding his fist slowly up and down his cock, which looked slightly longer and thicker than Steve's.

As they edged toward each other, they turned to me and said, "Hey, Bill, what are you waiting for?"

"Um, I was just enjoying the scenery," I stuttered as I started to shuck my clothes.

Steve and Jake sat on opposite ends of the big sofa and indicated the spot in the middle was for me. I didn't get a chance to sit, however, because Steve squatted in front of me and started sucking my six-inch cock. Jake started rubbing my ass cheeks and nuzzling my neck. He brings one of his fingers to my lips and I instinctively start sucking on it, making it wet and slippery. The slender finger is soon pressed between my ass cheeks and probes at my pucker. Steve slurps loudly on my cock, his nose buried in my pubic hair and his fingers busy fondling my balls. It feels great. Soon, Jake removes his finger from my butthole and presses me down toward the floor. Jake takes over from Steve on my trembling cock and I put my head between Steve's legs to lick his fat hardon. Steve completes the daisy chain by chowing down on Jake's precum-dripping rod. I feel Steve's hand on my ass and before long he's wedged two of his thick fingers up my butthole, sliding them slowly in and out in rhythm with our cock sucking triangle.

"I need a hole to fuck," Steve grunts, pulling his cock from my mouth with a loud "Slurp!"

He lays back on the floor with that spit-slick monster pointed at the ceiling.

Jake smiles at me. "Go for it, Bill," he encourages.

I straddle Steve's hairy legs and he grips my waist, pulling me forward and onto his cock. I slide on down his rod and start rocking on that saddle horn of his. He pulls me down into his arms to kiss me. Jake suddenly leaps on top of my ass, laying the head of his rock-hard cock on the shaft of Steve's ass-invader. As Steve bulldozes his way down my Hershey highway, I suddenly think, "I don't want my butt ripped apart!" But the two hot studs are intent on the same target. Jake manages

to slip his fat hardon into my ass while I squirm and fidget. They alternate strokes, shoving first one, then the other of their fat cocks into my very wet and open ass channel. Their urgent strokes force their cocks deeper and deeper into my bowels until I feel like they're up to my belly. With grunts and groans of pleasure, the two man cannons blast almost simultaneously into the pitch black of my guts. The recoil send a hot wave of jizm out of my cock onto Steve's hairy, sweating belly.

"Uh, uh, uh," I groan. "I'm cumming! Hot shit! Man, here's my fuck wad!"

I'm not sure which of the big guns has been left up my ass, but I feel it softening in the oozing, juicy confines of my butt.

"Let's get cleaned up," I suggest after a few moments when the only sound is our heavy breathing.

TESTOSTERONE TRIO;
A REALLY HOT TUB

Greetings! My name is Jake and I'm a retired publisher. No, not of pornography, but of legitimate literature. I now live in a small town in West Virginia and happily pursue many interests, not the least of which is sex, particularly with a good friend of mine who lives in a secluded country cabin.

Steve and I have known each other for years, but it was only within the past few years that we discovered each other sexually. Both of us were married for many years. He's divorced and I'm a widower now.

I've also developed an interest in the Internet and its many resources. Again, sex is not the least of them. I met Bill, a sexy married bisexual, online about a year ago. He lives in Oregon. We exchanged pleasant e-mails after he read a bisexual erotic story I wrote for an on-line publication. By a wonderful stroke of luck he had an assignment to attend a company training school right here in West Virginia. We first got together at Steve's cabin for a hot session of uninhibited sexual fun, a mind-blowing experience.

I then invited the two of them to join me at my home for another round the next day.

After a nice barbecue dinner from the grill, I suggested that we all go out to my hot tub for a little relaxation and refreshment. A few tequilas and Dos Equis with lime and we'd be in the mood for some more weekend entertainment. Once we were all three naked – Steve, a hairy and muscular stud with a nice long piece of meat and a set of low hangers he was proud to display; Bill, smooth and handsome with a beautifully shaped normal-sized dick, and me, still firm at middle age with a

slight paunch and, I admit with little modesty, an impressive package – we slipped into the hot water, ready for action.

Almost immediately, I slid my hand under the bubbling water and stuck a finger up Bill's moist asshole while I fed him my tongue. Steve worked on sucking and pinching Bill's tits until they stood out like little pencil erasers.

I didn't neglect Bill's hardening prick while I slid another finger up his tight butt, alternately stroking the shaft of his cock and tickling lightly against his balls and perineum with my other hand.

Then after a conspiratorial wink and nod, Steve and I lifted Bill out of the water, carried him up to the deck and began to towel him down. By now, our fat cocks were as stiff as they could get – my seven-and-a-half incher sticking straight out and Steve's thicker eight inches perked up at a 45-degree angle. I lay down on one of the towels while Steve guided Bill's hot ass to my hungry mouth.

While I rimmed him, Bill sucked hungrily on Steve's thick dark prick, which oozed precum like a motherfucker. When Bill lifted his ass from my slobbering mouth, I could look up and see Steve's hairy leathery balls slapping against Bill's chin. Bill continued hanging on to Steve's prick with his suctioning mouth as the two of us guided his ass down to my thick precum drizzling man fucker. Bill eased his hot ass down over my throbbing pecker and I watched it disappear, inch by slow inch, up his twitching butthole.

"Ah, oh, yeah, Bill, ride that fucker," I encouraged him. "Take it all. Oh, God, your ass is so hot. Mmm. Faster, baby, ride that thing."

His only response was "Mmm." because by this time Steve was jamming his stiff prick halfway down Bill's throat.

Bill had two fingers up Steve's butt, seeking out his hot button while he jacked himself off and speeded up his ass movements on my pistoning peter.

"Oh, shit, oh, I'm cumming!" Steve groaned as he spurted a hot load of jizm into Bill's mouth, sliding his cock out quickly so some of his juice flowed down across the younger man's chin and onto his chest. Steve flipped his spasming prick across Bill's mouth and lips.

Bill suddenly grunted: "Uh, here it cums, boys, ah, oh, fuck, yeah!"

Bill's cum load shot up and hit squarely where his fingers were pumping Steve's hot hairy butthole. The orgasmic spasms in Bill's sphincter and prostate throbbed against the swollen head of my ass-invading prick. It swelled up even larger and I geysered like Old Faithful.

"E!" I screamed. "Yeah, Bill, take my cum. It's yours. Oh, man, oh, man!"

I was stunned at the way Bill churned his ass on my still-stiff pecker. I felt my hot cum flowing out in gobs onto my pubic hair. Steve and I, breathing heavily and fully satisfied, pulled ourselves free to lie beside Bill, taking turns kissing him and tonguing remaining bits of Steve's spicy load from his mouth.

I look into Bill's gorgeous blue eyes. "What next?" I grinned.

IF THAT'S REJECTION...

Rick sat, working the keyboard. Andy knelt beside him supervising. They deleted some photos of his girlfriend's trip from the camera chip, formatted a CD and moved the remaining images there.

Sometimes Andy' muscular right arm lay across Rick's shoulders as he typed. When they conferred on some detail, Rick's left hand would rest in the small of Andy's back.

With the project finished, Rick start cleaning up the stray files and shutting down programs. Andy's hand stilled Rick's, keeping him from proceeding further. He needed help with his email, too. Rick's shoulders fell and his blue eyes rolled up doubtfully. Andy arched his blonde eyebrows, flashed a smile upon his rosy face and rocked his shoulders in encouragement.

He obviously needed to kiss up to his best friend a little bit more to extract more technical assistance. Inches from the older man's tan cheeks, he puckered his lips and made loud smacking noises. For just a second Rick's lips began puckering before he smiled and with a chuckle turned to the keyboard. As Rick brought up Andy's Yahoo profiles, his younger buddy went for the beers.

As they sorted the unread e-mails, Andy began rubbing the small of his back and massaging his left buttocks. A reoccurring complaint from an old injury. Andy suggested the Jacuzzi on Rick's back deck might offer some relief for his aching muscles. With a nod, Rick agreed. But it took a while to mail the photos to Andy's girlfriend.

The clock on the computer screen reported 11:07 p. m. before they stepped out the back door onto the icy deck. They were butt naked except for towels around

their waists, a bottle of Jose Cuervo and the single remaining long neck Budweiser. Rick reached the gazebo first, lit the candles, flipped the cover off and cranked up the Jacuzzi jets.

Rick was already soaking in the water when Andy crept out, leery of the ice and gloom dimly illuminated by the candlelit steam bubbling out of the gazebo around the hot tub.

Rick stood to help his buddy into the tube. He older man stood 6'1" and wore his 200 pounds comfortably. He had brown hair, blue eyes, and only a small middle age belly as he rapidly approached age 50.

He'd raised enough out of the water to reveal a heat-lengthened set of balls and average size dick. As Andy straddled the side of the tub, Rick admired his broad shoulders. His eyes dropped briefly to the younger man's cold tightened balls silhouetted against the light emitted by the study window. Andy was in his early 40s, the sort of blond stud that made young women sigh, older women pant, Marine recruiters smile and gay men…well, forget about it, because he would be unapproachable.

Rick, after admiring the view, grabbed the younger man and guided him to the little bench hidden below the boiling surface. Andy sat and made all those amusing hot tub "ah", "oh", "eh" grimaces while rubbing the goose bumps and heat off his legs. Finally, his shoulders fell, a sigh escaped his lips, he smiled and leaned back.

Rick let him relax a bit. They talked. Then Rick indicated a change in position with the whirling of an outstretched index finger. There were no benches in the opposite corners of the square tub. The men took those corners now, settling into the deeper water, their heels resting next to one another butts. Andy's big hands settled easily on Rick's knees. A deeper sigh and a "thanks" escaped the fisherman's lips.

Andy would be leaving for the Bering Sea soon. He'd be gone for four months. They needed to do a lot of talking. They took turns rolling backwards to dunk their heads beneath the surface while their legs, dick and balls dangled in the chill air. Andy stood and sat on the edge of the tub for a while, giving Rick a fine view of his muscular pale frame, his plump pubic package and the darker hair freshly grown on his chest and belly since the last time they'd gotten naked together – so long ago.

Andy leaned over Rick, his short, limp cock just inches from the other man's mouth and fumbled for the bottles adjacent to the hot tub. Rick helped him find the best place to set them. Andy opened the tequila, sipped it and handed it to Rick, then followed that with the beer. After putting them each in turn on the side of the tub, smooth-chested Rick stroked the hair on Andy's chest and belly appreciatively.

Andy smiled in response.

Rick's long-fingered hands flew up in exclamation and his mouth fell open like he had forgotten something. He grabbed Andy's left foot and pulled it over his

left shoulder, making Andy somewhat buoyant and floating in Rick's lap. His right hand crept under the fisherman's firm ass, groped his crotch, touched his man-hole and finally found the sore hip. That was, after all, the reason they headed to the hot tub.

Rick alternated kneading the offending buttock and applying pressure on the sore hip. Then he massaged large handfuls of flesh moving along the blonde's thigh to his knee. Rick kept working the area with instructions from Andy and an occasionally repositioning of the older man's hands. For Rick, the feelings were extremely sensual, if not erotic. Andy showed no sign of arousal, but he also did not complain or move away.

While Rick worked, Andy lifted the tequila to his own lips then carefully to Rick's. Then followed the beer bottle, poured lovingly into Rick's mouth, while Andy held his head back. He set the Budweiser aside and pulled Rick through the bubbling hot water to his naked lap.

They whispered in one another's ear of their friendship and kissed the nape of one another's necks. Andy's right hand pushed Rick into his left arm. The fisherman applied the bottles to their lips again followed by a kiss and a proposal.

Rick arched a brow and smiled in approval. They launched themselves back to their respective corners and each took up the other's sorest foot, wedging their free foot against each other's crotch. Andy's toes actually kneaded Rick's dick at first.

Andy drunkenly explained to Rick how to give foot massages. His instructions got loud by the time they finished, Rick was outlining the obscure mysteries of reflexology. They threw their heads back to laugh.

Andy told Rick about the romantic effects of a good foot massage on his girlfriend. His right hand jokingly yanked his cock beneath the waves. Rick followed suit. Rick started telling Andy about tantric sex and mapping the Kabala on his wife's body. Andy threw him a questioning look.

The thumb of the aviator's right hand touched the center of the fisherman's brow and all the doubt left his features. The thumb moved to the first eye and they both closed. It caressed the second and the fisherman's frame leaned closer into his best friend's body. It crossed his mouth in route to his shoulders and Andy's warm lips responded with a kiss.

The hand moved on to massage first one broad muscular shoulder, then the other. He rubbed the sparse forest of new chest hair sheltering Andy's big heart, moved on to the once aching hip and rubbed there hard for a while. His hand then moved to the other side. Before Rick could reach the more erotic Yesod or Malkuth of the Kabala, Andy wanted to demonstrate the technique he used on his girl friend.

He spun the taller man around and stretched the lanky frame across his more muscular body, settling Rick's butt atop his own hardening cock. Rick was surprised – and delighted – by this first sign of arousal. Andy pulled Rick's left arm up and arched his hand around his own muscular shoulders. The left hand held his

buddy's body while the right rubbed his chest and belly and dick. His lips whispered in Rick's right ear. Rick sighed and leaned back into Andy's arms, writhing there, stretching his other arm up to join the first. Andy asked if his technique worked.

Laughing, he pushed Rick away. Rick grinning, blushing and shaking his head, waggled an admonishing finger at his young friend and nodded appreciatively. Andy would be leaving soon for four months. Their friendship would need a lot of conversation tonight to last through such a drought. He pulled Rick towards him again and poured the last of the tequila down their throats. They each pretended to drink of the empty beer bottle his hand offered them.

It was late. It was time to get out of the water. Rick enticed the drunker man from the hot tub and led him into the house. Once Rick got Andy inside, he returned to the gazebo, turned down the tub and blew out the candles. Andy waited for him in the study, his beige towel barely wrapped around his stocky, milk-white frame.

Rick ushered Andy down the hall to the walk-in shower in the master bedroom where they could shower together. Andy shook his head at this, shrugged his shoulders and waved his hands. Rick calmed him down, drew him a shower and sent him in.

Andy apparently changed his mind – his right hand grabbed Rick's left and drug him in. They kissed and caressed there in the hot stream. Andy turning them so Rick stayed warm. They laughed and kissed one another as they whirled about the shower. Andy stepped back and smiling said something about his dick. His fingers trailed into the strawberry blond locks of pubic hair, then hefted his balls and dick up for the taller man to see. Rick put his left hand on Andy right shoulder and knelt on the shower floor.

Andy's strong arms cupped under the other man's arms and lifted him into an embrace. Andy wagged a finger at him and turned him towards the wall. Andy lathered up a wash rag, leaned Rick into the wall and reached across his prone friend's frame to wash his back. You know where his dick was. Rick reached under his balls to brush the slightly swollen tip of Andy's short-stemmed peter.

With a drunken giggle, Andy knelt on the shower floor, spread the taller man's ass cheeks and scrubbed his crack and then reached between his thighs and gently rolled the wash cloth around Rick's balls and stroked his dick. He cleaned Rick's legs and left the shower. He waited for Rick to come out, then pulled his short dick out straight from his body to gauge it against Rick's slightly longer member. Rick moved forward and laid his dick beside Andy's. Andy absentmindedly started stroking their cocks. When he discovered Rick's getting hard, he jumped back with a laugh and a blush. It was time for Andy to go.

Andy dressed hurriedly and departed with a quick hug and handshake. He would be completely sober by the time he hiked the half mile to his small temporary apartment.

Still naked as he watched Andy veer down the pathway, Rick let his mind spin over the amazing events of the past few hours. He wanted to etch them into

his memory. As he lay down to sleep a few hours before his wife and son returned from their holiday visit to grandma's, his cock rose unbidden into an almost painful rigidity. Suddenly, he couldn't imagine how it had behaved so primly in the presence of his best, his most Platonic friend.

He slid his hand down to grip the straining shaft while his other hand kneaded his tightening balls. One finger slid into the smooth, clean crack of his ass. He began to pump and in seconds his aching crotch signaled his orgasm. He pushed his index finger far into his asshole just as his twitching cock spurted his man juice for a shocking distance. The first shot hit his left cheek. In lessening tremors, his anxious dick unloaded the most cum he could ever remember.

"If that's rejection, I want to be rejected more often. If that's refusal, it was the most romantic refusal in history," Rick said aloud in the empty, darkened, echoing room.

Rick dropped the CD and printed photos by Andy's apartment at lunch time the next day. They ate homemade soup. They talked, or didn't talk as a the case maybe about the night before. They ate in the silence only old friends can enjoy. Then, back to work for Rick. Andy walked him to the door and shook his hand. As usual their free hands fell on one another's sides.

"Thanks for a fantastic evening," Andy called as Rick ran down the steps.

It was going to be a very long four months.

A NIGHT IN THE TIJUANA
OF SOUTHEAST

So last night there's a soft knock at my hotel room door. I open the door wearing nothing but boxers.

Paul's thinning hair betrays a hint of gray. He appears older than I'd expected as he silently slips in the door. Then I realize it's his lack of expression that confuses his age. His eyes aren't glazed with lust nor round with excitement. His lips barely move in greeting. I try to embrace him, but that's hard to do when the other person's arm lay limp at their sides. I walk him across the room and lightly kiss him until he smiles, but he still seems uncomfortable; ill-at-ease rather than nervous or shy. We start kissing and touching. He's a little shorter than I and wearing baggy pants, but I can feel his dick getting quickly hard. The chest hair curling up out of the collar of his shirt is turning me on. We strip him. His boxers are tenting and he thanks me for wearing boxers too.

"Want me out of these?" he asks, grinning.

"Yes, I want your boxers off," I said and dropped to my knees.

He had a dimpled chin with a couple of days' growth of beard, long black hair all over the front of his chest almost hiding his soft pink nipples, and now I discovered a thick bush of long hair guarding a curved, pink, gnarled 7 inch rock hard cock. I slurped on it a couple of times. The head of his dick was salty with precum. I tried pulling his shorts off his stocking feet.

"I'll take them off. You take yours off."

I watched mine hit the floor. When, I looked up I was shocked to see him jerking away with wild abandon, eyes glassed and knees bent. He spewed on the carpet before I could stop his hand.

"Don't worry it'll get hard again."

I threw myself on the bed and began stroking my dick. He paced the floor nervously.

"Come lay by me," I said finally, patting the mattress.

He did. Not even looking for a pillow, just staring straight at the ceiling, his eyes dark with ill ease. All the suggestions of what we could do next, the erotic topics I proposed, my discovery that the mirror on the opposite wall gave us a view of ourselves, none elicited a response. A quivering "Fine" or "I don't know" is all I got. Finally, I climbed atop his fine firm body and began rubbing against him. I kissed him every time I slid up his hirsute torso. His hairy chest hugged my smooth one, his hairy thighs massaged my balls. My semi-hard dick plowed thru his dark bush. His body began to respond. His dick began to grow and I found my semi rubbing up against a full blown coarse gnarled cock. His eyes came alive with a smile. His hairy hands each grabbed a white ass cheek and he started masturbating himself with my entire body. He kneaded my nipples and I returned the favor by manhandling his fur forested mountainous biceps.

"Got any condoms?" he asked breathlessly.

I rolled off to the side, pulled some out, rolled one on his steel-stiff erection, lubed it, and mounted.

"Won't go in?" he asked.

I smiled knowingly and readjusted my hips. He quivered his hips to help get his rock hard cock in. He shoved it all the way in, then moaned with delight. He kept hold of my cheeks and kept working my body back and forth in shallow strokes on his sturdy man cock. After 15 minutes or so of slow fucking I leaned back to get his invading prick further in. He reached under my thighs and started playing with my asshole and balls all at once.

I grabbed my cock and rode his train all the way to Cum City. He wiped my load of white stuff from his furry belly and kept fucking me for another 15 minutes. I asked how I could make him come. "I usually don't come the second time," he said.

Eventually we tried for another position and ended up sprawled on the bed. But I slipped and fell over the side. When I got up off the floor, he was pounding away.

"Want to put it in again?" I asked.

"Let's save it for Saturday," he replied pleasantly. "I got to get back to work."

It took him another ten minutes of jerking before he blew another somewhat smaller load of cum. Wow!

ANOTHER NIGHT IN TIJUANA

I had mixed emotions about calling Jerry when I got to the southernmost of Southeast; the Tijuana of Southeast. He's a good fuck, but I find him sort of annoying. Small, hard bodied, thick-dicked, balding, a face aged by cigarette smoke and attitude. He's a professional activist and his conversation is limited to his wonderful exploits in his current social endeavor.

So, I didn't call, not that I had much of a chance. My co-worker wanted a beer after work one day. I suggested the Brown Derby because I've always wanted to check it out. We walk in at 3:30.

"Bill!" Jerry warbles from the bar.

We had some drinks while he caught me up on the details of his life and promised (in front of my co-worker) to get together with me sometime that week.

A few hours later he calls the hotel room where I'm staying.

I say "Come on up."

I answered the door in the nude – 6' 1", gray hair, blue eyes, much-reduced pot belly from hiking across the muskegs to work each morning. He slipped into the room and started stripping. As he stripped, he caught me up on the details we couldn't share in front of my co-worker earlier. Namely, he told me about a boyfriend with a 10-inch cock and a live-in girlfriend who knew he was bi- and didn't ask where he was going tonight.

Jerry brought condoms but no lube. He wanted a smoke, so as he stood naked, with his back to the window and his cigarette dangling out into space, I started sucking on his impressive dangling cock. Tasted nasty! Just the way I wanted

it. I squatted before him and within seconds got him so hard, I had to protect my gag reflects.

My right hand rested on his little butt or cupped his hairy little left thigh. His cock is thick and eight inches. When the cigarette was done, he laid his little hands on my head and started facing fucking me. I wedged my tongue down my throat and let him go for it. His pelvis bounced back and forth between the window and my mustached mouth for a long time.

My hard-bodied little buddy then pulls me to my feet and guides me to the bed. He lounges there in all his naked glory and I take the opposite head-to-foot position so we can slurp and suck one another's cocks. My tongue chases his dick back and forth across his lap. He just deep throats mine and starts applying the vacuum to it.

It's hard for me to pay serious attention to my work when someone is working my six-inch hard-on so erotically. Jerry appeared to have the same problem. So, we took turns enjoying one another's mouths. I rolled him over on top of me and his hips started pounding my face. He was getting harder and longer. His eight-inch baby-maker was slamming furiously straight down into my throat and...

"Ugh!"

I swear the soft head of his very rigid rod slipped past my tonsils (or what remains of them after my childhood surgery). I lifted him off and sat up to catch my breath.

I laid back on the bed. Jerry straddled my shoulders and fed his cock to my hungry lips. This left my right hand free to stroke my own cock while the left played with my long balls. It had been months since the last time I had any sex and it wasn't long before I shot a thick white load all over my belly, tension sliding from my body in the process.

"Roll over," Jerry said, slipping his hairy buns down my body. He worked the middle finger of his left hand up my ass while jerking himself with his right. "Does that feel good?" he asked, in a husky baritone.

Honestly, it did. But without lube, even two fingers became a little painful. I put up with it for the pleasure to come.

Unfortunately, without lube, Jerry couldn't get his bulky rod into my puckered ass. He repositioned himself higher astride my ass, attacked from the small of my back and forced me onto all fours. Still, no luck.

"How about shaving cream?" I inquired with a note of desperation.

"Shaving cream! You sure?" He started lathering up my ass like he intended to shave it. "Nice ass," he muttered more to himself than to me. It worked great and in a few minutes he was in me.

"Oh God! It's been so long," I whispered so as not to draw the attention of the co-worker housed in the next room.

I buried my face in the mattress, rolled my ass back and forth to meet his lunging cock. I memorized the feel of his hands on my shoulders and the touch of his stiffened nipples on my back.

My cock and balls were mashed against the bedspread and being rolled back and forth in his thrusting passion. His grunts and all that motion started getting me hard again, a rarity for me after such an effluvial orgasm.

"He stays in the saddle longer than he used to," I thought.

He somewhat roughly pulled me to all fours, prying my cheeks apart with his small hands so he could drive that rampant charger between his thighs deeper down the muddy road to my heart. I was loving it.

Eventually – after an extended period of pure erotic pleasure – he whimpered, shuddered and collapsed atop me, his creamy load filling my ass and dripping down onto my shrunken balls.

I can't wait to work in Tijuana again!

KEN

"Did you know we cancelled your flight?" the woman behind the counter asked.

I turned to see the ferry departing for the far island.

"No."

They'd rescheduled me for a diverted flight that would depart from Southeast four hours later than I planned. I called my boyfriend Ken to warn him I'd arrive much later than expected.

"You know I'll still be there waiting for you!" My boyfriend spent a fuckless summer hiking the length of British Columbia. Well not totally fuckless, he got cougared by the woman who hired him to do yardwork. During several phone calls he'd promised to throw me down and fuck the shit out of me. He made the same promise over the phone this night. Only now there was a chance it would happen.

Naturally, I arrived 1-1/2 hours later than their revised estimate. Yeah, Ken was there, but I had to look twice. Instead of the giant Russell Crowe look-a-like with long hair, I saw a substantially thinner outdoorsy looking guy with pork chop sideburns, short black hair, a working man's build and shoes.

"It's my red neck look," he explained after my initial "wow!" of shock.

We hugged. He nearly lifted me off the ground as usual. I'm 6'1, but Ken is 6'7". He's ten years my junior but looks twenty younger.

We taxied to my hotel and dragged my luggage into the room. I put my glasses on the decorative shelf by the door and Ken drove his tongue down my throat like it was headed for Thursday. His body pressed forward with me in his

arms. I'm not good at two stepping backwards, but I did the best I could to keep us from crashing to the floor. By luck, we landed on the bed.

We made out madly, trying fruitlessly to get our hands into one another's clothes. With a grunt, Ken hoisted himself off me. His knees pinned my shoulders to the bed and his hands freed his familiar dark nine-inch cock to invade my waiting mouth. I don't even have my coat off and I'm sucking cock. I tried to enjoy the view while nudging his sparsely haired balls and attempting to suck his stiffening cock back into my mouth. Was that a lot more chest hair I saw? Hiking all summer had definitely turned him into a bear.

"Take off your clothes," he asked, pleaded, demanded.

I happily complied and more. When I climbed back into bed he was on his back, playing with the fully engorged dick he had pointed straight up. I kissed him deeply. I deep throated the head of his rod, licked the shaft, probed his man eggs with my tongue, licked the "taint" – that stretch of skin that tain't cock and tain't asshole. Then forced my tongue into his asshole. He groaned loudly. Did I mention he'd been waiting at the airport all evening? My tongue couldn't play there long and worked its way back to his cock.

"I want to be in you," he hoarsely whispered.

I rolled the condom on him. He groaned loudly. I lubed up his cock. He groaned loudly again. I shoved two lubed finger up my butt and then straddled my big buddy bear.

So, I started sliding down the shaft. It hurt. I tried wiggling around. It hurt worse. Damn, did he exercise that thing to a wider girth? I wondered. Finally I figured, fuck it and pushed through the pain. Instantly, I settled all the way down the shaft and the pain began to subside.

I was going to ride him, but Ken hadn't waited all summer to be patient for me now. He began driving up and out forcefully, bouncing me in the air and driving back in as my butt fell. He was getting us into a real rhythm. It must have felt even better on his dick when I lean back, because he pushed my shoulders back. We clasped fingers so I could go even further back.

"Fuck it! Get on your back!"

He flipped me over, folded me in half and while his tongue explored my mouth his cock again found my ass. Ken pounded away in wild joyful abandon. His green eyes searched mine desperately for pleasure and pain. I was loving it.

When he began losing traction he hoisted my feet into the air, plopped my ass on his knees and went back to drilling my weeping hole. He readjusted our position another four times and kept on fucking.

"Doggie style?"

I rolled over on all fours, feet off the bed. He stood on the floor, his wide thighs spreading my hips apart to help his big hands to open my hole and position my ass. He drove his dick in and kept at it until we tumbled forward on to the bed.

"On your back again."

I'd forgot to push a pillow under my behind and the small of my back was killing me. Plus my intestines felt like they would come lose it any minute.

"I got to go to the bathroom," I managed in a breathless tone.

"I don't want to stop," he pleaded.

"Then don't," I conceded.

"I'd better," he finally agreed, pulling his slimed-up prick out of my ass with a loud "Plop!"

When I came back he'd removed the condom and I asked for a taste of his load. We stroked and sucked until he was ready to shoot and I positioned myself above his cock.

"Here it comes, baby," he yelled. What was I thinking? This guy can shoot enough to give you a cum bath. I got a mouthful in the first two squirts and started choking.

"Who do you think you are with?" he laughed.

I gurgled, swallowing fast. "Judging by that explosion, you must be Ken

LAYOVER AT THE AIRPORT

The slightly taller and much heavier man stood waiting for Bill in the lobby. Big-Ray was in his early to mid thirties, bound in heavy black leather coat and open light vest. Big-Ray wore a tee-shirt reading, "Speak to the paw!" a clue that he was as hairy beneath the shirt as he was big. He was unshaven and sporting a graying goatee and thinning short brown hair.

Bill, a 6'1" Southeasterner said "Hi!" and beamed while extending a hand.

Ray's face lit up. His unshaven cheeks blushed, his blue eyes sparkled as he grinned back. They scooted across the busy street to enjoy a few cheap beers at the casino. Bill discovered that Ray's "aloofness" was shyness. They discussed the breakup of Ray's long term relationship. They smiled at one another as they chatted, eyeing up the other's frame and figure, their thighs rumbling beneath the bar. They left the bar right after finishing the second beer.

The hotel room door barely closed when they were in each other's arms. It's a good thing people kiss with their eyes closed. From the way Bill's face squinted up and shoulders rose, it appeared that Big-Ray had forgotten to brush his teeth. But, the bottom's body relaxed as Ray's thick fingers massaged his back. His eyes glassed as the stubble on Ray's face raked his smooth cheeks. Big-Ray had doffed his leathers at the door and Bill could wait no longer.

"I've waited two years to see this chest!" he reminded Big-Ray while dragging the taller man's tee-shirt over his head. A full broad chest and belly thoroughly and evenly covered with brown hair appeared before Bill's appreciative

eyes and groping hands. "Oh my God!" He bent to tickle a nipple with his long pink tongue.

Ray smiled in delight and stripped Bill's shirt from his own smooth chest.

They returned to kissing and pawing one another. Swinging his right hand into their crotches, Bill felt a long hard cock aching to pop out of Ray's Levis. He knelt and struggled with the belt. Big-Ray had to point out he was left handed. Then the buckle came open, button-fly flew apart and a long, bulbous headed, thick cock shot straight out. Bill choked the shaft and gave the head a wide appreciative lick. His left hand rose up the wide furry treasure trail, to the wider fully furred chest, up Ray's beard and then lifted his head back to let more light fall on the fabulous bear body.

He licked the shaft and tried to get to the dangling sparsely haired balls. Tried. He gave up and returned to kissing as the ringed cock head pocked at its owner's abdomen.

Out of breath, Bill finally pushed away, "Let's get naked and get in bed."

Bill barely had his cowboy boots off when Big-Ray towered nude and expectantly over him. Big-Ray grabbed him in his arms again as soon as Bill stepped out of his pants. And they returned to making out. Bill's hand returned to stroking Big-Ray stiff rod. It had looked to be 7-1/2 compared to Bill's 6 incher. But as Bill pushed his hand down the staff more of it revealed itself at the base. It was wide! Bill's eyes widened in excitement when he realized he almost could not wrap a finger and thumb around it. Ray broke his lips from Bill's, smiled and dove backwards onto the bed. His almost 9 incher stuck straight up and Bill fell on his knees to worship it, washing it with his saliva and polishing it with his tongue.

Ray couldn't have gotten any harder. Bill climbed atop him on all fours. As he returned to kissing the "very versatile" top, he wedged his ass against Ray's cock and let the bulbous head bang blindly at his bunghole. They kissed passionately all the while Bill's hairy butt crack first stroked the shaft and then wiggled atop the head.

"What's your favorite position?" Bill asked astride Ray.

"The bottom on top. You control it, pal. You control it."

They returned to kissing.

"What's your second favorite position?"

"From behind. What do they call it; doggy style?"

"Yeah, that's one of my favorites too!"

They returned to kissing. Bill's ass continued to rub Ray's upright rod.

"You want it. Don't you?"

"Yeah."

"Let's do it."

Bill grabbed the lube and rubbed some on Ray's stiff veiny prong. Then after two attempts they got the condom on. Big-Ray stroked himself as Bill bent beside the bed and lubed up his love canal. Straddling Ray, Bill hooked his ankles

under the thick hairy thighs and tried to lower himself on to the big dick. With some effort and experienced skill, the bulbous head plopped in.

"Ah," Big-Ray sighed with a smile.

Bill tried to press down. He grimaced a little but not excessively at the pain. It was a tight fit. He pushed down a little and then lifted. Ray sighed. Bill pushed down again, then rose. Big-Ray grinned and writhed enthusiastically. Bill started a rhythm that got him slightly further down the long, thick shaft with each attempt.

"Oh, yeah," Big-Ray cried.

"You've got such a thick cock. I'm putting all my weight on it and can't get all the way down," Bill marveled in a raspy voice.

When Bill's balls finally flopped onto the top's furry belly, a grunt escaped from Bill's upturned face and a great sigh from Ray. The bottom rested a moment and then began to rise and fall with Ray's throbbing rod wedged inside him.

Ray smiled up at Bill with his eyes still closed.

"Bill you are so good! You've got a great ass."

When the juices finally starting flowing Big-Ray took over the ramming, taking long slow strokes up into Bill's willing bottom.

"You are so good," Big-Ray affirmed again, as Bill's hands played across his furry broad belly and chest.

Ray kept poking at his buddy until he couldn't resist any longer and pulled Bill down into his arms for another make out sessions. Bill returned his tongue wrestling enthusiastically, while grinding his ass back and forth on the still hard rod. When they broke from their embrace, Bill spit on his hand and applied the "lube" to his littler dick and began dry humping the furry belly beneath his balls, while grinding his hips into Ray's crotch.

"Oh, yeah, Bill. You are so good!"

But, Big-Ray could not resist Bill's willing lips and pulled him into his arms again. A guttural groan escaped from Bill's mouth as the divine rod popped from his ass. They kissed madly. When Bill's tongue and mouth found the small of Ray's neck, he sighed and groaned with the same ecstasy as when he was fucking his buddy. The crack of Bill's butt began to stroke against the shaft again.

"You are so good! You want more don't you?"

"Yeah!'

"Get on all fours."

Ray crawled out from beneath, off the bed then stepped onto it and knelt behind the bent bottom. He pulled Bill's ass further down and tried to ease his cock in again. Bill writhed, arched his back and raised his ass in order to help the anal assault. Big-Ray put both his hairy paws in the small of Bill's back and pushed the white bubble butt back down. Then he drove his cock slowly in.

"Wow! That feels so good," Bill assured him with no sign of grimace or pain.

Ray eased all the way in then slowly pulled nearly out. Then back in again and out. A slow long fuck.

"Bill, your ass is so fucking good!'

Bill only sighed in response.

"I'm…going… to… cum, uh, dude! I'm gonna cum!" Big-Ray began rapidly ramming his hips on and off Bill's butt.

"Ah!" he hollered as he unloaded, sending both men into shivers with his explosive climax. "Oh, oh, oh, yeah!"

As Bill collapsed belly down on the bed, Big-Ray staggered off to the bathroom to clean up. When the hairy hunk returned, his nearly flaccid cock slapping wetly between his legs, Bill rose and kissed his goateed buddy before taking his turn in the bathroom.

When he returned the bigger boy was sitting on the edge of the bed waiting for him, that soft plump dick resting on his drained balls. Big-Ray took Bill in his arms kissed him gently and began to stroke his nearly limp pecker. Bill looked down in apparent surprise at his rising cock. Ray's tongue engulfed his mouth. A saliva-soaked paw wrapped around his member, rigid and reddened from its long ride on Ray's hair-roughened abdomen. The hairy top's embrace crushed and moved him back onto the bed, where he was wrapped in the hot embrace until his little soldier hurled the hot liquid ammunition across his belly and his buddy's hand.

"Ugh, oh, God, yes, uh, man!" Bill gurgled into Ray's hairy chest.

Ray hadn't even gotten out the door when he exclaimed, "We have got to do this again!"

LODGE THAT GRAND ROD

I wondered why I'd come to the Grand Lodge meeting.

Ages ago I agreed to serve as the local lodge's representative to the state-wide convention. I had not been too thrilled about the idea. And after I said yes, they said oh, and by the way, you'll need to attend the pre-Grand Lodge convention with just the local lodges. "Whatever!"

But, when the time came I had just gotten back from two weeks of training in LA (Hi, LAX) I was way behind on my personal and professional life. There seemed no way out of it. I could get away at lunch time. I called Jack to make lunch plans. "What are you doing? Cool. Who you staying with? No way, I just bought this big house. Stay here." So he picks me up at the airport. We have a great evening. He drops me downtown on his way to work.

My meeting is surprisingly good. Not too much business, inspirational speaker, some interesting addresses by famous men in the state. At lunch in the midst of a good time, Jack says, "You know John Jones moved up here." I didn't. Jack borrowed my cell, called Jonesy and made my lunch plans for the next day. Spent the night with Jack, had a great lunch with Jonesy and finally got to meet his four kids and his super wife. Jonesy takes me back to the evening session and says, "Jack and I are going to take you out afterwards." "It gets over at 10pm." "That's okay." We had a great evening. I thoroughly enjoyed myself. I friend suggested that now that Fate had set the hook, I was being reeled in.

So, there I was headed towards the baggage claim in the state's biggest airport wondering what the hell I was doing there, when my forever-relocating, boyfriend Ken strolled through security headed for my gate. He was late, and his

eyes moved back and forth across the concourse bright with emotion. His habitual smile fluttered about his lips. His features might have betrayed concern, but his body reeked of self confidence. It was the first time I'd seen him in his TSA uniform. His lapels were ironed out flat against his shirt revealing a bit of the hairy chest beneath and the white tank top that covered it. The white short sleeves of his shirt were rolled up to show off the muscles of his upper arms. He'd spent all of last summer hiking British Columbia and he still had a bit of that hiker's gait. In his wake stood slack jawed women and blushing men. Did I mention my boyfriend is 6'7" and looks like Russell Crowe with a neatly kept black beard? I, on the other hand, am almost old enough to be Ken's daddy and have gray hair.

When his eyes fell upon my 6'1" frame his face turned into a blushing grin. His shoulders fell as did the worry upon them. I always seem to have a really positive effect on him. When I call him on the phone and he answers all gruffly and business-like, you should hear the volume fall and warmth ooze into his voice when he knows it's me.

"Bill!" he crowed as his massive right hand engulfed mine.

"Ken," I replied shaking his hand resisting the temptation to hug him right there in front of his co-workers.

"We got a lot to catch up on," he informed me.

This was going to be our only night together. My meetings ran until 10 p.m. and he worked till 1 a.m. after this night So we talked about his new job, took the bus downtown, met his new roommate, shopped, talked about the difficulty of meeting people in a new town, made dinner, went for a beer, discovered his roomie was gone for the evening and then he said, "Wanna fuck?"

My hunk takes me by the hand, led me to his furnished room and encloses me in his arms. His tongue forces its way down into my mouth. I wrap my hands around his shoulders and pull his face down to mine. My boyfriend breaks our embrace with a gulp and a sheepish grin. His big hands drop to my belt and fly, pulls open my Levis, drops his butt to the queen size bed and starts sucking my little six-inch cock.

"Oh, yeah, Ken. Ah. That feels good," I whisper, leaning my full weight on my open hands on his broad shoulders. He's making slurping noises as his lips run the length of my saliva-drenched white dick, glancing up at me with an arch of his left eyebrow as the pink head comes to rest in his mouth. Then it's a big gulp and he slowly lets my manhood slide from his plush lips again.

With a smack of those lips, he suggests we get naked. By the time I get naked; he is already nude and stretched out on the bed. His left elbow props up his massive frame so he can enjoy the sight of me stripping; his right hand dangles his dark nine-inch slab of meat straight up at me. I kneel on the bed and my mouth goes straight to work, but Ken is not satisfied with just a blow job. His large caressing fingers work their way up my left leg to my thigh where his hand encourages me to bring my dick to his lips. I comply. Sixty-nining I can never deep throat the whole

thick shaft, but his cock was already hard anyway. He moans encouragingly as I alternate licking the shaft, mouthing the head and sucking on his balls.

He keeps moving his big brown ass, so I can eventually work a finger up to his bung hole. For his part, Ken goes right back to slurping on my dick. His ever aggressive fingers steadily search their way to my ass. First one, then the others pried my checks even further so they can double penetrate me and it seems like those thick digits are going for a gang bang when my boy friend jumps up. "On your back!" he hisses as he reaches for the lube. I wedge a pillow under my butt. My boyfriend splashes lube on his cock and presses the head against my bung hole. He always takes it easy so as not to hurt me. I have a surprise for him. My fingers had been "gang-banging" my ass every morning shower this week in preparation for this moment. My long white arms shoot out around his thighs. I barely grunt as I impale myself on his huge brown rod.

"Oh, Billy. You okay?"

I nod and he slowly pulls back and then shoves back in. Another couple of strokes and I is relaxing and smiling. "Oh, Billy," he whispers again and then starts thrusting the full length of his shaft. His face takes on a determined grin, his big hands press my thighs down and he leans over my folded frame to frantically kiss me. His big slab of meat keeps slamming in and out of me and I just submit to the pounding.

My hands stroke that forest of hair on his chest and pinch his nipples enough to get him to suck air. "Yeah, fuck me, Ken. Lodge that grand rod up my butt. Fuck that ass," I encourage and then start grinning.

"What?" he whispers.

"Your roommate is gone, no one lives around here, we ain't in your old apartment or a hotel room. We don't have to whisper." I shout, "Fuck that ass!"

"Yeah!" he shouts back, now huffing and puffing, the sweat beginning to form on his brow and amongst the hairy growth on his chest. His eyes are glassed over and he blindly drives in and out of me, bouncing my bent-in-half bottom across the bed. He pops out, we gasp; he lifts off my ass by pushing off my thighs with his left hand, guides his cock in with the right and away we go for more fucking. He pops out occasionally; "Damn," he shouts, lifts my left leg in the air and re-attacks my ass. The third time he pops out: "Damn!" He demands I roll over on my belly. I elevate my ass with a pillow under my prick, but Ken tosses it aside. He straddles my thighs and slides his rod up the crack of my ass into my hole. He grabs my hand from behind and passionately interlocks our fingers. Then he bangs away so hard and directly that he scoots us across the bed towards the wall. He rolls me on my back again, folds me in half and goes back to fucking his favorite way: long and hard, his tongue in my mouth and his sweat pooling on my chest. Another fifteen minutes of that.

"Damn!" when he pops out and then: "On your belly." This time I hear a spring in the mattress pop when he jumps off me. When the new position wasn't

getting him any closer to cumming, he grabs me and starts to roll me on my back again.

"How about this? On our sides."

His long arms and wide hands move my shoulders at ninety degrees to his body. He shoves in deeper and harder than before. But that still isn't cutting it and it's back on my back where the weight of his enormous body begins to make my legs ache. I straightened them out with the intent of easing the ache, but...

"Oh, no, you don't! Your ass is mine. I own you." And so saying he clamps the back of my legs to his chest, stands on his knees and keeps pounding my dangling ass. Eventually he pins me back on the bed. We wrap one another in our arms, with sweat flying everywhere, tongues wrestling, his ass rising high and rapidly down. "I want you to take my whole load in your mouth. I want to shoot it."

"Okay."

He flings himself on his back beside me. Lifting my upper torso with his left hand, he aims his cock at my mouth with his right. Ken is famous for the volume and force of his load so I didn't clamp down on that purple head but just let it fly my way until his massive eruption is spent. I bend to kiss him, releasing back to him his load. Our tongues feverishly clean one another's mouths. Then I collapse on to his left side. My dark skinned giant rolls over me, keeping his weight on his elbows and his lips, softly pecking at my face.

"I want to see you cum. Jerk for me. You like it when I fuck you, don't you? You like it when I'm plugging your ass, pinning you to the bed." My right hand has my whipped dick in its palm, rubbing my swelling shaft. "Come on, daddy, shoot for me. So I can fuck your ass again," Ken orders gruffly. With a grunt and a spasm, I let loose. My Russel-Crowe look alike's thick lips are around my spurting cock to soothe me. He shares my smaller and sweeter load of man-cream with me and thanks me with soft warm words. We cuddle there with him whimpering and sighing above me. I melt into the sweat-drenched warmth of his embrace, feeling loved and protected and fully sated. "I love you," rises to my lips, but stops there. Not the thing to say at such a moment. I push my thoughts elsewhere and when he asks me what I was thinking, I can report something else.

"What are you thinking?" I retorted.

"About having no sex drive as of late." My shoulders straighten beneath me and I turn to look at him quizzically. "Until you come to town and then I can't get enough." I start rambling on about old friends being the best and the stress of the move and new job and just keep going without considering the more obvious reason I just came up with.

The next morning I dressed in the dark, brushed my teeth with a harsh new toothbrush, kissed my boyfriend "good bye" until Sunday, and caught a cab to the convention. First day was a workshop on the gifts God gave us for the good of the Order. Good, thought provoking course. Second day began the long drawn

out initial readings and politicking for the resolutions. The second day also began my toothache.

By the afternoon the tooth was roaring. My head was pounding. The room was hot. The resolution requiring full public disclosure of all pertinent information like: marital status, sexual orientation, health and disabilities was read again and presented for discussion. I probably would have been okay, but everyone who got up spoke in favor with just glowing words, following the company line, one right after another. And my tooth was killing me.

I stood up and went to the mike. "I'm speaking against the resolution for two reasons. 1) What does this tell the possible brothers who might want to join our fraternal organization? And two, what does marital status, health or disabilities have to do with being a member of this Loyal Order? Many of our early leaders were afflicted with disabilities."

No one seemed to take much notice. My tooth was killing me. I sat down. The next speaker was a homophobe and the final speaker before he started said, "Bill you made a good point about that list being discriminatory." Afterwards one of the Governors talked to me about amending the resolution. At dinner a couple of gentlemen said they liked my comments. The first item the next day was amendments to the resolution and the final decision to just remove the entire offending paragraph. By then my tooth wasn't hurting any more. A few more presentations, dinner, entertainment, sound sleep and then off to the airport to meet Ken.

The brother, who was housing me, dropped me off early at the airport and I waited in the sunshine out front for my hunk. He appeared on time. We settled down to a table at the nearest restaurant.

"So, I got something to tell you," I started. "My best friend and I both travel a lot on business and don't get to see one another. So we write one another. One time I signed my note to him `Love, Bill `. Next time I see him he says that real men don't say `I love you' to one another. I think about that for a couple of days and then I tell him, `So, it's okay for me to love tequila. I can love my dog. But I can't love my best friend. Isn't that the definition of "best friend" the friend you love best. I love you. Deal with it'."

"And you are telling me this story why?" Ken asks with a grin.

"'Cause I love you, Ken. Deal with it."

"I love you too, Bill. It just took me longer to get here is all."

We chat, order, drink, rub thighs beneath the table, lean into one another, make eyes and then I say, "Did I ever tell you about Ray's trip to California?" Big-Ray was a mutual "acquaintance" of ours in Seattle. "Apparently he hadn't been getting any in Seattle and decided to make up for lost time when he and his buddies went on vacation. They started calling him `The Whore of Babylon'. Even got a blow job in Disneyland."

"What?" Ken whispered intently, his eyes squinting as a slier version of his habitual smile crept onto his face. He leaned towards me to hear and his outer thigh pressed more warmly against mine beneath the table.

"Yeah, some guy was checking him out on 'Main Street USA', so much so that the next thing Big-Ray hears is a postcard rack hitting the ground when the guy ran into it. That broke the ice. The guy says, 'You want a blow job? I know a place.' He had a key to some room." I casually went back to eating my lunch.

"I don't know of anything like that around the airport," he whispered. "The only keys I've got are for inside the security area. And I'm still new enough, I wouldn't know about any other places. Sorry."

"Cool," and we continued chatting and picking at our lunches.

"If you are done. Let's go for a walk," he suggested, thumbing towards outside where he could smoke.

I thought about stopping to relieve myself, but didn't. We ended up in the basement of the open air parking structure. He lit up and kept strolling. The concrete structure was cooled by breezes passing thru its chain link fence walls. The sunlight came in so forcibly on the sides of the structure that the flowering bushes and grass had worked their way in, perfuming the air and tinting the light. We walked through the few cars parked there and headed toward the open stairwell at the back. I thought… "Nah!"

As we walked through the open doorway into the stair well, Ken grabbed my left arm and swung my backside into the corner, he sandwiched me against the wall and his wet lips descended to mine. I couldn't believe it. My puckered lips were forced apart by a grin and then his tongue. The bittersweet taste of tobacco overpowered my mouth. The cigarette smoke still clung to his beard and collar. I grabbed him by the shoulders and held him as tightly as his enormous frame pressed me against the cool gray concrete.

"This is going to be one hell of a make out session," I thought.

But that hard thing in his pants pressing insistently into my abdomen told me that was a lie. I managed to move my right hand between our thrusting bodies and felt his hard cock tearing at the sheer fabric of his black TSA dress pants. "Okay, blowjob like in Disneyland," I thought, as Ken continued to press our bodies and lips together.

I began fumbling with his belt and sliding towards the floor, but when he eased his body off of mind it was to unbuckle my pants.

"Turn around," he said.

"No way!" burst out of me as the grin burst on my face.

"Yes!" he laughed.

He turned me to the corner. I pulled my Levis and shorts down over my ass and lifted my shirt tail. He pulled his slacks and bikini briefs to his thighs, spit on his huge cock, spit on his hand to lube his cock, grabbed it and started guiding it in. My ass was still wide open from the reaming he'd given me three nights before, but I should have squatted over the toilet before following my big hunk out here.

He didn't seem fazed by the extra "traction". His cock plowed its way into my hungry butt.

"Yeah, yeah, Bill." he grunted

His cock in my tight ass, his massive hands on my thigh; it felt great! Pleasure flowed through my veins. I put my hands on the wall and pushed off as I arched my back so he would reach that perfect spot.

"Oh, yeah!" I crowed when the huge knob of his invading prick crushed against my prostate.

Ken reached around my pelvis for a better grip and found my hard dick waiting there. He stroked it with the palm of his massive paw thru the fabric of my tighty whities. Then grabbed my hips and started with short, urgent, frantic strokes here in the open air stairwell rather than his long hard ones of his bed.

A car door slammed nearby. We stopped. I reached for my pants. "No, no, no," Ken whispered. His hands moving to my shoulders, massaging them, bend me over more. Distant footsteps moved further away from us. My boyfriend went back to his fast and furious short strokes in and out of my ass. I couldn't stand it any longer. I wedged my shoulder into the corner of the wall, braced my galloping body with my left hand and reached into my shorts. My cock was harder than it had been in years. I wrapped my fingers around and started stroking the shaft while the head trapped in my shorts made out with the soft fabric. It wasn't long and I was shooting hot sticky globs inside my briefs. I could feel my sphincter muscle twitching around Ken's thick pole.

"We got to go," I panted.

"No."

"I'll miss my flight."

"Damn."

We dressed and headed for security, hitting the bathroom along the way so Ken could take two soapy hand towels into the stall and clean himself up.

"That was great!" he told me as we headed for the gate. "You must have loved it. You were hard. You're never hard when I fuck you."

"Sorry, we didn't have longer," I felt guilty about me coming and him not.

"I could have hurried it this time. Damn, that was great!"

We got to the gate in time for Ken to meet the benevolent and loyal brothers who'd traveled with me. As they loaded on the plane, it gave us one last moment together. We fumbled through a handshake and then gave up and hugged. He walked me the final steps to the gate.

"I was great spending time with you. I wish we'd had more time together," he said in his warm soft voice.

"Yeah, buddy, except for the time I spent with you the whole trip was a waste."

"Oh, I don't know, sounds to me like you got up and said a few things to the Grand Lodge convention, 'cause that toothache made you cranky. Then they removed the stuff you complained about."

"Oh…yeah…that."

NOT IN MY NATURE

PART 1

Tuesday Night

"Oh, oh, no teeth. Okay?" Tom whispered.

Bill mumbled, okay, as he continued to deep throat Tom's eight-inch member. It tasted surprisingly clean considering the heat. He tried to get a better angle for his oral assault on the big guy.

Bill bent over about as far as he could go in the tight confines of the oven-like booth. His dress shirt grew wet from exertion and the heat. With his free hand he lifted the standing man's t-shirt and ran his fingers across the fuzz on Tom's chest and belly. By the flickering light of the booth's video screen, Bill saw blonde hair covered the bigger man's body.

Tom pulled Bill to his feet, squatted and proceeded to suck on Bill's wiener with such vacuum-like intensity that Bill squirmed in pain. Tom's thick fingers first cupped Bill's ass cheeks then spread his crack and began probing for his hole. Looking down at the big man in the flickering light, Bill massaged his shoulders as he slurped away.

"I so, want you in my ass, but..." then Bill's whisper faded.

"You know we have a policy! Only one guy in a booth. There are two of you in there! Come out!"

"Okay. We're coming out," Tom responded quickly, pulling up his pants.

"I'll meet you out front," he whispered to Bill's nodding approval. Tom had had this happen before.

Bill froze in surprise at first. Then quickly buttoned the shirt Tom had opened, pulled his Levis off the floor and got dressed. He kept his eyes firmly on the floor on the way out.

"That was embarrassing!"

"Yeah! Beer?"

The two tall men went to a restaurant overlooking the market and slid into a booth opposite one another. Tom appeared probably 40 years old in contrast to Bill's 46 years, short blonde hair, green seductive eyes, and broad shoulders. He was beefy and lounged in the booth sensually. His gold earrings gave him another touch of something enticing.

Bill was in town for minor surgery. Tom's backpack revealed his homelessness. Bill didn't know if it was his age or the age in general, but during the last three trips to an arcade homeless guys hit him up on. He blushed in shame when seeing the pack, but homelessness like shortness turned him off. Half of Bill's delight in getting laid was that someone wanted him, not his hotel room.

Besides, during the layover in route to Seattle, the night before, he'd gotten an hour-long fuck from a 6'7" Russell Crowe look-alike. It wasn't in his nature to say "No, thanks." But Bill paid for the drinks, made some plausible excuse, thanked Tom for the fun and continued his tour of Seattle.

Next stop, "The Bond". Bill walked through the sparsely populated front bar for the patio.

"Hello," said a smiling open-faced big boy with a shaved head and big grin.

"Hi," Bill replied with a smile. "How's it going?"

"Fine."

Bill leaned against the wall admiring the man's lean frame. "Can I buy you a beer?"

They walked to the bar and straddled two stools. Steve's hand immediately went to Bill's crotch. Bill's eyebrows popped up in surprise.

"When I see what I want I go for it!"

"Really?"

"Did you notice my orange bandana?"

"I thought it was a red banana in your left pocket."

"Yeah, I'm into peeing and fisting. It was the best moment of my life when I finally got a fist up my ass. You'll see," he assured Bill with a gentle pat on his thigh.

It wasn't in Bill nature to say "I can't be your huckleberry." But he made an exception in Steve's case.

Final stop for the night; Seattle Baths, just to check them out. After all who'd expect any action early on a Tuesday night. Bill walked up the terraced seating above the big screen television, checked out the playrooms and shower and then circled back to the locker rooms. As Bill suspected nothing going on – until he

walked by an open door where the proverbial corn-fed farm boy laid on his back and was getting it from an older gray-haired guy.

The top proudly waved Bill in and twisted his buddy's bottom around so Bill could get a better view of his six-inch cock sliding in and out. Bill took every opportunity to suck the bottom's thicker six-incher that their positions allowed. The top played with Bill's ass during such moments, but never too aggressively. Finally, Bill stepped to the far end of the bed and Farmer Jones returned the favor for a while, slurping away at his precum dripping hardon.

Bill gave up his spot to a young Latino long, dark, thin erection and took a walk. When he returned the old timer was pumping away in a climactic frenzy. "Uh, oh, yeah, boy, take my load. I'm cumming!" he grunted as he finished in a red-faced sweat. He spun the farm boy around, so the Latino with his broad shoulders, flat top haircut and that eight-inch hard dick could start up.

Bill got a little more head from the writhing blond, who was obviously getting his prostate prodded by his swarthy ass-fucker. Pulling Bill's cock from his mouth, he breathlessly rasped at the Latin. "Oh, baby, fuck me hard. I'm ready. Yeah, yeah, give me the load."

The Latino pulled back on the young blonds hips, purred through his ass-flooding orgasm and grabbed the farm boy's waving, half-hard pecker. A few quick strokes and the boy's dick rose and spat. Within seconds, Bill jerked to climax and spewed thick, white juice on the boy's face. "Mmm," the bottom lad moaned, leaning into Bill's crotch to suck out the last drops.

Bill thanked the athletic pair for a great show.

It was not in his nature to be impolite.

PART 2

Wednesday

Bill saw his doctors during the day Wednesday and they planned on his minor surgery for Friday. That evening Bill planned a few beers at the Bond before attending the special event at Club A.

The rump ramming he'd gotten from the Southeastern giant two nights before had almost worn off. However, he'd enjoyed a great blowjob last night, so Bill wasn't particularly horny and gave his thoughts over to the soul searching that usually accompanies planned surgery, however minor. He absently spoke with these neighbors on the Bond's back patio. The closest one, wore a faded plain green t-shirts and old shorts. He told Bill, "I dumped my lover last week." With a perplexed twist of his brow he added, "He seemed happier about the whole thing than me."

The sad tale-teller was over-weight and slouched. Neither he nor Bill talked excitedly nor seemed particularly interested in the passing parade of manly beauty. Someone rather annoying joined them. He wore an orange banana in his left rear pocket. Bill said, "I need a new beer."

Shortly after that, his neighbor needed to use the bathroom. When resettled at the front bar Bill saw his former neighbor across the bar. They nodded to one another. And Bill went back to exchanging admiring glances with the passing man meat.

When Bill actually needed a beer, he stopped to ask his old neighbor, "Leave the patio because of the company? Or for this better view?"

His neighbor mumbled something inconsequential, commented, "I'm tired and it's late." Then added, "If you want to, we could go to my place and jerk off. I'm too tired to fuck."

"It's not in my nature to say, no, thanks, but that's the least enthusiastic proposition I've ever gotten."

"Sorry, I'm really tired."

"Let's try sometime when you're not so tired."

When Bill made it to the bar for the beer, someone said, "Hello. We spoke on the patio."

Joe was loud and funny, drunk, sinewy and tan, and eventually asked, "Want to go to Club A with me?"

It wasn't in Bill's nature to say "no, thanks." When they checked in at the bathhouse, Joe of the hairy chest wrote his phone number on Bill's pass, "in case we get separated inside." Once changed into their towels he suggested they start in the video room. A nice cross section of guys prowled the carpeted halls. Some big-muscled guys graced the outer chamber of the video area.

Bill and his buddy found a carpeted bench. Bill was just getting comfortable – and a bit aroused – watching some bronzed god on the screen laying on his side, knee in the air getting it in the ass. Joe pried open his towel and stared sucking Bill's hardening six inches. Bill watched the guy on the screen start sucking the cock of someone off-screen while continuing to get it up the ass. Joe was already totally nude, so Bill flipped around and much to the delight of the gathering crowd started sixty-nining with Joe.

Bill being a bottom and Joe too drunk, nothing climactic came of their crowd-arousing efforts, so Bill suggested they check out the playroom.

"Yeah, I want to see how they remodeled it."

The major improvement was glory holes on a raised platform. Joe went promptly to the long curved thin dick offered there and started slurping and licking.

"Bill!" he called, pulling his buddy over. They took turns. one sucking the head, while the other licked the shaft. Soon the love Popsicle started shoving itself in and out of their faces. Big balls with curly pubes tried to slam themselves through the hole after their cock.

"Hey, you guys going to be here for a while?" A sandy-haired jock with dimpled chin, muscular frame and a well-formed chest covered in curly brown hair peered from over his cock at them. "This is great, but I gotta fuck."

"We can help you there."

"No, I gotta meet someone. You guys gonna be here?"

Joe assured them they would. Behind them two black guys; one with big muscles and a ridiculously huge dick were trying unsuccessfully to fuck on a small bench. Joe collapsed there and Bill knelt between his thighs. Other guys leaned over Bill to watch him lick Joe's dick and long hairy balls.

"Maybe we should go to the maze," Joe said, rising and leading Bill into the darker corridor next door. There they were free to suck one another off without a crowd towering over.

"Let's go down again," Bill suggested.

"Ah, okay."

But at the bottom of the stairs, Joe wasn't there. Bill went on into watch the video and wait for Joe. The film was at the exact same place as his last visit. Two other patrons shared the room. One from the rough trade completely covering his cock and the fist stroking it with his towel. The other was a big dark-haired boy, twenty years younger. Bill assumed there would be no interest from that side of the room.

Realizing he'd seen the film before, Bill got up to leave. The big boy was now stretched out naked. With a smile and a wave of his wang, he offered his hard cock. Bill curled up on the bench next to the big smooth body and went down on the hard eight-inch clean cock.

"Wow!" he mumbled between slurps, sucks and licks. He moved to David's face and did the one thing almost forbidden in a bathhouse, kissed the boy. David responded likewise.

"So you like to kiss. What else do you like to do?"

"Want to come to my room and find out?"

It wasn't in Bill nature to say, "No, thanks."

In David's cubicle they quickly decided on doggy style with Bill on all fours gleefully smiling into the mirror at the head of the bed. David stood behind with a glob of goo on his sheathed rod. "Lower your ass a little, Bill. I'll just put it in and let you do the rest."

He pressed the head of his rock hard cock down the crack of Bill's big white ass and forced it in Bill's hole. David rocked his cock in and out slightly while keeping his slim thighs rock solid. Bill groaned and squirmed, eventually pushing into David's thighs.

"Yeah, oh, yeah." he said encouragingly as David's guiding hands landed gently on his ass cheeks. They kept gently rocking towards one another.

"Okay, all the way in now," said Bill, turning to see the younger man's pleasure twisted face. He sighed with relief when David obliged, sending his thick eight inches right in past Bill's prostate.

"Oh, Bill, You've got such a great ass." Bill looked in the mirror. David's eyes were glassed and staring down, watching his thick white cock pound Bill's brown hole. His breathing was ragged and huffy.

David kept up the rhythm. Bill wiggled and writhed beneath him making appreciative noises.

"Bill, that was great," The big boy gasped, while continuing to pound away.

"You came?" Bill asked.

"Couldn't you tell? Oh, I'm wearing a condom," the top said still driving in and out.

"You're still hard."

"Yeah. But I got to lay down."

Bill made room on the narrow bed for David and the hot clammy body fell into his arms. They kissed and cuddled waiting for the young man to fully regain his strength.

"Wow, Bill, you are great. Most guys are just, 'Wham bam, thank you ma'am'."

"Then I'd miss seconds," Bill whispered back.

As they spoke, the gents in the neighboring booth had gotten louder, the bed began to bang rhythmically against the dividing partition. The air and their loud efforts were punctuated with "Suck that cock, bitch. Suck that cock."

In unison Bill and David reached for their units. Between David's long passionate kisses and the rising symphony of lovemaking next-door, Bill's smaller pecker spewed in no time, unloading its initial burst on David's chest with the rest running down his pounding fist onto his tight balls. David with determined strokes came again soon after. Bill, feeling the drowsiness overpowering him, started to speak and then thought better of it.

"Go ahead, baby, say it."

"I didn't want to go and spoil the moment by saying something stupid. But would you like to go to my hotel with me?"

By the time they got there it was 3 in the morning. The drowsiness that prompted their journey promptly ended it in their mutual slumber. They woke early to kiss and cuddle. Bill moved to the foot of the bed kneeling over David's long white body stretched out in the morning light. He began by licking and kissing the top of the top's rising dong while pinching hard on David's nipples. His lapping tongue began to work its way down the hard white shaft towards the long sparsely haired balls. Bill hefted David's light thighs onto his shoulders exposing his balls above the little brown hole.

"Go for it. Please do it." David moaned.

As Bill 's tongue continued to work downward the young man quickly grabbed his own knees and pulled them up and apart to rest above his shoulders widening his ass for Bill's attack. Encouraged by the moans of delight inspired by his tongue's probe of the top's bottom, he spit on the middle finger of his right hand and worked the digit up as far as the whimpers of pleasure directed. Then abandoning his drilling operation with finger still in place, Bill went back to sucking the top's perfect cock.

In a short time either because he was close or overwhelmed by his pleasure, the big boy eased the finger out of him, pried the tongue off, rolled the bottom onto his back, penned his shoulders to the bed, lifted the older man's legs with the pressure of his lean hot thighs and – the phone rang.

Bill had to take the call; it was probably his doctors about his surgery His lover laid back down beside him, Bill quickly dealt with the call and said, "Where were we?"

A few long kisses and strokes from Bill and they were ready. "I want you on top this time,." the top told him. Bill straddled the younger man and almost effortlessly slid down his fat cock. The headboard swayed to and fro as Bill rose and dove on that hard slab of meat. He leaned back to improve the angle of attack. They laced fingers and he leaned back even further. The bedsprings began to creak and David grunted over the fucking. "Oh, yes, oh, Bill. Your ass feels so good. Mmm. Feels…so….good…"

He began rapid thrusts into Bill's well-lubed ass while Bill enjoyed the ride and concentrated on dry humping David's little round belly. When David's breathing rose to a fevered pitch he pulled Bill down for one final kiss. "Uh, uh, uh, gonna cum…yeah, Now!" His thick cock spurted hotly into the condom in Bill's ass. His cock popped out of Bill, who gasped. David pulled him to the bed snapped off the condom and stroked Bill's throbbing cock to climax before releasing his lip lock on his lover.

Bill began fasting and visiting his doctors. David went to work, but not before promising to meet Bill at "Hour Place" to help him prepare for the surgery.

It was not in Bill's nature to refuse the ardent attentions of his new friend.

.

ON THE WAY TO SEATTLE

Where to start? I suppose I can begin with the morning I got ready to fly.

I was surprised Jerry's front door was unlocked. I wasn't surprised to see him bound down the stairs, naked, water still clinging to his tight muscular little body, his thinning dark hair with the streak of white still wet, his chest and body flush from the hot caress of water coming from the shower upstairs. What did surprise me was the blush on his cheeks (the upper ones) and the delight on his face.

I was surprised, after I'd stripped and we'd poked a video in to the VCR that his glance fell more often upon my 6'1" frame stretched out on his couch than on the big-breasted babe and long-haired jock on the screen. Ends up I'm not the only one he's bonking regularly. He confessed to having an affair with a local woman.

"Want to see her picture?" he said, leading me to his computer. I knelt beside his chair as he moused his way to her digital photo. We both praised her big round tits while our hands found one another's cocks. He's got a thick 7 incher, me a lame 6 incher. My lips replaced my hand quickly enough. Fresh from the shower, his human popsicle was flavorless and it took me a while to work a taste of precum out of him.

Jerry was hard when his hands slipped under my arms and urged me erect. I assume he was guiding me into his favorite position – me bent over the couch, him kneeling on a cushion behind my ass. Instead he raised my lips to his. He kissed me full and long, then went to nibbling at my throat and neck.

I returned the favor, growling in the small of his neck and slipping my tongue in his ear. Our hands ground hard into the knots on one another's backs, forcing groans from our busy lips. He reached below and adjusted his dick to slip beneath my balls. I squeezed my thighs together and he began to stroke his pre-cum covered cock against them as my peter ground into his belly. Our cocks grew hard, our grip on one another grew tighter and more forceful. Our lips met more often and longer. His worked their way down my chest and licked lightly at my left nipple, then kept heading south.

I rolled back on the floor against the couch to accommodate his mouth's walkabout. So imagine my surprise when he forced his cock straight down in my mouth. His right hand then reached for my groin, squeezed my cock and balls tight, and began stretching and stroking the whole package away from my body the opposite from the way my cock wanted to spring. His left hand held my head firmly against the couch and he squat thrusted his tasty meat down to the back of my throat.

My tongue followed it out on each stroke, sucking all the juice and flavor it could. I couldn't resist grabbing my cock from his hand, as he pounded my longing face furiously, I jerked off.

My body thrashed in ecstasy as I convulsed with each spasm of cum, but he held my head tight and kept face fucking me. As the cum on my body began to cool and the taste of his rod grew stale, my body began to ache and I had to get up. He drew me into his arms and we began to kiss again. He hugged me desperately as I stroked his cock, the slippery head wedged up against my thigh. The mushroom at the end of his rod flared with each stroke, his breath becoming more rapid, his whispers of "yeah, yeah, yeah" becoming shouts and cries. And then a gush of cum, gush of cum, gush of cum until the upper half of my right leg was covered and Jerry leaned exhausted in my arms.

A couple hours later I was on the jet headed to Seattle.

PRIAPUS:
SEVEN SHORT ADVENTURES

Chapter 1: Paul's Untrampled Tranquility

Paul stretched out his naked left arm and placed the folded flannel shirt on the conveniently located branch of the pine that shaded them. The new born sun spewed hot shafts of light into the meadow before him. The wet grass steamed in its embrace.

Somewhere a bird twittered, but nothing trampled the tranquility of the moment or disturbed the grass. Well, nothing except Chubby-Ray's face sliding back and forth on his six-inch schlong and the sounds of hungry slurping. Paul's pants laid at his ankles making him appear totally naked in the rising sun. Chubby-Ray was fully dressed on his knees before the younger taller man.

What a perfect way to start the day. And the best part of having Chubby-Ray as a playmate was he enjoyed getting his face fucked. His thick moustache and bushy goatee made a great cushion to bounce a beer belly and hanging balls on. Chubby-Ray had one hand playing with the taller man's ass (he liked that) while the other hand's thumb and finger stroked the shaft.

The bottom's tongue rolled the head of Paul's rod around inside the cave of his words. The sun stirred the air above and the air lifted the scented pollen off the pines curtaining the still meadow. Paul sucked it deep into his lungs as he gasped in delight.

Paul leaned down, and with arms outstretched put his whole weight on the modern day satyr's stout shoulders.

"Oh, yeah, just like that, buddy."

Then he started rolling his hips as erotic scenes rolled through his mind's eyes floating wistfully above the lush green park before him. He mumbled encouragement as his balls started rapping the bottom's goatee and his belly slammed the satyr's face.

A stubby finger tentatively prods his ass.

"Oh yeah!" Paul shouted to the mountain above which echoed back with encouragement. As Paul's pounding became more brutal, the satyr placed his free hand on the fairer man's thighs for bracing and let Paul's hands keep his head in place for the repeated assaults.

Paul liked the experienced cocksucker's complacency, liked that finger up his ass.

"Oh yeah," he moaned again.

He bent his knees and pulled the head in his crotch into the perfect position for a rapid ramming. His ardent fellator complied and let Paul shove his stiffening rod to the back of throat.

"Oh, yeah. Oh yeah." Paul muttered over and over. He pulled the curly black head tight in against his cock and unloaded deep inside.

"What a way to start the day!"

Chapter 2: Ricky's Rumpus Room

Right in back of the men's upstairs bathroom, a door provides access to the water heater, but that bathroom is often used. The janitor's closet is out as a locale for clandestine sex because it's in the middle of a large open office area. There are no back rooms, not even a little used storeroom attached to the main office. There are a few private offices, but Bill and Ricky couldn't use them without drawing attention to themselves.

There is however, the little used main warehouse across town. Bill had to lug equipment in and out of there on a weekly basis. Ricky, the new guy in the office, got stuck overseeing the contract used to rent the place. Nothing odd about them being there at the same place.

"What're you doing Bill?" the taller black man asked.

"Putting equipment back." answered the tall Swede wearing a flannel shirt.

"You all need some help?" Ricky asked with practiced voice.

Bill handed him a few swivels. They were the cleanest of his equipment and least inclined to spoil the other man's expensive winter coat. One in flat black shoes and the other in cowboy boots, the two men climbed the stairs, deposited the rigging on the appropriate shelves, and then Bill lead the way.

It was an out-of-the-way office in the mostly abandoned warehouse. Anyone walking by, not that anyone did, would think it a closet. Bill pushed open the door, then stepped back so Ricky could enter. He actually had to guide him in. A little "oh" escaped the newcomer's lips. Bill turned on a dim desk lamp and closed the door behind them.

"Aren't you worried someone will hear us?"

"Not if you stop talking and start…"

Bill's thin dry lips pressed into Ricky's large wetly erotic lips. He grabbed the lapels of the other's down coat and pulled the black man closer. Ricky was a wet kisser. That settled, Bill's calloused right hand reached beneath the heavy winter coat and felt through the soft fabric of his slacks for Ricky's cock. Bill broke from the kiss with a smothered laugh.

"Oh, you are ready to go!"

With that he leaned back and started unbuttoning the cuffs of his shirt.

"Honey, we shouldn't undress," growled the black man. "Just in case. Turn around and drop your drawers. I'll do the rest."

Bill complied, his belt less pants hitting the floor noiselessly. Hands out he leaned forward against the wall opposite the desk. Ricky raised his shirt tail to view a round white butt ready for ramming. Over his shoulder Bill could barely see the kinky pubic hairy sticking out from under Ricky's dress shirt, the balls hidden below in the darkness of his thighs, his cock tenting the dress shirt above.

Large black hands pulled Astroglide out of the coat pocket. In the semi-dark Bill heard and smelled Ricky fumble with the lube one handed. A second later Ricky's long fingers pried Bill's ass cheeks apart allowing the lubed up forefinger to enter. Bill made no sound, but his smile assured Ricky.

Two fingers were a little more painful, but the white guy rode them gleefully in a very short time. Then came the tug-of-war as his big toothy grin and his gooey hand tried to tear open the condom. It took both the large man's hands to roll it on and the same pair to force his slicked up 8 inches into Bill's waiting backside.

The ensuing grunt was somewhere between a gasp and a sigh. Bill hid the pain from Ricky by turning his face to the wall. The coat wearing top was too busy staring heavenward in delight.

A guttural "Oh!" escaped Ricky's thick drooling lips. As his hips began rocking back and forth the "oh" turned into a truncated howl with each thrust. Each howl growing loader than the last as his black dick grew harder. As pain gave way to pleasure Bill realized that the guys working down stairs might eventually hear this.

"Ricky!" he admonished.

"Sorry man. I'm a howler."

Bill bent over even more to find something in the desk draw, then turned back to the bigger man. The thick black rod popped out of the tight hole eliciting a gasp from Bill and "ah" from Ricky.

"Bite this." It was a pencil. Ricky obeyed. Bill kicked out of his pants and cowboy boots. Then ducking under the overhanging cupboard he scooted under on his back, until he was resting comfortable on the desk. Ricky lifted the bottoms left leg and forced his thick rod back in.

With Bill's ankle on his right shoulder, Ricky went back to rocking his rod in and out of the tight ass, his howls turned into hisses of joy by the pencil.

The sweet aroma of sweat wafted out of Ricky's coat. He rested his tottering head against the overhanging cabinets to brace himself and started pulling Bill towards him with each lunge of his cock.

He salivated like crazy, his drool dripping onto Bill's bare smooth chest. One of Bill's hands was playing with the nearest nipple and stroking the stubble field of kinky hair on Rick's chest.

The excited irregular thrusts moved Bill further under the overhanging cabinets and Ricky didn't have enough leverage on the one leg to pull him out.

Ricky spit out the pencil. "Get down on the floor, darling," the 6'7" black man requested. "All fours."

His own pants fell, his belt or something hit the garbage can and now half naked, he squatted over Bill's ass and penetrated him from above. Bill grunted in pain this time.

"Sorry, darling. You'll be okay. Okay?" Ricky asked without really meaning it. He grabbed the underside of the desk and started driving his full weight in and out of Bill's hole, driving deeper than ever before.

Bill started stroking his short limp cock below. "No, sugar. No, wait until I'm done." Prying Bill's right hand out and pressing it to the floor with his big black hand on top.

"Here, I come honey. Here I come." Ricky's thighs clamped onto Bill's body to hold the quivering bottom in place, while waiting for relief. The jizm came in waves, each accompanied by Ricky's body's trembling groan. Bill could feel his love canal getting juicer.

When Ricky got his breath back, he asked Bill to come. They lay on their sides, spooning, Ricky's big black cock still wedge way up Bill's behind. They took turns jerking his dick until he complied with Ricky's request with two spasms of white cum on the floor.

As they crawled up off the floor and started putting their pants on, Bill noticed the condom all ready in the garbage can.

"Honey," Ricky whispered. "I've got to go clean up now. But we've got to make this a regular thing, okay?"

Chapter 3: I'm Going to Call you 'Ill

"I'm going to call you 'Ill," I slurred.

"Why's that?" he asked with that grin that always seemed to grace his face when I was around. He stared at me straight on, his pointed chin and pointed nose down, showing off his buzz cut.

"Well, originally when we met, I thought your name was Bill Gates. Hence you are buying the tequila tonight." There'd been 5 shots of Jose Cuervo lined up for me when I met him in the lounge of our hotel. "Of course, your name is Gill Bates. But I have Bill Gates in my head, so I always screw it up. I'll just call you 'Ill and that will solve everything."

"You can call me anything you want, buddy. Just don't call me late for dinner – or sex. Speaking of which…I'm buying you dessert, too. Anything your heart desires."

"Nah.," I objected.

"No, no. It's just the new guy's way of saying thanks. Your friendship has meant more to me than you will ever know." I almost teared up at that. "What's your fave?"

Somehow, I let slip my fondness for Kahlua and cream. I might have also mentioned the aphrodisiacal affects it had on me. Kahlua and cream came with my Black-Forest dessert. 'Ill shared it with me. Feeding me with his own fork. His piercing steel-blue eyes stayed on mine, ignoring the looks and movements of everyone else in the dining room. The Kahlua and cream kept on coming.

"I hear you are going back to college?"

At which point he let me ramble on and on about the degree I intended to get in classical studies and my interest in Greek mythology.

"Tell me some stories about Aphrodite," he requested. Which I did with him warming to the tale of she and Ares caught in the net and the other male gods getting to enjoy the show. Priapus got mentioned somewhere in there and I had to tell all about the scarecrow that doubled as a dildo. Then Ganymede and Zeus. Achilles and Patroculus.

Gill giggled throughout, but his eyes gleamed with each telling. He'd pat me on the back or slap me on the thigh at all the best parts. There's nothing like an appreciative audience to get me going.

He regaled me with a tale about getting caught with a honey, him and one other guy, when the rest of the fraternity came home early from the game. So, with a little tickling I bragged about me, the manager and the waitress behind the salad bar.

Gill straightened out the fabric in his crotch. "It's time to go. They want to close."

I had a hard time navigating through the chairs and tables in the lounge and Gill gladly hugged me to his side to keep me up right. In the elevator I fell back against the wall, pulling him atop me. His face smashed into mine, nose to nose, lips to lips. He laughed. I laughed. He bent his lips to mine, I pulled his head closer.

The doors parted. He parted our embrace with a fake jab with his right and tickle to my ribs with his left. His right arm held me up as we advanced on his room, his left grabbed at my balls and gave them a shake, pinched around in search of my nipples, gave me a wet willey and slid his middle finger in and out of my mouth, jokingly.

He unlocked the door, held it open with his right hand and pushed my ass in with his left, drilling for my hole in the process.

"Damn you are fine," he muttered in the dark. With his left hand in the small of my back, he pulled my crotch into his while his right hand searched out my face and index finger marked his place up on my lips.

"Everyone must want you! What a great body!"

His lips advanced on mine. His right hand kept my head in place. His left hand went back to feeling for my asshole thru the denim.

"Yeah!" he shouted as he broke from out kiss with a gasp.

"Here," and he ripped my shirt over my head.

As my hands fell back down, his muscular shoulders were already bare. He worked my belt loose, unbuckled my pants, yanked my fly open, his left hand snaked down the crack of my ass, his right grabbed my chin and his tongue dove for my throat.

"Ain't this fun! I know everyone at work wants to do this with you. Come on!"

In the dark he grabbed my hand and skipped to the queen size bed. I think he was squatting barefoot on the bed; I fell dizzily on my back. He lifted my right arm while holding onto my pants with his left. His little pink tongue found my arm pit. I screamed jokingly and tried to wiggle away.

His tongue next found my left nip and I wiggled even more, only succeeding in wiggling out of my pants. I could hear Gill digging around in the bed stand in the dark, maybe taking off his pants. All I really heard was how much fun we were going to have. How much he'd been looking forward to spending time with me. How manly I was.

He slid between my legs. His shoulders rolled my knees up towards mine as his tongue made its way from my cock to my lips.

"You are going to be so much fun."

I knew his cock was trying to get in my ass, but my whirling head was overwhelmed by his tongue in my mouth, his shoulders pinning me to the bed, the smothered giggles coming from our mouths' embrace, our bodies wrestling around on the bed.

I didn't notice until he was all the way in and beginning to fuck me. The last of the Kahlua took effect about then and the tequila caught up with me. I woke to Gill spooning me, with his cock still up my ass. He said we did it three times. We've definitely done it that many times since that night – and I remember the feeling much better.

Chapter 4; Andy Hunting Love

"Bill! What were you doing out there shivering at 4:30 in the morning?"

"Didn't want my wife waking up when this rattle trap old Volkswagen van of yours came around the corner. So, I took my shotgun, duck decoys and pack out front under the eaves of the house, to wait."

"Jesus! Your teeth still chattering? I should have given you this when you got in the van. Spread your legs. Got them nice and wide? Let me check. Hold still. Here you go. A nice warm thermos of coffee all for you."

"You want some, Andy?"

"Nah, finished off a pot before I came to get you."

"Wow! Lot more than just coffee here!"

"It's Kahlua, you love that, I know. Down that first cup. That'll warm you up. Let me help tip that cup for you... Chug a lug, chug a lug, buddy. Damn!"

"What?"

"I'm not trying to hit on you, Bill, but, damn, I am so horny. I got to adjust my shorts."

"Roads kind of rough, Andy. You need a hand with the wheel while you are playing with that thing?"

"Yeah, you can give me a hand alright. Ha ha! Yeah, take the wheel, so I can unbuckle my pants. Yeah, I can stroke this thing with one hand and drive with the other."

"Looks like it might be best with two hands on that thing," I said, staring at the long fleshy tube poking upward from his open fly. "Just past this rise, there's

a little overgrown road on the right. Why don't you drive in there a bit and shut off the engine?"

"Hey, you got your hand on my leg, why don't you get to it, while I'm driving?" Andy said, his husky voice betraying the sexual thrill he was feeling." I wrapped my hand around the thick, hot hunk of meat, feeling it twitch with excitement.

"Whoa! T'aint much road. Okay, we're here and I'm turning off the lights."

"Now what, Andy? You want me to just keep pulling on your cock?"

"Remember that trip we made to the state capitol together? How we made out on the ferry on the way up there? I took my hands and put them over your ears like this and turned your head and told you I loved you and kissed…like that. Then turned your head and… like that. And then kissed… you…for… a…very… long… time…."

"Sorry buddy, this ain't doing it. I'm still horny. Remember that time after the hot tub when we were taking a shower and you got down on your knees cause you thought I wanted a blow job? Remember that?"

"Yeah."

"Let me scoot my pants down to my knees and turn in the seat, because this time I want that blowjob. I know you want to do it. Come on. It's kind of dark, I'll guide your head over. Pull your pants down, so I can play with your little dick too. Oh yeah, Bill. Oh yeah. Whole thing in your mouth. I love that. Oh, oh, I love you licking the shaft, too."

"Mmm…" It was all I could respond with that fat hot cock deep in my mouth.

"Oh buddy, oh buddy, Bill, I love you. Know what though, I can barely play with your cock in this position. Let's get in the back. I'm taking off my pants. You, too.

"We can get on these sleeping bags I laid out. What a buddy! Lick that thing. Yeah, yeah. I'm going to drag your ass around here. I'm going to slick up my hand with Astroglide and massage your balls and cock at the same time.

"…Like that? I know what you really like. I'll finger fuck you. Yeah, you love that. And I love you Bill. This is great, but this ain't doing it. I'm still horny.

"The only way, I'll be happy is in you. We've got little dicks, it won't hurt at all. Come on, we'll take off all our clothes and get in these sleeping bags I zipped together.

"On your back. On your back, buddy. Oh, fuck, you are so hot! I'll kneel down here, put your knees on my shoulders and ease in. I'm so tiny, you probably won't feel it. Oh, oh, that feels so good. It's okay, buddy. I'll take it easy. Okay, okay. Hey, I'm fucking you. You've wanted this right?"

"Right!" I said, giving my ass to him as I've fantasized about so many times while jacking off in the shower.

"Let me hug you. Don't squirm so much okay? Oh, oh, this feels good. Oh Bill, that tongue in my ear. You know that drives me crazy. Oh, man, what a tight ass. Oh!"

"What?"

"Knees are starting to kill me. Lay back. I'll assume the position, like they say and so some pushups on you. Like that? Like me doing squat thrusts into you? Not really. I'm being silly. Damn, wish I threw a mattress in here."

"Let's change positions."

"What?"

"Get on your back and I'll slide down your pole. Here, let me push it back in. There! now I can just jump up and down on it or grind my dick up against your beer belly. How's that feel?"

"I'm just going to put my hands behind my head and relax. This is great. You've done this before! Oh, oh, I'm going to cum. I don't want to come inside. Lay down beside me and I'll dry hump the crack of your ass. Yeah, yeah, ah! Hold still, let me slip in the crack, back and forth, back and forth. Oh yeah! Oh yeah! I'm coming, Bill. I'm shooting on your butt."

I could feel the warm spurts of his cum. His big load dripped down my ass cheek and onto my balls.

"Ah, oh, that was great. But, I want more. I want you to cum. Cum on my hand. Come on buddy, I'll put my right arm under your head and left hand under your dick.. Come on shoot for me. Come on! Oh yeah, buddy. I'll put my tongue in your ear that will do it. Good job, buddy. Now look, now look, I'm going to lick it off my hand. You know why?"

"Why...?"

"Because I love you, buddy. I love you."

Chapter 5: Produce Guy

He was a distinguished looking gentleman; tall and broad-shouldered. He looked good in his tweed jacket. His white hairline receded with time exposing a high well-formed forehead and sharp attentive eyes. His round face accented by a white goatee carried a bemused expression.

His grocery cart held cold medicine, 7-Up, tissue, and orange sherbet. He was headed towards the bananas when the back of the produce guy caught his eye. The taller produce guy wore a tight gray uniform, stretching from his impossibly wide shoulders and muscular upper arms to narrow waist, then cut to show off his tight ass and thick thighs, clinging tightly the length of his long legs.

Tan immaculate hands moved produce from his cart to the display. As Simpson and cart approached, the produce guy turned: a square dimpled chin, 5 o'clock shadow (it was around 5) sparkling light blue eyes and a shock of shorn chestnut hair on his head just beginning to show curl.

"You're, you're…" Simpson stuttered out.

"The produce guy." The other finished with a wink while pointing at the title on his nametag. Underneath was written "Ted". He glanced about knowingly to let Simpson know to be discreet.

Simpson reached for the bell peppers as his fingers admired their firm flesh his well modulated voice continued sotto voce.

"I must say, the photo in your escort ad does not do you justice, 'Ted'. Nor does it represent your obvious intelligence and charm."

"Nor does your photo, Dr. Simpson."

Simpson's eye rose slowly, eyelids aflutter, one eyebrow raised in question. "I read your recent piece in American Classicist about Paeon healing Ares. Humor in Homer! Who could have guessed!"

"You're a classicists? I mean, thank you." Simpson's eyes had popped open big in pleasant surprise, he seemed unable to speak. Ted began to, but Simpson held up his hand requesting a pause.

"As a matter of fact there is a symposium at the university tomorrow and I'm reading that paper. My wife won't be able to attend," he said indicating the medicinal contents of his shopping cart. "So if you'd like, you can go as my guest," he finished in a rush.

Ted took his turn at looking pleasantly surprised. "A symposium among classicists. Shall I wear my toga?"

"Well, the English department joins us for this dinner, so we had to go modern. I'll be wearing a tux."

"Then so shall I."

"I'll pick you up," Simpson blushed at the expression "The university is sending a car for me."

The next evening went off like a dream for Simpson. Ted met them outside the club he'd given as an address.

"A limousine? Wow! And don't you fill out that tuxedo nice," Ted smiled.

Entering the banquet hall, Ted's height, physique and physical charm caught the attention of all the women and a good portion of the men. Everyone assumed he was one of Simpson's grad students. He was introduced by Simpson as a friend with mutual interest in classical mythology.

Ted observed that they were seated at the head table and Simpson, blushing, admitted he was the guest of honor. They sat with thighs touching the whole evening. The reading of the paper was a big hit and generated lively discussion. Simpson claiming concern for his sick wife at home, arranged for him and Ted to leave early.

"It's been a special night for you, Dr. Simpson," Ted commented.

"And I'm hoping it's just begun," the older man replied slyly.

He instructed the driver to head for the "Old Mill Room," part of the Boar's Head Resort and at the same time slipped Ted his usual fee, in crisp hundreds. Ted offered to buy the first round as they sat. Simpson excused himself momentarily and then was back, pressing a room key into the pocket of Ted's tux. Not too much later they slipped from the bar, slipped the card-key in the door and slipped into the room.

"Now, it's my turn to excuse myself."

Ted headed to the bathroom, while Simpson fiddled with the lighting and doffed his jacket. As he paced back and forth in front of the curtains, he realized that Ted had left the bathroom door open. He heard the shower running, and he felt the steam tumbling into the room.

By the time he worked up the nerve to go look, Ted was out of the shower. Droplets still clung to the curly chest hair fronting his muscular chest and rippled abdomen. A broad hand stroked the thick cotton towel across his manhood.

He was staring dreamily at the floor. The awed look on Simpson's face caught Ted by surprise. He dropped the towel, shook his wet head with a laugh, and stretched out his hands to grasp the shower curtain rod, thereby showing off this muscular arms.

"Let's make this a special night for you."

Simpson was still speechless before such naked beauty. The nine incher on his escort was already getting hard. Ted grabbed him by the suspenders to pull him closer, but Simpson had something else in mind.

The distinguished gentleman dropped to his knees and began licking the clear water droplets off Ted's brown pubic hair and impressive member. Breathing deep, Simpson lunged upon Ted's rod, trying to "deep throat" it. The back of his throat literally bounced off the hardening shaft. After gasping for air, he joined Ted's good-natured laughter.

"Let me try that. I'm a trained professional."

Ted's strong arms pulled Simpson to his feet. His hairy right hand slid into the middle of the professors back, his left hand lifted behind the professor's knees and Simpson found himself being carried to the bed. Once there, Simpson frantically fumbled with his cummerbund, much to Ted's amusement, until he had it off and his pants open. The professor had an admirable thick eight incher, which Ted promptly went down on. Cupping the long balls in his left hand and holding the shaft erect with his thumb, he expertly took the whole thing into his mouth and throat.

"Ah!" Simpson sighed giving up on the struggle to free his ankles from the pants. Ted took care of undressing the older man completely as he continued the expert blow job. Simpson got a peak of the nine incher being stroked against the bed with each stroke down of Ted's mouth. The cock was hard and glistening with pre-cum. The index finger of Ted's right hand began playing around Simpson's hole.

"I should mention I'm a virgin," the professor said with only a shadow of trepidation. Ted responded with a wink and kept on sliding his lips up and down that white slab of meat. He fiddled with Simpson's balls a bit, slid a finger in the entrance of the virgin ass.

The next thing Simpson knew, "You're sucking my balls and cock at the same time! I want you to bust my cherry tonight!"

Ted let Moby pop from his mouth. He grinned that all too charming grin, crawled up the bed so their lips could met.

As their lips parted, Ted sighed, "Dr. Simpson, lie on your side."

The professor complied. The escort began dry humping the smooth round ass, using only the pre-cum for lube. Both his arms were wrapped around the bottom-to-be. His manly hands were well lubed, one stroking the classicist's cock

and the other working his hole. In all the action and excitement the professor could smell himself breaking into a sweat, but Ted was cool, calm, passionate and persistent.

They'd already worked up to two fingers with no pain, when Ted asked, "You ready?"

In a dreamy voice the doctor begged for it. Ted rolled on one of the condoms from the nightstand and scooted in closer. Simpson cleared his voice nervously. Ted when back to massaging Simpson's knotted back muscles and dry humping his ass. As Simpson's "oh's" and "ah's" got more encouraging, Ted lifted his knees against the back of the professors knees forcing him into the fetal position, opening up his ass more.

Ted pressed the head of his long curved cock in the hole and left it there, offering words of encouragement and promising not to rush things. Simpson gasped, but assured the bigger man that everything was fine. Ted never hurried or thrusted. He just provided constant pressure until his big cock eased in with a "Thump".

"So, this is what it feels like," Simpson panted.

"It gets a lot better."

With that Ted's long frame began to ease his cock further up and then back inside the professor. Breaking his ass in slow, urging on the primordial juices, hinting at things to come, never taking his thrusts too far or too rapid.

"That's feeling good," Simpson assured him.

"Then let me show you what it's really like to get fucked in the ass."

With that he turned Simpson's face to the mattress and forced his shoulders that way too, leaving his not quite so virgin ass up in the air and exposed. Ted mounted up and started taking longer thrusts, sliding further this way and that until Simpson shouted encouragement.

"Okay, let's roll you on your back now," suggested the pro.

Ted pulled Simpson right leg up and over, turning the amateur 180 degrees below him. He moved the doctor's legs into a certain position. He lowered his heavenly tan and hairy chest upon the white field of chest hair below. His lips reached for those below. His thick, experienced rod began to pound the surface once more with lightning strokes.

Dr. Simpson was going to remember this moment for years to come. His arms rose up to embrace Ted. Ted's muscular arms pushed down into the bed and wrapped themselves around Simpson. Simpson felt himself sinking to the mattress, felt himself engulfed by their passion, felt the hardness of his own white rod waving between them, the pleasure in his ass.

It was almost an out of body experience.

"Oh my God!" he gasped.

"What?" Ted asked knowingly, his cock still steady pounding Simpson's butt.

"I can't believe it! I've read this in porn stories! Oh, my God! I'm cumming."

Chapter 6: Uncle Gene

"Gull darn! My back is flaring up on me," he groaned, as he gave me a wink they didn't see.

Uncle Eugene reckoned on getting out of dinner at his mother-in-law's. Or maybe coming up with an excuse to be alone with me. Uncle Gene wasn't actually my uncle, you know. He was my dad's best buddy and according to my mom and nana, the cutest guy in the senior class. He'd always been big (even before the arthritis) with Latin looks, an easy smile and a solid frame.

"I probably couldn't have sat thru the whole thing anyway," he sighed adjusting the pillows under his arthritic back.

I'd known Uncle Gene and his family my entire life. My brother and I spent weekends with them when we were in grade school. We shared a room with our Cousin Scott.

One visit, I don't know where my brother was, but Scott and I decided to play "you show me yours and I'll show you mine" Scott never heard his father behind him. Uncle Gene was on his way down the hall towards the bathroom. He laid his thick index finger across his lips; telling me to keep quite a while, and then watched as we stroked one another's "boyhood" and played with our hairless balls.

He gave me a wink and walked away only to return noisily. He pulled me aside later and gave me a lecture on sex. Said it was okay to check things out, but to only do it with friends, not strangers or adults. As to what he saw, that would be our little secret.

He still wore his thin white bathroom when we talked. At the end he lifted his knee up calmly revealing the dark alley of his golden thighs, his goose egg size balls rolling on the couch where he sat, his thick, purple-headed dick flinching on a bed of curly black pubic hair.

He put his leg down after I got an eyeful and reminded me; no strangers or adults. Then he winked and was on his way.

"No, you all go on and go. Bill can stay and keep me company. He doesn't know any of those people anyway."

It was Christmas break, my freshman year of college. I doubt if many of those folks would have recognized me. I stood at maximum height of 6'1", flaming red hair, a respectable start on a patriarchal beard, an albino white body covered in copper colored hair, and a wild look in my blue eyes.

I was still a bean pole, but my cock was thick, hard and nine inches long. Yeah, I could keep Uncle Gene company. As oldest of the cousins, it seemed like I was always the one appointed to help him with the manly tasks around the house and at dinner parties. His thanks was always a wink or a sip of his Kailua and cream. Nothing more. But I was an adult now and "no strangers and no adults" didn't apply any more.

When I got done helping load our share of the pot luck dinner into the car and got Aunt Barb and my folks packed in I found him still in his bed. Only there were drinks for each of us.

"I thought they'd never leave. Help out of this pajama top, will you?"

He rolled back and forth a bit as I pulled it over his head. He was still as handsome as ever. Heavier, of course and his hairline had receded "thanks to his wife's tight nightgowns." That was his joke. But, he still had that easy smile and Latin charm. He had a respectable stand of black hair on his brown chest. I sat on the bed next to him. He handed me a Kailua and cream, "Cheers!"

Then an awkward moment followed as we both tried to figure out how to do it. They wouldn't be gone all that long.

"Well, I know what you are thinking," Gene said, his broad brown hand grasping my bony shoulder, which was kind of amazing because I didn't know what I was thinking at that moment. "How's that old guy get any pussy, as big and bummed up as he is?"

I smiled and laughed soundlessly. I shook my head but didn't exactly deny that had crossed my mind.

"Well, I'm here to tell you that 'little Eugene' works as good as ever. It's just the back that's out of commission. But, your Aunt hauls a couple of these pillows out from behind me so I lay flat out more, mounts up and away we go."

I must have been blushing purple. Just shook my head laughing.

"You are a good looking guy. You must be getting the girls. Ever do it that way?"

I wasn't all that experienced. But, I shared a tale or two. Making sure to leave out a tale or two while I was at it. This conversation was making me hot. My

shorts were in a knot and there was no way to hide the fact when I kept adjusting myself.

Uncle Gene didn't say anything, just watched me do it and then winked at me.

"Ever try anal sex?"

Now, I know I was blushing. I also know I had to sit up straighter because my cock was pushing its way past the elastic on my tighty-whities. Had I ever tried it? Shoot, that was about all I ever had!

"Shoot, the wife loves that! During that time of the month, your Aunt takes it up the poop shoot and even cums doing it."

I had to lift the hem of my shorts so "little Billy" could peek out.

"Got a big one, huh? I ain't seen it since you were little. Help me get my pajama' off would you. It's hot under these covers."

He tossed back the white quilt and began squirming out of his pajama bottoms. There was no mistaking the wet spot on the sheer fabric nor that stiff big brown cock poking thru the slit in the front.

"Hello, little Eugene." I chuckled as I leaned over my uncle to help pull the fabric off his buttocks and down his long brown legs. I heard it slap against Uncle Gene's able belly as it came clear of the waist band.

"Little Eugene says hi back." He pushed that long thin shaft till it was aimed at me and then let it snap back again. "And if you noticed, he ain't so little." I suppose he expected some smart aleck reply, but I was too busy staring and to my embarrassment drooling.

"Let's see what you got." I pulled open my button fly britches and started to show him what I got. "Hey now. Here I am all laid out butt naked. Only fair you be naked too."

I pulled my stripped tee off over my head. "Nice chest full of hair. Let me rub my hand thru it." Which he did, taking the liberty of pressing his thumb against the head of my cock which was peeking out of my shorts and just oozing pre-cum. He was stroking himself with his left hand.

"Let's see Bill." I dropped "trou" and his hand swooped in to grasp my thick, hard, nine inches. "Feels just like a big rhubarb curved stem; wider than it is thick. Just like your dad."

I'm been dying to ask this for years. "You and my dad ever do this sort of thing?"

"Oh, yeah, all the time when we were kids. Of course, he always wanted to be on top."

"I wouldn't mind playing Aunt Barb," I said taking a sip of my sweet sticky drink.

He already had the lube out and was greasing up. I straddled his girth with my long skinny legs and settled on that thing. "Little Eugene" wasn't as long as "Little Billy" but it's thinness made it look long and it was going places that hadn't been filled in a couple of months. "Oh, good, Bill!" He looked almost in as much

pain as I, but then again he was smiling too. I started gliding up and down that solid steel shaft. "Oh Bill." he uttered with a shiver in his voice that told me he wouldn't be long in cumming. I kept bouncing up and down nice and easy, so as to not throw out his back.

My butt juices were flowing and no more lube was necessary. Uncle Gene had some more lube in his hand though and he was stroking my rhubarb. That was feeling good, but I was a long ways from coming. Not him.

"I'm cumming, I'm cumming."

His broad hands pressed my thighs down on his and he held me in place while he unloaded in smiles and groans. When his breathing returned to normal and he could talk, he told me "Thanks, Bill. It's been a while. Did you enjoy that?"

Rather than wait for an answer he went back to stroking "Little Billy" and rubbing my hairy chest.

"I sure did," I sipped on my drink, groaning appreciatively as he stroked my cock and my ass wallowed in the wetness of his softening dick.

"Well, Bill, I want to know if you are as good as your old man down there. Why don't you shove a couple of pillows under my ass and let's see if we can introduce 'Little Billy' into a place only your dad has been before."

He didn't have to tell me twice. I rolled those pillows up under his ass, bent his knees back a little out of the way and pushed that big purple head on my wide dick into the sweaty crack of his large brown ass. I took it slow cause of his back and he had to redirect where I put his legs sometime, but I kept the pressure on. In a little bit my copper pubs were clutching at his iron black thatch.

Truth be told, his butt was so big, that it was mostly his cheeks that were squeezing my joy toy. But they were doing the job just fine. And the head of my dick and the few inches in his hole seem to be doing it for him, cause something was oozing out of his whipped dick.

I have a hard time restraining myself once I get it in there. I don't know if we had the pillow just right for his back, or he was determined not to complain and ruin our first time. Either way I was up on my knees giving it to the that big brown boy and he was telling me how good I was.

It felt like I shot a gallon when I finally came. I was thanking him and telling him how good it was, half leaning over his sprawled frame when we heard the car pull up.

"Shit! What are we going to do?" I groaned, looking at the wreck we'd made of his bed and mess we'd made of his sheets.

"Get dressed Bill. Just get dressed." As I complied, Uncle Gene poured his drink on the floor, slipped out of bed and into the nearby shower. "Grab the sheets and clothes. Put them in the washing machine and start it."

"Hello," came Aunt Barb's voice as I headed to the basement with the laundry.

"Barb! Can you come help me!" he whined from the shower.

I was out of earshot by then, but heard all about how he'd spilled his drink all over himself and the bed, how I'd been such a saint to help my crippled old uncle into the shower and even had the mess half cleaned up by the time they got home.

Chapter 7: Seventeen

"Seventeen. Yep. I ate seventeen of the things. And you know, after I finished my coffee I think I could have finished a couple of pancakes. That guy makes some pretty good ones. Crustee's mix I think. Well you probably don't care about that. Anyhow…"

Rod continued with a shake of his head and lift of his pointed chin. He fiddled with his portable "ipod stereo" before continuing. He'd sworn the battery would last the 45 minutes they had to wait for their ride. I put on country western music to please Bill.

"That's how I got stuck with the handle of 'Seventeen'."

"And all this time I thought it was the length of your cock."

Rod jumped back in his chair, his blue eyes suddenly wide, his feet pushed off the floor and lifted his knees to meet the down stroke of his open palms. At the sound of the ensuing slap his jaw fell open, a choked "Ah!" popped out along with a toothy smile. His drawn sun-burnt face blushed bright red. His eyes watered up. His right hand slapped his thigh again as he tried to regain his breath.

Still blushing he took his eyes from his companion and stared at the ground while admitting, "Shoot, Bill, if that was the case, I'd be a big time porn star in Hollywood."

He grinned at his own joke.

"Most people think I act like I'm 17."

"Well, you've got the energy of a 17 year old. I know you can work concrete 17 hours a day."

Bill waited for the compliments' effect, and then added. "And when you are trapped in the office, I've seen you drink 17 cups of coffee in one morning. Boy, you are always on step."

"Gotta keep up, Bill. Don't want people thinking I'm slacking on the job."

"Well, as fast as you talk, work and walk in the woods, when you're fucking you must cum in a matter of seconds."

Again Rod's jaw fell open. Again he looked away with a smile. "I ain't got no complaints in that area."

Rod was in his mid twenties, all sinewy from a life of hard work; thin with broad shoulders and sledge like fists, long gangly legs that carried him easily. His face was always smiling which belied the intensity of his eyes and normal tightness of his thin lips.

"What you say?"

"I haven't had in complaints in that department." he said standing, adjusting himself in the process.

"You got something to brag about in those 'Kick Ass' jeans?"

Rod wasn't blushing any more. He simply struggled knowingly, letting his suspenders lift the loose fitting jeans that hung on his slim frame. He glanced out the window of the little shack giving them shelter from the weather. The shack stored the logger's unused chainsaws. A couple of skinned logs stood suspended in the air a couple feet of the ground with slits where they inserted their long, well-oiled bars.

The dirt floor was covered with bar oils and spruce shavings. The boat coming to get them probably hadn't left Papke's Landing yet and they'd be able to hear any logging trucks intending to drop loads here.

Bill pulled off his "Four Stages of Tequila" tee shirt as he stood and dropped it in the chair. His pants fell shortly after. "Is it bigger than this?" he asked stretching out his six incher.

Rod stared at the older man intently, his eyes glassing over. He wore an old, thin, provocative "Alaska Bush Pilot" tee-shirt, which laid close to his naked skin and moved with the slight heaving of his chest. "Come see for yourself."

Bill hopped over as fast as his dirt dragging Levi's would allow. He unbuttoned the button on Rod's pants, found the zip and pulled it down. He could see a growth down the right pants leg. He looked from the treasure at hand and into Rod's eyes.

His hands rose to the once red suspenders, slid underneath and slid them off his bony shoulders. Bill's eye's fell as the pants did, revealing a "beer can". That is to say a cock the length and roundness of a beer can. Bill's right hand grabbed it and began to stroke it as his left did the same at home.

"That's amazing! You can get this thing in somebody's hole?"

"I've gotten it in several some bodies' holes," Rod affirmed in a deepened guttural voice.

Bill stacked his cock atop Rod's and began to stroke them both.

"Okay, that's about enough of that."

"Yeah," Bill agreed continuing to stroke. "Don't want to look like a faggot."

"I'm not a faggot," Rod replied, lost in the moment, as he cock grew harder.

"Then you won't mind me doing this."

Bill dropped his knees to the dirt floor and glommed onto the wide pinkish head of Rod's rod.

"That's cool. A willing mouth is a willing mouth."

Bill let the just the head of that beer can slide in an out of his face. His features were stretched by the tension like a big yawn. His bristly gray moustache turned straight out. His eye watered with the effort. But each stroke of Rod's bony hips were met by a thrust of Bill's face, as he tried to ease the big cock further and further down his throat.

"Yeah, that's pretty good, Bill…"

Opening his jaws even wider, Bill eased his face on the thick round rod, licked his lips and said, "Think you can do better."

"Well…"

Bill rose. Rod dropped to his knees. Rod slurped up Bill's dick in one movement of his jaw. His tongue worked the purplish head, while his right hand rolled and played with Bill's loose nuts. Appreciative "ah's" escaped Bill's thin lips. Rod's left hand reached around to cup Bill's right ass cheek and then started searching for the entrance of his man-pussy.

Bill gasped as Rod sucked in first one and then the other of his balls. Open-mouthed Rod worked his long pointed jaw around Bill's genitals!

"You're sucking 'em all at once! Oh, my God!"

Another gasp escaped the older man's mouth as Rod's right hand slipped around him and began prying apart his ass cheeks to give the roaming index finger of his left hand better access. Breathless, Bill slumped over a bit, leaning on the shoulder of the energetic younger man. Rod had now worked two fingers up Bill's poop-chute.

Shaking his face free of Bill's basket, he said, "You want to see what else I can do?"

"Sure."

Rod stood and reached for his day pack. There was a half-used jar of Vaseline inside. Bill's eyes grew eyes in surprise. His mouth fell open in shock as Rod stared lubing up his "rod."

Rod with eyes a glaze said, "What you think me and my buddy Jack do nights when we are camped out in the woods working of trails?"

Bill began to shake his head at the "beer can" now pointing straight out. "Yeah, I can. Let me show ya."

So saying, Rod turned the beer bellied bottom around and laid him over one of the naked poles used for sheathing the cutters' tools. He curled a glob of goo around his right point finger and inserted it up Bill's ass.

"Hey, you've done this before."

"You're not the only one that fools around with his best friend."

Two fingers brought on heavy breathing, but no grimace.

Three fingers: Bill panted, but with slow and steady pressure Rod got them all in.

"Looks like it's time." Rod slapped another glob of Vaseline on the head of his thick round cock and pressed it up against Bill's hole.

"Now reach back and spread your cheeks."

As Bill helped on that end, Rods left hand pushed his shoulders further towards the floor and with his right around the shaft he pushed. Bill sucked air. "Over more. Let's get your head down more." As Bill's frame rotated forward, Rod kept rolling on over the top of him, Rod's body weight forcing his wrist size tool further in.

With a further gasp and a sudden clearing of his head, Bill realized that Rod was all the way in.

"Now, let's do something about that music."

Bill could feel Rod's weight shift as he reached for the little stereo. He fiddled with the controls until he found dance music.

"This is better for fucking!"

The lanky top then proceeded to pound the beat on Bill's butt there in a tiny shack barely hiding them from the scenic landscape of Southeast.

"I can't believe it," Bill mumbled.

"Oh, Bill-buddy. It only gets better. Wait until you loosen up."

Bill laid across the thick log his arms dangling down almost to the dusty ground. His ass perched up high and with each stroke getting shoved a little bit further forward and over the log. His boots barely touched the floor and his legs dangled as helpless as his arms on the other side of the naked spruce log.

"Let me change the tunes." Rod fiddled with the equipment and then wedged his own equipment firmly in Bill's ass before helping him slide off the log. Bill now stood bent at the waist, pulling his cheeks apart, mumbling praise and amazement at Rod's performance.

It was a lot longer than 17 minutes when Rod unloosed his load in between Bill's now rosy ass cheeks. He had the bottom's butt licked clean when their boat ride home finally arrived.

RENDEZVOUS WITH RUSS

He rapped at the door promptly at 7 p.m. which surprised me due to the lack of enthusiasm and luridness in his voice when we spoke over the phone. I opened the door. I smiled more broadly at his large size and stature. I sighed in relief that he wasn't 10 years my junior like I'd worried.

"I'm Russ," he said, advancing into the room and offering his hand.

Russ weighed at least 230 and stood 6 foot. Curly, short-cut, salt-and-pepper hair snuck out from under his baseball cap. A full short-cut beard graced his solid chin. He was big boned with a big belly. And, yes, a hairy chest revealed itself in the "v" of his flannel shirt. I could smell the soap from his recent shower even at the awkward distance we stood apart inside my motel room.

"Not watching the World Series?" he inquired.

"MTV usually provides better background noise," I replied.

He smiled in response.

"I didn't expect you to be so big. I like that."

"And I like you," he responded.

His left hand reached for my crotch. His lips suddenly pressed against mine. His beard didn't scratch. His lips felt like silk. The embrace of his tongue with mine was like the kiss of a butterfly. We began to caress one another's chests and play with each other's nipples, then quickly stripped. His chest was adequately hairy. His dick was short and stubby to the eye, but I knew with these big bellied boys that all I have to do is press against their flesh and a full rounded hard seven-inch cock will slide into my hand.

He sat me on the bed, knelt on the floor and began some serious sucking on my cock. I looked down my hairless chest to see his blue eyes glazed with delight and rosy cheeks concave with suction. But there was something else I wanted.

I pushed him erect and bent from my sitting position to suck his pudgy pole. We found the position pretty ineffective.

"Here." he grunted and tossed himself on the bed.

I rolled his knees up to his shoulders. By reflex, his hands pulled his thighs even further apart. My tongue licked up the conical shaft of his cock, tickled his little round balls nestled in a nest of pubic hair. But I decided not to move further downstream. He was definitely hard, but I could move his prick to any position, which told me we would have some ass-fucking fun. I was ready to mount up when he pulled me up onto the bed, kissed me deeply for a while, then put me on to his head. He pulled my hips to his lips and went back to lapping and licking with his butterfly-soft tongue strokes.

I thought, "What the hell! I like to fuck face."

I wrapped my ankles under his arms and start pumping away on his silky lips. My wife hadn't done this in ages. I went for it, crumbling into a ball at the head of the bed as I squirted into his mouth. I had to do my part though and crawled over his belly to find that solid little soldier still waiting. As I started deep-throating Russ, he spun my butt around for some sixty-nine kind of action. I sprawled over his belly and the distance from the tip of my tongue to the base of my crotch was stretched to the max. I wasn't really ready for seconds on my cock, but I did want him up my butt. As I turned to suggest it, something warm and soft struck the fist I had wrapped greedily around his cock. Lunging back I barely got a mouthful, gagged (after all I'd just eaten dinner) and lapped up as much as I could. We collapsed side by side. When he got up to clean himself, I tossed him a towel from the bedside stand. He cleaned himself while grinning at me shyly.

"How long you here?"

"Until Friday."

"Could we get together Thursday? Late?"

"That sounds good," I assured him.

"Really?"

I guess I can wait that long to have that plump pole inserted into my hungering butthole.

SATURDAY NIGHT HOT

The bar was crowded, hot from the heat of the congregated bear meat.

Bob arrived a little late at Sprags. He took up a spot of the wall with a clear view of the buffet provided during the Northwest Bears monthly social gathering. The food was sort of "bear bait" and he was the trapper. A large selection of hairy hunks, hulks, cubby chasers, bears, polar bears and bear trappers prowled the place.

The thickest part of the throng was out on the back deck. Bob decided to wait until the boys had a few. He'd check out the show then. A small group of men invaded the bar not long after Bob got settled. They took up residence a few feet away.

"Bad choice of hats in a gay bar," Bob thought to himself noticing that the couple (in their proverbial matching outfits) had chosen yellow baseball caps to accentuate their Carhart pants and new embroidered jackets.

It didn't go unnoticed by the twosome that they were being checked out. Lance, the thinner, slightly taller of the two, a black man, turn to repay the eyeballing compliment to Bob. Lance took several long slow glances from the thick salt and pepper hair atop Bob's head to the brown cowboy boots. His infectious smile, arching eyebrow and knowing look made it clear he liked what he saw.

Bob almost coughed up his beer in response. Soon they got to talking. "Hey, I like you," Bob assured Lance, "but I don't want to cause trouble for you with your lover."

"That's not my lover. That's my best friend, in town visiting. That's my lover over there."

"You got people, I don't want….", Bob stammered, but his eyes were on Lance's ample crotch bulge and his left hand on Lance's hip.

"I'm all grown up. Let me arrange something. I'll be back," Lance said.

Bob talked with a few folks while Lance worked his way out of his previous engagements with some difficulty. Bob talked to a few passing bears, then (after letting Lance know) he drifted off to the back deck.

Bob found a seat on the bench/table and was entertained by the mocking hilarity of one of those stereotypical "New Yorkers". Kenny was hairy and outrageous and funny. Bob and the crowd had talked him into dropping his pants when Lance showed up.

"What's going on out here?" Lance asked knowingly as someone snaked his hand into the open fly of Kenny's teddy-bear-decorated boxers.

"Where you stayin'?" he whispered to Bob, then asked for the room number. He'd try to work something out. Meanwhile, the group of bears had worked Ken's eight incher out. Everyone's hand took a few appreciative strokes of Ken's big brown tool. Ken's smile seemed broadest and cock got thickest when Bob slid his hand seductively up and down the upward-pointing cock.

Happy Hour ended and Bob headed to the Bond to meet Mike, his new friend from the night before. Mike was probably 210, 6'1", like Bob, and probably 50 to Bob's 45. They kissed lightly in greeting, spoke over beers with their arms wrapped around one another's waist. They decided to check out the action on the back deck of the Hawk on their way to Bob's hotel.

No action on the back deck, but while cruising upstairs and down, they ran into Ken, wider eyed, drunker, and hornier than ever. Bob introduced them and then lead the way as he and Mike drifted off.

"I liked him," Mike commented. Bob stopped, turned, smiled, took Mike by the hand and led him back to Ken's side. Taking both men in his arms, Bob said, "Mike likes you." Mike and Kenny kissed deeply. Kenny and Bob kissed deeper. Then Bob and Mike. After a long make out session blocking the aisles of the Hawk, they ended up in Bob's hotel, having lost Kenny along the way.

Mike took Bob's face in his hands as soon as the door closed and kissed him square on the lips, forcing his tongue against the inside of Bob's cheek and then all the way to the back of his throat. When they broke for air, Mike said, "Let's get naked."

Then he strode to the bathroom leaving Bob to strip. He returned in nothing but his undershorts and took Bob's face in his hands again. Kissing Bob, he forced him on the bed, spreading his legs apart as he knelt over him. Bob's stiff dick pressed into the Mike's underwear bulge and he sighed loudly.

Mike held Bob down with his left hand as he yanked his own whitey righties off with his right. A nice thick six-inch boner flopped out, bounced off Mike's belly and came to a hard upright erection. In a swift motion, he installed the condom he had tucked into his right hand.

Mike cupped his hands under Bob's muscular buttocks, wedged his shoulders against the bottom's knees, spread his own knees even wider to get his cock closer. He pried the head of his cock down and pressed it against Bob's brown hole. He shoved just a little.

"Like that?" he said.

"Yeah," Bob sighed as he threw his arms back and relaxed for a pounding. Mike began a slow steady full in and out fuck. Eventually settling into a rhythm and stretching his arm out to keep his weight off Bob. The sweat began to form on the patch of hair in the middle of his chest, and Bob could feel his lips quiver with exertion during their occasional kiss.

Mike gripped the bottom's semi-erect cock in his left hand, pumping it up to full erection with a few strokes. "Uh, oh, cumming soon," he grunted, his movements speeding, his breathing rasping loudly in the otherwise silent room. The rapid-fire jacking of Bob's cock and the urgent stroking of the dick against his prostate sent him over the edge. "Oh, yeah," he panted, cum spurting down over the black fingers encircling his twitching prick.

The spasms running through him set his cock twitching and his asshole clinching against its welcome intruder. Mike unloaded into his condom, fell on Bob, cuddled for a while and departed.

But, the night was young. And Bob needed more. He was dressed before Mike made the elevator. Down the stairs he went and out the building to Club A for some real fucking.

It was the usual – cruising the halls, checking out what was available in which room, talking to a few guys then off to the play room for groping and rubbing and…. "Hello, sir. Whatever you need, sir. I'll do it for you sir."

The whiny voice in the dark sounded southern, maybe black, but it wasn't Lance. This guy was thin, but short.

"Sorry, I'm a bottom. What I need is a stiff dick up my ass," Bob informed the formless voice.

"I can help you there, sir." And the voice began to deepen. "I got what you need right here." Bob could hear the whack of a condom being snapped on. The little man stepped behind him.

"You shy?"

"No."

"Lean up against the wall."

Bob compiled spread his feet wide due to the height difference, leaned forward and grabbed the chain link fence. With Bob's wet crack spread wide open, the little black man got his cock in quickly and began fucking like a bunny. The crowd murmured in appreciation and scooted closer, but in the darkened hall could see little.

"Scoot over here," the man at his rear whispered to Bob, leading him to the bench in the middle of the play room. "Get on all fours" Bob obliged. The top climbed up on the bigger man and began pumping enthusiastically away. A rapidly

increasing grunt and rate of panting gave away the fact he was about to cum, but as he exuberantly did just that, there was motion behind Bob and the black man. Someone standing penetrated the little man's black ass.

"Yeah, yeah, fuck me!" he drawled.

Bob climbed out to watch the show, mesmerized. He stroked his white dick and watched a hairy, well-muscled dude of about 35 shove a thick white dick into the black man's narrow butt.

Appreciative fans poked at Bob's oozing hole and one hairy muscle god rubbed Bob's cock with his own thick tool.

Ready for a rest, Bob adjourned to the television room. A little relaxation and a little pornography had his asshole twitching again. Looking around he found an older blonde teddy hair stroking a hard eight-incher admiring him. Bob admired back. A hairy blond hand fell upon his shoulder. The blonde moved next to him and pulled Bob's lips around the shaft of meat. Bob's towel fell from his well worn ass now hoisted in the air as he bent to suck cock.

Suddenly, he pulled his thick meat out of Bob's mouth with a loud slurping noise. The rubber he pulled out slid on the huge tool with amazing ease. The aged teddy bear got to his feet, spun Bob around, forced him forward at the hips and began plunging his cock into Bob's well-primed ass. He kept fucking and forcing Bob's head down, then swiveling Bob's hips he offered those lips to several appreciative cocks watching the show.

"Want some?" the teddy bear growled Someone stepped forward and Bob hungrily gobbled his cock.

"I'm gonna cum. Wanna?" the teddy bear said to the unknown man, indicating Bob's ass. The teddy bear pulled out, they spun him around. As the other cock cramped up Bob's ass, the teddy bear slid the messy rubber from his throbbing man pole and slammed the tangy thick meat into Bob's mouth. Wedging the engorged tool against the back of Bob's throat, he kept coming until the spew and the drool rolled out of his lover's lips.

Exhausted, Bob wandered off, stumbling into Mitch's room. Mitch is the angel of fucking with the wings tattooed on to prove it.

"Looking to get fucked, Bob?"

"I just did two guys at once," Bob muttered.

"Good timing," said the angel. "I'm ready again. Hey, you've been fucked tonight, haven't you? It feels good tonight."

Then this bathhouse legend went at Bob's ass until he'd fucked him dry and Bob's knees collapsed under him.

Bob made it back to his hotel room, well fucked on a hot Saturday night.

TARRYING WITH TERRY BEAR

He's picking me up after work tonight. Just like last night only he'll bring a big tube of lube and a new packet of condoms.

When I walked out of the office last night he was waiting for me in the parking lot with that sweet smile of his. We'd been leering at one another for days as I passed thru the lobby. He says the nicest things to me over the phone.

I should mention that Terry is about 6'1", just a little shorter than I am, arching eyebrows, seducing blue eyes, the sweetest little smile, hairy body and heavy frame. Terry's big, maybe too big for his health's sake. But I love bears!

We went to the hotel where I stay and where he works, "for a drink". On the way to the lounge, we stopped in my room to drop off my briefcase. I'd never advise you to try to take off a tie when someone else is unbuttoning your shirt and sucking on your nipples. Terry and I were naked just feet inside the hotel room door.

When I finally got a look at his hard dick, I thought, "Not too long, but nice and thick." I pulled on it a few times and then pushed. His enormous belly gave way before my hand and my fist slid down an ever broadening shaft, to settle at the base of a thick, smooth, 7 incher.

"Let's get comfortable," he said encouraging me to finish stripping. He then pushed me towards the bed when I was nude.

It was a blur for a while after that of a mad make out session, rolling one another around the bed and then finding myself on my back with his tremendous girth pinning me down and his pecker tapping at my asshole.

"You want it, don't you?" he grinned.

I responded by reaching for the condoms and KY in the bed stand. He rolled over on his back. I rolled on the condom, greased it up, settled down on it, and started rocking back and forth.

"This your favorite position?"

"Just for starting. Now that I'm comfortable, we can do it anyway you want."

Terry smiled up at me, "Lean back."

As I leaned back he pulled himself up to his knees and started to give it to my ass. Each pounding shoved me a little bit closer to the foot of the bed. I started looking back to see where we'd end up.

"I won't let you fall," he promised.

"I was worried about where WE would fall."

"Scoot over here," he said pulling me easily along.

I indicated closer to the side of the bed and he slid us over, pulled my ankles up in the air and went back to pounding away.

"Look up," I directed.

I followed his gaze to the mirror opposite us. There I was upside down, dick and balls bouncing, legs dragged up into a V. Terry's hairy belly and furry tits jiggled and glistened with each stroke. He smiled at the image and started hammering my behind.

"Uh, oh, oh, God, I'm close," he grunted, his full weight slamming his rigid prick far inside me. "Uh!"

He came quickly, his twitching dick depositing a very noticeable wetness in my quivering ass channel. He fell into my arms for another make out session.

"Want a drink?" Terry grinned when we ended up back in the hotel bar.

He bought me several and encouraged me to have more. Then he took me to a neighboring restaurant and insisted on paying the tab. I was never into the "Daddy" scene, and even though we were the same age, here I was playing the part. It felt good. I knew I was in for some serious butt reaming.

He took me home. His younger slimmer roommate met us in the living room.

"Will's going to work on the computer," Terry said, a little too loudly.

I saw the knowing lift of the roommate's eyebrow, the secret smile of happiness for his buddy and the bite of the tongue not to say anything. I went to work on the PC. Terry joined me. The net was slow and we started making out again. When I reached for his pants he said we needed to wait till the roommate left for work.

"He doesn't know." I too bit my tongue and went back to work. Terry discovered that the roommate had decided to give us some privacy, er I mean walk to work. As Terry called to apologize, I stretched on the couch and waited with anticipation for the show to begin.

I heard Terry get off the phone to his roommate and pad down the hallway. He leaned over the couch and started kissing me upside down. He wrapped his

hairy arms around my torso. His hairy hands mauled my nipples. His broad palms rubbed my belly. I tried to return the favors but Terry is so large and held me so tightly that reaching back of the couch to grab him was impossible. When his hands began to invade my pants he broke from our lip lock and said, "Let's get more comfortable."

We walked to the bedroom. He apologized for the mess: "Bachelor, you know." Tossed piles of papers and clothes covered the floor. We stripped and jumped into his bed. Another blur of action followed. His harsh five o'clock shadow aroused the blush on my cheeks and chin. His tongue took over my mouth. He rolled us around on the bed, trying different positions. Eventually he ended up on top of me his hairy huge frame squeezing the air from my lungs, his lips sucking the breathe out of me. His thick knees spread apart my willing thighs, his pecker tapped again at my already-aching asshole.

He rolled a little and lifted my left leg over my head, spreading my cheeks wide open. He settled his weight back on my leg and moved the head of his 7-inch cock into my quivering crack. I thought he was going to shove it in bare, but he lifted off of me when I reached for the condoms. Once we had him sheaved and greased, in it went.

Another blur of lovemaking. Sometimes I was pinned helpless into the mattress while he laid atop me and his cock lunged in and out of me. Sometimes, Terry would yank my ankles into the air and his whole big hairy body would pound at my butt. I learned to hold onto the backs of this massive thighs so we didn't pitch off the bed onto the cluttered floor. He switched back and forth, back and forth for 30 minutes until we collapsed into a sweaty sticky mass of exhausted man meat.

"I need to rest," he explained. "I was thinking you might want to face fuck me."

He didn't have to ask twice! As he rolled onto his back, I climbed on his chest, wedged my legs under his shoulder and shoved my dick in his mouth. What a vacuum he was! He kept a constant suction as I bent over him more and more to drive my dick in deeper. His hands played with my nipples and chest and belly and ass again. I started moaning as he touched my asshole. I said, "Yes, yes." as he slipped a finger in and began swirling it around in my bowels. I drove my hips back and forth as my throbbing prick slid wetly between his tight pink lips and his impaling digit did a sensuous number in my ass. He could tell I wanted it. He slipped another finger in there. "Terry! Yes! Oh Terry!"

It felt like he was getting another in. My hips whipped frantically back and forth. "How many fingers do you have in there?" He could only hum in response. It was incredible. Then I stopped.

"I've got to go now," I said.

I looked between my smooth thighs to see the concern in his eyes. Spitting my dick out of his mouth, he asked, "You okay?"

"Yeah. We've just loosened up my bowels too much. I'll go to the bathroom and be back."

I assured him everything was fine when I returned.

"So how many finger did you have inside me?" I asked again.

He grinned and showed me "two thumbs up." I jumped in bed with him and suggested I needed to suck his cock, so we could get it hard again.

"Kissing you gets me hard faster," he advised, that smile lighting his face again.

A hot make-out session followed and we decided it was my turn to be on top. I wanted to make him come. I slapped that cock up my butt. I jumped up and down on it. I ground my crotch into his abdomen; stroked my cock against his hairy belly. I rocked and pounded my pelvis into his, until he started groaning and gasping for air.

"Ah, oh, yeah, baby, I m shooting!" he shouted. I had no doubt of it as his thick spasming rod unloaded again inside me. After he came, he told me how great I was.

It was time to rest. Time for wine and a video. Time to get some "juice" into us to replace the juices we had spent and get them flowing again. I suppose we watched the boys on the screen for awhile. But we quickly returned to make out again. And Terry was quickly aroused again. But this time when I laid pinned against the bed and his knees spread my thighs apart, he said. "Can you get on top again this time. It felt so good. And lube me up so I'll last longer."

He routinely lasted 30 minutes, but I wanted him so madly in my butt that I complied gladly. I greased the rod and slide on down. It felt good. I leaned back as I rocked my hips to get his dick deeper in. It felt really good. But what felt even better was my cock sliding through the dimple on his prodigious belly. The thick fur caressed the sensitized head of my cock, setting me wild with a newborn lust. My balls rolled up his abdomen, tightening against me as they pressed into his thickly matted pubic bush.

"Yeah, baby. Yeah, baby. Do it!" Terry moaned as I reached down for my own cock. I pulled on the shaft aiming the head towards his five o'clock shade while I slammed harder on his shaft. I fingered the place where my foreskin should be and show Terry my precum. I licked a sample from my finger and continued to pound his cock inside me. I started pummeling my twitching hard prick, listening listened to his shouts of encouragement as globs of white stuff splattered across my fist and his furry belly.

I tried to stay in the saddle for my bear boy, but I'm one of those guys that wives complain about. When I cum, it's all over. I tried to stay awake, tried to keep pumping his prick. But we'd been at it for two hours now, it was midnight and I was exhausted. I apologized and fell onto the pillow next to him.

"Roll over on your side so I can cuddle with you," he whispered sweetly. "Will you be warm enough?" he asked wrapping his arms around me. "Wrapped in my own bear skin rug? Yeah," I mumbled my eyes already shut.

"I love you," he said as I drifted off to sleep.

Ogden Nash said, "Candy is dandy, but liquor is quicker." Terry had bought me several drinks during dinner and gave me a big glass of wine while we watched the porn flick. At 3:30 in the morning all that booze reached my bladder. I snuck out of Terry's bed. But returning from the bathroom I stumbled around and woke the slumbering bear.

"You're awake this time of night?" he asked.

"Laying next to a good looking man like you? Of course, I am."

"I love you," he said again before crawling to my side and kissing me.

He kissed me long and hard, then pushed me back down in the bed. He turned his tongue and lips to my dick.

I giggled when the bristles on his chin touched my inner thighs or small round balls. I moaned as he sucked on my cock or tried to gobble up both balls and the cock. Knowing my appreciation for ass play, he worked a finger up the crack of my ass. I jumped. "We're going to need a lot of KY to do that," I protested mildly.

"Give it to me," he pleaded.

I handed him the now flat tube. I heard it fly against the far wall, when he'd squeezed everything he could out of it. I braced myself when the finger went back in but couldn't keep from jumping.

I wanted Terry to fuck my ass again so bad. I considered telling him to forget the finger and to just rape my ass no matter what. But, I knew the reality would be him or both of us ending up on the floor. "Please don't do that," I said in frustration.

"Tomorrow, I'll buy a big tube of KY," he assured me with no indication of frustration or bitterness. He pulled me into his arms again. "I love you," he assured me as we drifted off to sleep.

In the morning he dropped me at the hotel. He promised to buy a "big" tube of butt lube and another pack of condoms. He wanted to pick me up from work again.

Later in the day he called to make it later and eventually called back saying he was exhausted, could we make it the following night. I should have been disappointed but with only three hours of sleep and an asshole that winced every time I sat down, I could only think of one thing, "Thank God."

But I'm sure looking forward to tomorrow night.

THEIR FIRST TIME

"That's not nine inches."

Peter looked up from soaping up his oversized balls, thick dick and little pubic patch of curly brown hair. Bill stepped forward pulling his own six incher straight out. As Peter watched Bill lifted his cock up with the palm of his left hand to compare the two side by side. Grinning Peter looked at his best friend and said, "It would have to be hard."

With a mischievous lift of his right eyebrow, Bill began to stroke the two cocks wrapped in his left hand. In two strokes they were both hardening. Beyond the plastic curtain of the little shower room, they heard the bathroom door open. Both men stepped back to their respective showerheads.

Peter was a jocular jock with sandy hair, broad shoulders, a barrel chest, stocky frame, nice butt, and thick thighs. He was given to wearing tight jeans and loose tennis shoes. His most striking feature was his ever-infectious smile.

Bill stood a little taller, blonde-brown hair, lean frame and long muscular legs. He wore cowboy boots that made him that much taller than Peter when they weren't naked in the shower.

They had known one another for years on the Coconino National Forest Firefighting Crew. They'd only become intimate when they both signed up for an intense four semesters at the School of Forestry at Northern Arizona University. They spent all day side by side, their outer thighs and knees gently touching, their hands casually laying on one another's inner thighs when they turned to speak to one another.

Bill had wanted to make the friendship "a little more intimate" for a long time. But, barring the occasional day hike or trip to Oak Creek Canyon, Peter's wife kept him on a pretty short leash, particularly since the baby.

A few days before this pleasant shower interlude, Peter's wife and daughter went to California preparing for his sister-in-law's wedding.

That day, Peter moved into Bill's room in the dorm Bill's roommate didn't mind. He was used to Bill's firefighting buddies crashing on the floor on weekends. But, Bury Hall was noisy, dirty, crowded, and Bill's roommate was always there. So, it was no surprise when Bill suggested spending a quiet night at Peter's. Bill thought he saw a little twinkle in Peter's eye at the suggestion.

Peter and his wife shared a small one-bedroom daylight basement with a standard living/dining/kitchen area. Their bathroom shower was notoriously oversized for one showerhead. Bill made sure the cooked carrots were on the menu. (His girlfriend had once suggested that it was a powerful aphrodisiac. His girlfriend also liked to get ass rammed occasionally, particularly when she was on the rag. She'd even come once getting it up the ass from Bill.)

As the men cooked and scurried about the kitchen making dinner, Peter pulled off his shirt. "Too hot." Bill nodded in agreement. Smiling into Peter's eyes he unbuttoned and pulled out the tail of his own short-sleeved shirt.

After dinner with glasses full of cheap red wine, the boys moved onto the small couch across the room. Bill admired his buddy's broad chest and then squinted at the sofa where they sat.

"Didn't you tell me you were sitting here once with your shirt off and the baby tried to get a little milk off of you?"

"Yeah!" Peter admitted with a chuckle and his usual grin.

"What's it feel like?"

"Good," Peter replied still grinning, "a little weird, but good. Let me show you."

He pulled back Bill's shirt, leaned forward and took the whole right nipple in his lips. The only chest hair Bill had was around his right nipple and Peter's bristly moustache now hid it all. As his tongue flicked across Bill's nipple and his lips sucked at Bill's tit, his hand rolled into Bill's inner thigh and Peter's knuckles rolled against his buddy's crotch.

"How's that?" Peter asked sitting back and licking his lips.

"I liked the tongue action. Your turn."

Bill stretched out across the couch, his mouth encircling Peter's nipple. Peter held the taller man's head with his right hand, his left snuck beneath the cotton shirt, slid over the small of Bill's back and came to rest on his hot ass, then cupped the nearest cheeks and pulled his buddy closer. Later, he pried Bill loose and suggested they hit the shower.

"Hey, tonight you can show me your wife's favorite position," Bill suggested while following his host. "I never get it, when you describe it."

In the shower they took turns lathering up, while they rinsed in the shower stream. Then, arm in arm, they scooted around one another, their semi-hard cocks poking at one another's dangling balls, patches of pubic hair surrounding their dicks and upper thighs.

Occasionally through the "swat, swat, swat" of the shower on the tile and on their muscular bodies, you could hear the "thud" of their wagging cocks whacking one another as their masters passed beneath the showerhead.

"I'll wash your back," Bill offered with a cock of his head.

Peter turned spread eagle to the tiled wall and began to "oh" and "ah" as Bill's long fingered hands worked Peter's broad shoulders into a lather, then dragged the bar up his butt crack. But, Peter's moans really got going when Bill went back to kneading and pushing his hands into the huskier guys shoulder blades and shoulders.

"You know what would work even better?" Bill asked, a hint of glee in his voice.

"What?" Peter sighed.

"If I used all three hands!" And with that he dropped his dick into the crack of Peter's butt and began pushing with his pelvis as he did with his hands.

Peter grinned and laughed, maybe even pushed his ass into Bill's thrusting cock.

"My turn," he said, spinning Bill around and sloppily scrubbing his back. "Oops."

The bar of soap hit the shower floor in front of Bill. Legs straight he grabbed for it. Peter grabbed his ass and drove them both forward so Bill could get out of the shower. His thick cock slid back and forth between Bill's butt cheeks showing plenty of its pink head above the bent bottom with each up thrust. They started laughing. Bill slipped. They both ended up in a pile on the shower stall floor.

Once composed and dry, they raced one another to the bedroom, yanked back the comforter and upper sheet and plopped onto the bed.

"Look!" Bill lied. "It actually is 9 inches long."

His open palm, fingers down pressed Peter's rock hard 8-1/2 inches. Peter grinned. Both men now had raging hardons. Peter grabbed his bud and threw him on his back towards the head of the bed.

"She lays like that." Lifting Bill's legs he crawled underneath and turned his body perpendicular and facing Bill. "Then I get like this and…" He rocked his hips back and forth. His cock wagged and occasionally poked impotently at Bill's thigh. Bill laughed.

"It's great cause I can play with her titties."

He stroked Bill's right nipple.

"And then play with her pussy." His fingers slid down Bill's chest and wiggled his hard on back and forth.

The six incher was rock-rigid and pale, with a bright red head just starting to ooze.

"And rub the little man in the boat."

His thumb lifted his buddy's ball sack and then rolled the two testicles back forth across his flat abdomen. This lifted Bill's legs a little but not enough to give his striking cock a hole to enter.

"Show me your favorite position," he shouted when he became frustrated at the effort.

Peter knew perfectly well to get on his hands and knees, previous conversation having revealed "doggy" as being Bill's preferred fucking style. Bill put his knees inside Peter's thighs and spread the broad-shouldered boy's knees further apart to lower his ass to the desired position.

"This ain't exactly the way I do my girlfriend, but…" He reached under Peter and between his legs, pulling his over-size balls to one side, then slid his own cock between Peter's sack and thigh, grabbed his ass and began to push. "…it'll do nicely."

Bill began pushing his pelvis off Peter's butt as he guided his buddy's butt away, only to quickly slam the two together again. He kept up a heavy rhythm His breath came loudly. Unbeknownst to Bill whose head was thrown back and eyes closed, Peter was looking over his shoulder, grinning with pleasure.

Suddenly, Bill stopped, his hands and thighs aquiver. He was careful to keep his sensitized cock from further contact with the bottom's body. A string of sticky precum stretched from a wet spot on Peter's thigh to the pee hole in Bill's dick.

"Maybe you should show me your second favorite way."

Peter spun around to a seated position then threw Bill back on the bed face up. Bill panted heavily as he lay beneath his pal, his breath making sucking noises as he waited for Peter to climb on top. Peter lifted Bill's long legs to his shoulder and fell on top of his pal. He started a mock-lewd humping, his hairier oversized balls rolling across Bill's and their hard cocks crossed, rubbing and stroking one another.

As the pace increased color rose to his cheeks. He pressed harder and harder into Bill's abdomen. Bill continued panting and started rolling his hips to push his own erection into Peter's.

The top's eyes began to glaze over and sweat came to his brow. He stopped suddenly pressing all his greater weight on Bill, pinning him to the bed. He stared straight ahead at the shelves of the headboard. He gulped.

"You'd better show me your second favorite."

His voice sounded distant. Then he grinned at Bill and blushed as they both looked down at his throbbing red prick and all the love juice it had spread on their bellies. Bill laughed at their predicament, then pushed the broad-shouldered buck back to a sitting position on the bed and gave him a quick kiss.

"Put your knees on the floor and your belly on the bed."

"What?" Peter giggled.

Bill motioned for him to get down and Peter knelt at the side of the bed.

"Now stretch out up there and relax a minute. I'll be right back."

Peter rubbed his still dripping pecker into the mattress and did stretch his arms across the bed in a yawn of pleasure while Bill hit the head. But rather than hear the toilet flush, his ears picked up the click of riding heels on the kitchen floor. Peter turned to look and burst into a grin.

Bill walked in wearing nothing put a hardon and pair of Tony Llama lizard skin boots. His white socks stuck up above the top of the boots.

"What'?" be asked in mock surprise.

"It's for the additional height," Bill explained with a wink. He licked his lips appreciatively. "Nice ass. Is that 'eye' winking at me?"

Peter wiggled his butt, which sent Bill stomping across the room. He straddled the stockier man while laying his cock in Peter's crack. His hardon, now smeared with their precum, slid slowly forward. Bill's hands slipped under Peter's shoulders for a better grip.

"This the way you butt fuck your girlfriend?"

"Yeah," Bill sighed. "Better angle of attacking."

He rose in the saddle a little to demonstrate. He noticed that Peter wasn't grinning. His burly buddy stared straight ahead at the shelves of the headboard. His muscular right arm stretched out and pushed his hand into a decorative basket there. He pulled his arm back behind his back and handed Bill the tube of lubricant he had retrieved.

"Go for it." he said with his usual grin.

Bill didn't ask "Really?" He didn't question the opportunity. He just gobbled up his aching cock with the lube and aimed into his buddy's bunghole. Bill applied gentle steady pressure. Peter arched his back and ass to make it easier to fuck him. Bill couldn't believe it was going in.

The warmth and tightness of Peter's bowel was almost overwhelming. It had such a grip on the top's rod that he was moving the two of them rather than his seeping cock. Bill was eventually back to breathing hard, and walloping on Peter's loosened ass. Peter's body rocked forward with each pounding, rolling his thick cock and big balls across the bed sheets. Bill dropped a convulsing, lengthy load into his buddy's belly. He dropped, pale and panting, on the bed beside Peter.

Peter looked up. Bill smiled at him. Peter grinned and said, "My turn." Bill smiled even more. Bill came once more that night; Peter, three times total.

The remainder of their college careers the occasional day hike up some spent cider cone or skinny-dipping session in the Oak Creek got a lot more interesting.

THREE TIMES IN THE COUNTY SEAT

The First Time

"Honey! I'm home!" warbled a drunken voice from the back door of the small cinderblock apartment.

Bill was right around the corner in the bathroom, his long lanky frame standing in front of the toilet taking a leak. The shower, getting hotter, ran full blast behind him, muffling Roger's stumbling footfalls. When Bill looked up from his business, Roger was holding onto the doorframe checking out Bill's six-inch pecker.

"Welcome home, boss," Bill called above the noise of the shower.

He shook his dick a few more times than was absolutely necessary and was delighted to watch his supervisor's drunken face nod in like motion. He took the two steps to the door, folded his long arms over his naked chest and leaned against the door jamb, too.

Roger straightens a little, all the while giving Bill a knowing look.

"I like what you did to my place."

Bill had covered for his boss at the office and stayed at Roger's government-issued apartment in the county seat while Roger was away to law enforcement training in the state capitol.

"You had gun powder from re-loading all over the place. Drop a match and the place would have gone up. I had to clean up a little."

Roger's head was nodding again as his eyes studied the room, slowly turning back to Bill's blue eyes.

"Nice hot shower. That's what I need."

"Go for it. I can wait."

"No, you're already naked. Just shout when you get out and I'll jump in."

"Okay," Bill bent to pick a bar of soap out of his toilet kit lying on the floor.

"Bend over again like that and I'll jump you!" Roger hollered with a laugh. He was pulling off his shirt as he spoke.

Bill stood slowly. "I'll keep that in mind. Long time since you saw the wife eh?" he asked as he stepped behind the curtain.

The only response was the muffled sound of Roger's Levis and heavy belt buckle hitting the floor. Bill didn't spend too long in the shower.

Actually, he'd sort of wondered if his boss would jump into the shower behind him. Nay! He went to shout as he stepped out, but Roger was standing there naked, flicking his cock around as though bored. Roger was about the same height as Bill, a little over six foot, 50, silver haired, cocky and with a reputation for really being able to use his nine-incher. He grabbed Bill's white hips to steady himself as he slid by into the small bathroom. His cock seemed to rise up on its own and slide all the way across Bill's thirty-something white bubble butt. Roger kept up the general chatter as he lathered up his front side.

Bill made funny faces at himself in the mirror as though thinking about shaving, but in fact was checking out Roger's right hand. He also noticed the open jar of Vaseline on the back of the toilet seat that hadn't been there before. Roger's right hand was particularly working the lather into his pubic hair and balls. Due to the partially closed shower curtain, Bill couldn't see Roger penetrate his own asshole with the middle finger of his left hand. He was grinding his behind and doing pretty well, when Bill bent to get something out of his toilet kit.

Roger leaped the rim, grabbed the offered ass, slipped his cock between the white cheeks and started pumping away. If Bill got angry Roger figured to call it a joke; otherwise… Bill only smiled back over his shoulder. Roger returned the smile, forced Bill's shoulders down with his left hand, grabbed some Vaseline with his right, plopped some on the straining helmet head of his cock next time it peeked out from between Bill's bottom cheeks and then pushed it into his asshole. The strokes were real short and soft. Bill positively purred, squirming his bottom into a more comfortable position for himself and offering Rogers tool easier access.

"Ah!" Roger gasped as his cock slipped in surprisingly deeper.

"Yeah, go, boss. Yeah, go!"

Roger started taking wild strokes into his subordinate, slamming them both up and back and side to side in the small bathroom. Bill's knee held them off the floor while his hands braced off the walls so they wouldn't topple over.

"Ah, ah, ah!" Roger grunted as he continued to bounce them around the room. He started pulling further out and the slamming into Bill's upturned thighs with a slapping sound caused by their wet skin.

"Yeah, yeah, I'm going to cum," he shouted as he dropped a load deep inside his doubled up buddy's bottom.

Good thing it was too early in the season for the campground outside the door to be occupied and too late in the day for the boys at the shop to still be at work. Roger collapsed upon the crouching bottom.

When his long cock popped out of Bill's behind, Bill took him by the shoulders and lead his to the tiny bedroom with two twin beds. Roger could barely walk, barely see. Bill laid him across his bed sideways, his head up against the cinderblock wall, his bottom hanging off the side of the bed. Roger's light blue eyes looked up into Bill's dark ones to thank him for the fuck. That's when he noticed the jar of Vaseline in Bill's free hand, the gleam of the goo sheathing the hardon he was now stroking.

"Buddy, I don't think I can right now, but…"

"Oh, I think you can," Bill assured him lifting his ankles off the floor and throwing Roger's two limp legs over his left shoulder. He leaned into Rogers's damp thighs forcing his bottom up off the mattress to meet Bill's cock. Roger grinned, squirmed a little, spread his cheeks with his rough long fingers and even helped guide it in. Bill's smaller pecker slid easily in.

"You've done this before." They both laughed as Bill began fucking his buddy like a bunny. Bill pumped in quick, full-length strokes. "Oh, oh, I'm ready…" Both men were breathing hard and Roger felt sensations in his ass channel that he'd never experienced. The prodding of his prostate forced out fluids left over from his recent ejaculation in steady spurts. Bill's climax came quickly. He plunged all the way in for the spurting finale. "Ah, yeah, baby!"

Within a few minutes, they both settled back on their beds for a short nap before doing it all over again.

The Second Time

"It's about time for mid-year review. Why don't we meet about 5:00?" Roger announced over the phone

"Five, p.m.? Kind of late?" Bill replied lowering his voice.

"Well, I tell you what, how often do you get over to the county seat anyway? If it's a good performance review, you can buy me dinner. If I have to give you bad marks after we talk, I'll buy dinner as a consolation prize."

Bill arrived to find the parking lot deserted except for Roger's truck. Bill used his key to let himself in and then wandered down the empty hall. He heard Garth Brooks playing on the radio in Roger's office. The door was closed but not latched. A yellow sticky note said, "Come on in, Bill." He pushed the door open quietly. Roger was bent over his desk concentrating on something. Maybe on the papers lying there.

Roger had heard him enter and he slowly lifted his chin. "Hi, Buddy. Come on in. Have a seat."

The door locked when it swung shut. They spoke of the weather and the drive over and almost even about work. Then he said, "Why don't you come look at this?" Then tapped the desktop.

Bill scooted around the desk peering down at the hand drawn diagram with chicken scratches for notes. Roger had pushed his chair back and stood to make room for the younger man behind the desk too. "What is this?" he whispered as he heard telltale sound of a heavy belt buckle hitting the floor.

"It's a diagram of what I want us to do!" Roger's arm shot up under Bill's. He launched himself onto his buddy's back, which knocked them both to the desk

top. Roger got to his feet, dragged Bill's body back until his bottom hung over the edge of the desk. Half-nelson, he yanked his subordinates underpants and Levis down without unbuckling anything, and worked his reddened cock into the exposed brown hole in Bill's butt.

Bill was grinning. The grinding he was getting in the seat seemed to grind his own cock against the polished desk drawer. Bill's cock thickened and lengthened.

"Ah, ah, ah," Roger started grunting as he plowed Bill's behind, straining to stay on his tip toes.

Roger has long balls and Bill liked the feel of them banging against his own small round balls. Bill's ball were swelling too. "Ah, ah," the older of the two panted. "This is great. I'm sweating like a pig!"

Roger shook his short hair to take the perspiration from his eyes. His thighs began to burn and knees to shake. "I'm getting tired, pal."

"Let me do some of the work then." Bill said pushing off the desk. "Sit back." He directed pushing back on his boss man so Roger ended seated at his chair behind the desk. Bill eased himself on down the nine-inch pole of loving.

"I didn't believe I could go in further!" Roger exclaimed as Bill began rocking his hips back and forth, driving his tight-muscled ass up and down the thick veiny shaft. He grabbed the armrest and stretched back over Roger's prone body, driving the cock even further up with each down plunge.

Roger reached around and began jacking Bill's flapping dong, until the excitement got too much for the older man. He grabbed Bill's hip and began lunging up to meet the strong downward drives. When Roger's throbbing cock unleashed his cum load deep in Bill's bowels, they almost ended up on the floor.

"That was great!" Roger whispered in Bill's ear. Bill's only response was to wait, breathing hard.

"I don't' mean to appear unappreciative, but let's go to dinner. I'll buy." Bill didn't respond. "Then you can fuck me in the ass."

"Sounds good," Bill finally answered, turning in Roger's arms to study the man.

He hammered Roger's butt hole twice that night.

The Third Time

Summer came and fire raged across the high country. Other firefighters came to help contain it, until the rains came. That's the way it is with the big ones. It's just a holding action until God arrives to put them out.

Afterwards Roger and Bill and the crew were left alone with weeks and weeks of patrols and rehab work in the burn. It was hot in that black desolation.

Roger and Bill had been doing paperwork down the hill, but were now in Roger's truck headed up the mountain. Bill had changed into his flight suit before they left the office. His hill-hardened thighs stretched the fabric in the legs as he sat next to Roger on the long hot drive. The tight Velcro at his waist cinched the orange Nomex tight to his skin. The sweat began to collect as a damp patch in the middle of his chest.

As they bounced about on the trucks vinyl seats, Roger's eyes began to note how tightly the sweat made the fabric cling everywhere on Bill's slender body. He sort of wondered if Bill was wearing anything at all under there.

"You look hot." Roger said with a smile from the shaded side of the cab. His right hand reached across and grabbed the zipper on Bill's flight suit. The bouncing of the truck naturally jerked his hand and the suit came open to the top of his buddy's belly. "Is that better?" Bill's only response was to pretend to be peering down inside his clothing.

Then he smiled back at Roger. Roger pulled on the zipper, down and then forward. He could see pubic hair and no underwear, but was afraid to fiddle with things further as the truck bounced along. He cast hungry glances towards the rising bugle beneath the fabric. His long tongue whipped at his chapped lips.

Bill's hand slid down his torso, inside the open zipper. With the next bounce he pried his erection and balls out of the suit, pressing the fabric flat against his inner thighs with his palms.

"Want some?"

Still miles for the crew and the burn, Roger, turned onto a dirt road leading to a thick clump of black jack pine.

"I'll help you out of that thing," he said tersely as he slipped out of the drive door and ran thru the blazing sunlight behind the truck to Bill's door.

Bill had shrugged his shoulders out of the suit. As Roger hastily yanked the door open, Bill swung his legs out and left them in mid air. Roger unzipped the cuffs at the ankles and they managed to pull the Nomex off without having to remove Bill's boots.

"Oh, that's nice." Roger said admiring Bill's sweaty body. He kissed him then grabbed Bill's cock.

Meanwhile, Bill was working the zipper and belt on Roger's green government issue pants. "Ah!" Roger sighed when Bill got the oversized meat out of the sweaty confines. "That's good buddy." Roger groaned as Bill lightly stroked the stiffening nine-incher. "Roll over on your belly."

Bill obliged him, dangling his right knee over the edge of the truck seat to widen the crack of his ass cheeks. Roger climbed in the passenger side, long rigid cock and long dangling balls hanging out of the crotch of his still buttoned jeans. He tried to jam the rigid monster in to the hilt. But his cock bounced maddeningly out of Bill's ass crack, slid wildly across his wet back and brought Roger down onto Bill. The sweat stains under Rogers's armpit were spreading to his side. He kept trying to wedge the dripping mushroom head in the brown hole of the younger man's seat.

Bill finally lifted his thighs off the seat of the truck and spread his white ass wide so Roger could get it. He pumped several inches in at once with a grunt. Bill squirmed on the sweaty seat beneath, the smell of dusty sweat and the occasional whiff of wood smoke filling the cab. Roger pushed and pulled his cock several times at Bill's puckered ass. "Damn," he cussed under his breath, shaking sweat off his head. Bill's ass had clamped down tight on the Roger's thick cock shaft.

Roger pumped a few more times, growling in frustration, then looked around and pried Bill's cheeks further apart and threw all his body weight into the attack.

"Ah! Ah, ah," Bill shouted through gritted teeth and the rest came out as a groan. Roger's weight pinned Bill's body to the seat. He began to madly jab at Bill's now loosened hole. The smell of sweat and shit began to overpower the wood smoke in the cab. The sun seared thru Roger's shirt just below his shoulders and seemed to drive him harder and harder as his skin began to redden.

"I gotta cum. I gotta cum!" he whimpered, whipping at Bill's butt. He gasped and the tempo of his strokes quickened. He gasped again and then his right

foot collapsed under him and he collapsed on top of Bill as his nearly spent cock spewed and leaked into Bill's body.

"That was great, buddy, that was so great," Roger panted.

Then he thought of Bill pinning to the seat, and lifted himself off the younger man. That's when he saw the mess he'd made and recollected his thought. "Oh, man, I was a little too… Sorry."

Bill lifted his naked raped body up on his forearms. He looked over his shoulder at Roger rather seriously. Then with a kick of his booted left foot he spun into a sitting position, back against the driver's side door, knees spread as wide as the steering wheel would allow, a scraped up, banged up, beet red boner bobbing upright in his crotch. "I think you can make it up to me."

"Shit," Roger laughed. He spit to clear the adrenalin from his system and smiled again.

"Less talk, more tongue." Bill directed, reaching down to tug on his six-inch hardon.

Roger was famous for the length of his tongue, a fact that he used most often to please his wife and other women. The older guy hesitated at the thought of licking a sweaty dick, especially after looking at the sticky mess on the truck seat in front of Bill's crotch. But once Bill dragged him across the cab by the collar of his green shirt, Roger was enthusiastic.

His tongue was so long, he could slide it down Bill's bobbing six incher, tickle his balls and roll his tongue around the shaft the long way.

"Ah," Bill sighed at the feeling of the soft cool tongue on his ravaged dick.

Roger kept his tongue in the position and slammed his skull up and down until he got a mouth full of creamy tart cum that chased away all the other smells they'd made.

Roger received a directed reassignment to the State Capitol not too much later. So, Bill figured three times was all he and Roger would get. But he was wrong. Just as he had been about his affair with his bald, muscular, broad shouldered, sledge-fisted neighbor, Brian. But, both of those fucks are one more story.

TRAILER TRIO:
F'CKIN'

I scraped the dirt off my boots one last time as I knocked, waited for the "Come on in!" and then entered the darkened trailer from the uninsulated mud room. My best friend Drew stood maybe ten feet away from the door in a faded light blue tee-shirt with blue trim and worn, cheap jeans.

For just a moment his blue eyes sunk back in the sockets of his weathered face, dark with worry. But the wide grin seemed confident of the surprise he planned for me. "How's it hanging, Bill?"

Before, I could answer the joke, a long wet tongue snaked down my throat, his lips locked down on mine, his wet and wild kiss rained on me. His long bony, hairy arms wrapped around my shoulders, his ribs poking against my chest, as always his forest of strawberry-blonde chest hair cushioned his on rush.

And that slab of meat in his worn Wal-Mart specials poked against my crotch. It had been a long time since my old friend and I screwed around on my living room couch after Saturday morning coffee. And we weren't going to, today either, he'd warned me.

We broke for air. His eyes were afire. His large rough right hand grabbed my ass and started drilling through the denim for my asshole.

"Ready to get *f'cked*?" He could never admit we'd been *fucking* one another. His thick sun-bleached eyebrows danced in excitement, shaking his shaggy almost orange hair. His dirty, scarred finger tips with their gnawed off nails began unbuttoning my shirt.

"Somebody anxious?" I asked, my palm stroking the hard ridge of fabric in his pants.

"Oh. It's not for me, Bud." His grin turning into a secret little smile.

"Ah, you want me naked when the mystery man arrives?"

My flannel shirt flittered floor ward. Drew folded his long skinny legs and knelt before me, fumbling hurriedly with my belt. He clawed my trousers open, slurped up my little six incher, grabbed handfuls of my "tighty whities" and denim, and yanked everything down to my socks.

I quit asking questions. I had been so long and even back then by buddy Drew rarely licked the lizard. My head felt light. My spine arched back. A sigh escaped. I grasped his bony shoulders to keep from falling. My dick started twitching. Drew rolled it and his thick tongue around the inside of his hot wet mouth; two pairs of wet shorts tumbling in the dryer at the Laundromat. He pulled the pants away from my feet, his mouth still suctioned to my crotch.

He looked up, his eyes glassed with pleasure, his freckles danced upon the blush red field of his high cheeks. His copper mustache slid in and out of the forest of my brown pubes. "Like that Buddy?" he garbled around my twitching dick.

His chapped lips kept working my weiner. Oh yeah, I liked that. His right hand knew its way around my ass. His middle finger tore its way in my asshole. I gasped. I arched my knees and he began widening the entrance. I held onto the back of his hairy neck. My dick stood half-erect and Drew's face bounced back and forth on my middle-aged belly.

"Aw," I moaned when his finger made it about half way up my ass and I could smell the butt juices starting to flow. We'd trained my ass up well in that intermittent fling of a few months back.

He shook his bearded jaw back and forth now, holding my erection by the purpled head and letting his tongue drag back and forth. His finger made it all the way in. I was panting.

"Ready for some *f'ckin'*?" he asked again. His finger popped out of my hole. He yarded himself up and caught me with his left arm as I started to collapse. His left arm herded me towards the back of the trailer.

"Is he here already?" I hoped.

"Bud, he's a really nice guy." My foggy, horned-up brain didn't have time to register "uh-oh". "He just don't look like a nice guy. Give `em a chance, okay?"

We were half way down the dusty carpeted hall. Drew's massive left hand wedged firmly in the small of my back and his right hand curled around my right shoulder.

Now, let me tell you about me and Drew. We are about as tall as a summer day in Southeast is long. Both as fair as the snow. Shoot, my red-headed buddy, Drew, would be an albino if he wasn't so hairy. I'm looking down the hall towards Drew's bedroom. I'm seeing a short dark man lying in his bed. Maybe Hispanic,

muscular, stroking his thick cock as he stared up at the ceiling, wide shoulders, and a curly black beard. Did I mention muscles and thick cock?

"Gomez," he calls guiding my naked body, my raging hard-on bouncing with our long strides to the foot of the bed, my knees shaking just a little. Drew's hand on my shoulder felt good. "Let me introduce my best buddy…"

"Bill!" Gomez shouted with surprise.

Gomez teaches boxing and carries an undeserved reputation for a bad temper. He rented a room from my best friend when his relationship with his girlfriend went south and the cops mistakenly showed up. His nose has obviously broken several times, from barroom brawls people say. Either his head is too short or his face too wide. We are talking mono-brow thicker than most guys' mustaches. His brown eyes are so dark, they look black and lifeless. His beard is scruffy and patchy; torn. His short forehead creased with wrinkles. His features expressionless. His lips habitually looked in a grimace. His jaw firmly locked. Scary. And then he smiles, he's just plain ugly.

"You two know one another?" Drew asks, delight raising the volume on his previously worried voice. His hand began to slide down my back.

"Gomez rented a room from Andy for a while." Our eyes locked. "I hear he can fuck for an hour straight." The walls in Andy's house are very thin.

"And I hear you'd like to get fucked for an hour straight."

His sledge like hands on his muscular brown hairy arms held up by his impossible wide muscled shoulders reached for me. His hard chest rose up after his thick fingered hands. His fat brown eight incher popped from the sheets wadded at his narrow waist, waving a string of glistening love juice that ran from the head of his perfect cock to his firm fuzzy belly.

Drew's hand continued to slide down my back and found its way to the crack between my ass cheeks.

"I'll leave you two fellers alone." He shoved me onto Bob. My lips fell on his, as my trembling body fell into his arms and my eyes shut. His lips played discreetly, carefully across mine, as though fearing to scare me off. His beard made sure to not scrape my smooth chin and blushing cheeks. He gently pulled me down atop his thighs. His whole frame shook with hesitation, anticipation and restraint.

"Drew, said nothing but safe sex. I've got all the supplies. I'm already." I'd guess that brown soldier standing in the hunk's lap felt definitely ready, by the way he unconsciously dry humped my inner thigh. "Drew says you like to start on top," he said cheerily, rocking his head and broad shoulders side to side.

I pressed an index finger to his lips, to calm his worried words, to quench the shudders of anticipation. "It's been a while. But once I get settled on that big cock of yours, we can do it anyway you want."

Gomez's mouth falls open in response, saliva curls at his lower lip, then slips over bounces down his chest and splatters the top of his cock. He never notices. I run my hand up and down his cock lubricating his rod with his saliva and pre-cum. His thick dick stirs in my hand.

He says, "Hm, you miss getting it from a big cock."

I say, "Yep." I lick his tiny nipples, little boy nubs lost in the black fur on his chest.

"My beam is wide, no? Not as long as Drew's but thick."

I chuckled aloud at that. So Drew had finally found someone to bone his butt, like he used to do mine. I get Bob to stand up on his knees. You can almost hear that brown, stiff cock go "Sproing" when it pops out of the sheet that snagged it. I grab it and start to lick it from my squatting position at the foot of the bed. The purple veins stand out in sharp relief on his fat fudge pole. The glans is the dark purple of most mature Hispanic cocks.

He kneels before me and I earnestly slurp up and down his prick while I rub his legs and play with his tightening ball sack. His leg muscles are so tight and thick, like he's been working out at the boxing gym all his life. He moans and his rock-hard pecker twitches in my gripping, pumping hand, and hungry mouth.

When I lift off his cock to catch a breath, he says, "How about you lying face down for a minute and I'll climb atop you with my dick rubbing your ass crack? I won't go in, I swear." He grew very excited – his cock gets steel-hard and drips.

I flopped face down on the bed beside him, grabbing the head of the mattress to keep the world from spinning. So, I know this is real. He jumps up to his feet and steps behind and over me. He eased his hard body onto mine, his cock sliding into the cleft of my narrow ass. It's wet there. My hole, kindly widened by Drew our matchmaker, leaked. Gomez is oozing sticky pre-cum. It's getting hot in Drew's room. Gomez was perspiring before I got there and now I'm sweating under his hard thrusting body.

By his whimpers and pants I'm guessing it gets to be too much for him. "My turn. Climb on top of me, white boy."

I roll over onto his smaller frame, and shake my hips around until my semi-hard semen-hose settles into his furry crack. I lift torso so I can watch the pink head of my cock poke out of his crack into the grove of black hair in the small of the broad plain of his back.

"Yeah, that feels good."

I lean down and stick my tongue in his little brown ear.

"Oh, God, Bill. You're killing me. You can plow my ass anytime you want when we're done." Oh yeah. "You ready for some *f'ckin'*?" he asks using Drew's expression.

I scoot back on my haunches. He flips over on his back-side and pulls a handful of supplies from the nightstand. As he squirts KY on the head of his rod and rolls it around with his thumb, I open the condom. We roll it down the shaft. He squirts on more gel; we both stroke it around. I take the little left on my hand and swipe my ass, then scoot up on my knees to straddle his hips.

"Yeah, yeah" he mutters as I reach behind me grab his cock from him and lower my ass onto the head. I slide the sheaved snake back and forth until promptly

finding the door to our own personal paradise. I settled on the head and just waited, not in pain, but sheer delight. It had been many months since Drew had done the honors. I love that feel of my sphincter stretching. Of my body being taken. Of release. Of joy.

Gomez shook with excitement below me. Arching his back in anticipation of the thrust and fighting his cock craving to violate me at the same time. I relieved him of his dilemma by lowering and raising myself, lowering and rising myself ever lower until my long hairless balls rested comfortably on his hard abdomen.

"Yeah? Yeah? Now can I?" A moot question, I suppose. He already was.

Gomez pulled me down to his chest, lifted his hips and began freely fucking my ass. I turned to kiss him. But, he knew no restraint now. His thighs rammed my buttock, his cock gave my hole no consideration. He no longer acted concerned about my comfort. His strong arms held my head and shoulders off to the side and he stared Heavenward in a world of his own. Or so I thought, until I heard him mutter, "Oh, that's so pretty."

I looked up. "Drew has a mirrored ceiling?"

"You want to watch?" he asked all concerned.

He yanked out. I gasped. He rolled me on my left side. He grabbed my right leg with his right hand and guided himself with is natural left hand. When I recovered, I looked up and saw us both on our sides, *f'ckin'*. We tried the view when we spooned. We tried with one of my legs straight up in the air. We giggled at my balls and dick bouncing every time he drove it home. Gomez pulled me close, ignoring the mirror, fucking fast and close. "Anyway I want, no?" he panted into my ear.

I pulled my sticky hand off my cock and patted him assuredly on the thigh. "Yeah, I'm all yours."

"Doggy style!" He held tight as I struggled to my hands and knees. My brown buddy managed to stay in and keep stroking as I pulled us into position across the width of the bed. That's not quite what my top wanted. He grabbed my hips and swung me 90 degrees so we both faced the foot of the bed and could peer into the mirror on the wall. We could also see Drew in the doorway; shirtless, trousers unbuttoned and rolled down to his thighs, pushing and pulling that nine-inch slab of white meat our direction.

"Hey, Drew!" Gomez laughed. Drew didn't even seem embarrassed.

"Three holes!" I called. "No waiting."

Drew didn't even wait to take off his pants until he planted his cock in my mouth. Once free of the costume he wore in the world, he rode my face and fucked my mouth with that big peter, rubbing my lips and cheeks with my own saliva before sticking it back in.

"Oh yeah, Drew!" Gomez called in encouragement.

Drew never stays long in the saddle. In a minute, he finished by jacking off rapidly while I held my mouth close to his cock head as Gomez's firm grasp on my shoulders would let me..

"Do it, Drew, do it!" Gomez chants from the back of my bleachers.

When Drew starts to leak precum pretty heavily, I take it in my mouth and squeeze out as much juice as I can. He jacks a bit more and starts spurting, a shot that almost goes up my nose.

"Yeah, buddy, eat that fuckin' cum!" our active Hispanic audience shouts.

I suck down the rest of Drew's huge load of man juice while I jack myself off, cumming in the wadded up sheets. Drew collapses back into the room's sole chair, apologizing to me for the deluge. I collapse on the bed, head to the mattress, arms useless, Gomez having his way with my post-orgasm ass.

"Bill, you've got a great ass. I'm going to shoot, okay?"

My jaw aches, my arms ache, thighs, back. I'm exhausted and loving it. "Yeah," I sigh.

He's banging me furiously, grunting, calling for Drew's attention, cussing in Spanish. He shudders, let's loose a few times and collapse on top of me.

My old friend Drew and I try to smile at one another across the foot of the tussled bed. I try to say thanks, him too. We are so drained; all we can do is stare. Gomez manages to pry himself off my sticky, stinky butt. He's kneeling behind me, trying to stand, shaking the perspiration out of his hair and lethargy out of his mind.

"That was great, you guys. I loved doing your ass, Bill. I gotta use the bathroom. When I get back, I'll *f'ck* ya, Drew!"

We didn't burst out laughing until we heard our handsome friend close the bathroom door.

UH, BUDDY

"Uh, buddy? I sleep in the nude," John Jones announces, a giggle in his voice and a blush rising to his cherub cheeks.

He's already nude, baring it all for Bill to see – beefy body, coppery body hair, small coral lips, fair freckled complexion, and broad shoulders. John's short frame poses in the middle of the room, naked from ruddy buzz cut to the closely trimmed toe nails on his left foot.

Bill already lies abed, reading. He tosses "The Odyssey," rolls the bedding and flips it back to reveal the upper thighs of his long legs, a hairless belly and a six-inch cock crouching on his long sac. "Me too, buddy," he grins.

The blue eyes beneath Bill's brown hair meet John's even bluer. There is no telling expression on the taller man's face, but Jones's sparkling eyes and sly smile do enough talking for the both of them.

"Well, scoot over then."

John pulls back the bedding on his side of the double bed. As the rosy knee on his left leg presses the mattress, Bills long arm shoots out and his hand comes to rest against John's chest in the fine fiery forest of hair there.

"I'm jealous," Bill admits with a toothy smile as he begins to stroke the coppery field of curling hair. Each swipe moves further down the field ever closer to the thicker, darker triangle of burgundy pubic hair floating above John's swollen cock.

"I've been known to share," Jones says. Suddenly serious, he nods again for Bill to scoot over.

These old friends and former co-workers came to the capitol city representing their local lodges at the statewide convention. They requested housing together and discreetly mentioned (in very concerned and considerate tones of voice) that they don't mind sharing. Their host's son is gone off to college. They received his efficiency apartment above the garage all to themselves.

Bill rolls away, reaching for the switch on the bedside lamp that lights the room. John eyes the plump full cheeks he seems to be proudly displaying in the process. His face flushes and cock jumps. But the light goes out before Bill rolls back. Of course, he sees the flush on John's face and the arousal of his cock in the mirror on the wall. John never actually lies down. One leg curled beneath, he props himself up on this left elbow, gazing down on Bill in the darkness. Bill lays back, long arms curl beneath his head, exposing the only hair on his upper torso, leaving himself vulnerable and exposed. Neither man bothers pulling the covers up. As their eyes adjust, beams from the corner streetlight slip through the blinds and fall softly on the scene.

"I have a question," Bill begins in a knowing tone of voice. With Jones's urging, he continues. "Why did Tom say burn those pictures?"

John responds with the prefunctionary "What?" Bill reminded him of his last trip to town, their round of drinking with Jones's best friend, Tom. Tom and John were recalling their bachelor days and a now legendary weekend in the Capitol City; staying at the State Hotel and Bar, sharing a hot tub with two lesbians that night and the foursome's trip to Mendenhall glacier the next day.

"Oh, he thought they sent me pictures from the hot tub."

Bill can feel the heat from Jones's cheekbones burning as the blood rose in blush. Bill enjoys teasing Jones.

"So, what happened in the hot tubs, Jonesy?" A long paused followed. Bill could see, John turn his head away in embarrassment.

"Hot tubs?" Bill's voice snaps as his fingers tweak one of Jones's soft pink nipples.

"So?" his knowing voice prods as his finger tips prod the left side of John's stout torso. The redhead giggles and rolls towards the tickle.

"Well?" Bill asks switching words as his tickling fingers switch to the copper-tops right side. A little lower this time. "And?" and back to the left, once again lower. "Tell…" Bill's finger tips touch the tip of Jones's fully aroused rod. They stop there, caressing the head. The first and index finger hold the helmet head while the thumb pushes down on the pool of precum there and smears it around, losing more juice in the process. Then the moving hand shifts on to the other side.

John laughs out loud.

"Well, we meet these girls at the bar; Rose and Ruby. They had a hot tub reserved in a room underneath the hotel." Jones begins gleefully. "They offered to share their tub with us." John hoots and nudges him in the chest.

"Rose had big tits. You would have liked her. Long brown hair. Big ole round nipples. So, they take us down there. We start getting undressed. They aren't shy at all. Well, you know Tom. Neither is he."

Bill knows Tom. He's blond and bulky now. But, Bill knows that in their youth, Tom and John were gorgeous little boys to behold. They experienced no trouble with the ladies. Everyone knows, too, that usually Tom led them into trouble.

"Once we all get in the tub, he reaches over for the girl with the short blonde hair. Ruby laughs and takes 'my girl' in her arms." Bill starts stroking his cock. "Tom says, 'So is that how it's going to be?' And like, instead of answering the girls start kissing. It was hot; we were both pulling our wangs."

Jones nods to where his left hand is active between his own thighs. "Then they break and Ruby says if we want to see more of that, they need to see some from us."

"I've already got my right arm across Tom's shoulders. He's so horny. I don't think he knew what he did. He turns in my arm, drops his cock, grabs my body with both hands and lays a wet one on me. It was hot. I'll admit, I enjoyed it. I kissed back. Rose and Ruby hooted and hollered.

"Tom and I break for air; the girls are sucking on one another's titts and licking the nipples. Did I tell you Rose had enormous hooters? So Tom goes down on my nipples. I return the favor. We go back to kissing, because Ruby tells us to."

Bill's left hand scales the darkness again to caress John's soft pink nipples. His right hand is flaying his cock furiously.

"Ruby is telling Rose how much she wants to get fucked tonight and asking her if she wants to get fucked. Rose is, like, 'Oh yeah,' and giving me specifically the eye. Tom and I are still holding one another. He whispers that we are getting laid tonight, then pulls both our cocks into his hand, so we are tip to base and starts stroking us.

"Rose climbs out on the deck around the tub and spreads her legs around the edge of the pool. Bill, she had a shaven pussy! Absolutely beautiful! I had to take Tom's hand and stop him, so I didn't lose it right there.

"Ruby gets down there with her little pink tongue and starts working Rose's pink hole, while wiggling her ass at us. Rose gives her directions and makes all sorts of appreciative noises. Tom is holding me even tighter and even with my hand fighting his goes back to jerking us off. Ruby is making a show of running her tongue up Rose's clit, curling it up at the end of the stroke and slurping up the juice. Tom is going crazy. Ruby says she's about got Rose ready and that we should get one another ready.

"Tom roars like a bull coming out of the water. He lifts me up out of the pool lays me back on the deck next to Rose, points my aroused wang skyward, opens his mouth and goes down on it. It was hot! Yeah, his mouth! He didn't like

work my tool with his tongue or anything, but he did it. He sucks me off; his best friend.

"I didn't know what to do, until Rose's cherry lips find mine. Then I don't know what is going on. Maybe Ruby took a turn on my wang. Then, I hear her say, `It's my turn'. Rose seems disappointed when Tom pulls me up. He tells me don't even think about it. I can feel Rose's wanting hands on my back and hips. I hear Ruby urging me to do it. I lick the shaft of his cock a few times.

"The fool coos in a high falsetto that he loves me and then tells me to suck it. I open my mouth wide and his rod jams between my lips like a salmon jumping a fish ladder. All I taste is chlorine.

"He takes three shallow strokes in my mouth. Ruby shouts hoorah. Tom jumps to her side of the pool. My sweet Rose pulls me back to her and in a few moments she is mounted up on my wang riding away. Next to me Tom is pounding Rose's pussy while winking at me. Rose and I spent the night together in their room; Tom and Ruby in ours.

"The next day with bloodshot eyes and bruised bodies we all went to Mendenhall Glacier."

John didn't explain the sleeping arrangements that night, but no doubt it was interesting. By now John's inexpert right hand is trying to jerk Bill off. Bill's taken over the duties on John's till John stops him.

Jones's breath is coming fast and shallow.

"I have a question." He tries to imitate the knowing tone used by his old friend. With a sigh, Bill lets his hand relax inside John's. That's the sign to go on. "Why did Jim Barnyard say if you like him now, wait until you take a shower with him?"

Bill's body goes rigid with surprise. His "What?" is unconvincing.

"Last time I was in town, we went to that party," John presses. "We talked to the wildlife guy, Barnyard? Big boy, hairy all over, real daddy type. You'd been teasing and flirting with me hellaciously. Your pager went off and you had to go find the phone.

"Jim's asking if I'm not offended by your behavior. I assure him that I really enjoy your company. He'd been drinking a whole lot of wine that night. Remember? Claret, I think. Then he says, if you like him now, wait until you take a shower with him. I don't think he knew what he said until he saw the shock on my face. He turned beet-red, maroon, scarlet, something I don't know. He asks me not to repeat that and leaves. Leaves the party!"

Bill lies still for a moment. John bends to kiss his hand. A sigh escapes Bill's lips as he begins.

"We stayed at Rowan Bay, the previous fall. I helped him with a deer darting project. As big and burly as he is you'd think he'd need no help hiking around a temperate rain forest, but I was pleased to help. You been to Rowan? It's a remote camp way east of town. We had the whole place to ourselves, took the best

trailer. It's nice, but the generator is tricky. It shuts off automatically, so you have to time your evening and showers."

"Ah," John interjects, absentmindedly fondling Bill's balls.

"Yeah, well. I'm taking a shower with the door open. He calls through the curtains: `You about done?' I say, `Yeah, you want me to leave the water running? It's temperamental.'

He says, `Yeah'. Then I hear him climbing in. I say hear because I'm all bent backwards trying to wash the soap out of my hair. But over the hum of the generator and rush of the water I can hear the curtain rustle and the tub groan under his 270 pounds. I can feel his presence, smell the hemlock needles stuck in his curly hair, the stink of a hard day on his body. I know he's looks down on my with that grin of his. I'm 6'1". Someone looking down on me is amazing."

Bill pauses in his story and reaches for his own cock. Jones cradles his aroused member in his open left hand.

"When, I straighten up, shaking the water out of my hair, I lean right into him. He's standing ever close with his big muscular arms folded across his hairy chest. `Gotcha,' he says and grabs me around the waist. No place for my hands to go, but atop his shoulders. `Wanna switch?' he says and grins. He whirls us around the little shower and starts rinsing off.

"We are talking about stuff. I'm handing him shampoo and soap as needed. He points out where I need to rinse off and pulls me under the spray with him. The generator shuts off. The lights flicker and die. Did you ever notice how people grab one another when the lights go out? The water pressure dwindles to a little trickle running down the crack of Barnyard's ample ass. I get woozy. He helps me sit on the edge of the tub. I start apologizing all over myself when he gets a little disoriented in the dark and leans into me.

"I'm jabbering away when his dick flops into my mouth. It's big! Even if I hadn't been in a state of shock, it would have been hard to spit it out. So, it rolls around in there for a bit. `Sorry about that,' I say. `No problem,' he says, hulking over me black against the starlight coming in through the window. `It felt good.'"

"I'll bet," John replies in a husky pant, failing to notice that Bill didn't explain the sleeping arrangements that night

His vermillion lips hang over Bill's. The crimson field shimmering on John's chest floats just inches about the buckled barren plain of Bill's body. Their lips touch like a bolt striking dirt. The flaming forest is crushed by the rush of their two chests together. The breath clashes between their locked mouths and crashes like thunder around the little isolated room.

Bill spreads his white thighs and lifts his knees. Jones settles between his legs rubbing his brick hard cock against Bill's. His tight furry red balls roll back and forth across Bill's sac. Brown pubes clutch at crimson. When Jones's cock slides further down and starts banging at the rose bud in Bill's butt, Bill gets out the lube. A condom hides hopefully in the back pocket of John's pants lying beside

the bed. John's thick eight incher gets easily into Bill's behind. Bill's long tongue wedges itself happily into Jones's willing mouth.

Soon, they ride the heat and hardness in matching rhythm. "Fuck, yeah, man," Bill grunts. "Give me that big rod. Uh. Fuck. I'm cumming!" Bill's load spurts into the mass of red hair on his fucker's belly and chest.

The rapid orgasmic twitching of Bill's ass muscles on John's pumping rod sends him over the edge.

"Uh, buddy, me, too! Oh, shit, yeah! Ah!" John roars at last, unleashing a gush of jizm deep inside his buddy's ass.

This was going to be a good convention and they didn't need to explain the sleeping arrangements tonight.

CARLOS IN THE VALLEY OF THE SUN

Carlos sat at his desk bored, waiting for five o'clock to roll around. Trying to decide if he should go jerk off in the men's room or wait and try to get a little off of Bill later in the night. Or both.

The phone rang. It was Bill, "Get your bags packed we're headed to Phoenix. We've got to fix a problem down there."

Carlos was up for it so he jumped at the chance to get out of the office. And an opportunity to jump Bill's bones all weekend. Bill was 6'1", long legged with a beer belly and a big butt just made for fucking. Bill could be annoying, but he got them work doing construction cost estimates and occasional contracts. Plus there was the added benefit that once Carlos pinned him down, Bill just loved to be fucked. Carlos, on the other hand, was a little shorter, darker of skin, black haired, handsome, hairy, stocky, hard muscled from swinging a hammer and hung with a perpetually hard 8-inch cock.

It was 110 degrees when Carlos got off the jet. Walking across the tarmac he could feel the sweat run down his balls. The crack of his ass was instantly wet and juicy. Just the way he hoped Bill's would be. But, Bill wasn't there to greet him. Carlos ended up waiting in the lung- searing sun for an expensive ride in a crumby cab with no air conditioning and a third world driver not worth looking at twice. And the driver got lost three time.

When Carlos got to the hotel room, Bill met him at the door wearing a pair of hastily donned tighty-whiteys. His tall body was wet with sweat. He had turned the air conditioner off! The sliding glass door to the little balcony must have been

wide open. The partial drawn curtain in front of it let the sickeningly sweet smell of car exhaust and orange blossoms waft into the stifling room.

"What the fuck did you turn the air conditioning off for?" asks Carlos. "It's flipping hot in here!"

"I'm not hot." says Bill. "I like it this way."

"Turn on the God damned air!"

"No!" Bill fidgeted and weakly smiled at Carlos.

"Fine." said Carlos. "Get your ass over here. Help me peel my shirt off."

Bill comes over and slowly unbuttons Carlos shirt. The bottom runs his hands over Carlos' chest and his fingers through the matt of black hair there. He reaches down and pulls the shirttail out of his partner's pants. Then his fingers are running down the brown stomach on the treasure trail brushing the stiffening cock through the khaki pants.

"Now get down on your knees."

Bill gets down as he's told and then looks up, his blue eyes meeting the other man's brown.

"Reach into my pants pocket and pull out what's in there. I got a surprise for you."

Bill reaches in, plays with Carlos notoriously hairy balls some, but finds a piece of plastic in there. He pulls it out and discovers a condom in his hand

"Now roll it on my dick."

"What?"

"Pull my pants down, get my dick hard, play with it a bit and then put the condom on my dick"

"What for?"

"Because I'm going to fuck your ass on the kitchen table for disobeying me. That's why!"

"Oh."

Bill pulls Carlos's pants down around his knees and proceeds to play with his hairy balls. When his cock starts to rise, Bill holds it in his hand rolling it in his fingers until it gets rock hard. When it starts to pulse from being teased Bill rolls the condom on.

"Now get up, bend over the table and pull your underwear down. Get them down around your ankles"

Bill gives Carlos a sneer but hesitantly obeys as Carlos kicks out of his own pants. Carlos walks over reaches around Bill, grabs his balls and then rips his underwear off

"Damn! Watch out, you son of a bitch. That hurt my balls," says Bill.

"I told you to get your ass naked and bend over the fucking table. I meant it.

Bill bends over again waiting for the feel of Carlos dick head sliding up his ass into position. He hears curtain behind them sway with breeze and feels a blast

of scorching air on his ass. Then a burning sensation makes him scream as Carlos' dick fills his ass.

"Fucker! You could have loosened me up some."

"Serves you right for making it so damn hot in here. Besides it went in nice and easy."

Carlos starts slamming into his ass, hard. He can feel his dick head slide out and then back over Bill's opening. Carlos liked to pull his dickhead almost out of his asshole before sliding it all the way back in. Bill groans with pleasure as his dick starts to leak some cum.

Carlos starts to moan. His thick cock is overly sensitive because it's been sitting in sweat between his hairy balls all day on the flight. He can't hold it any longer; he comes as he continues to pound Bill's ass.

"Ah, yeah, fucker, here it is! Take my cum up your hot ass! Uh, uh, uh!"

Bill starts to come just from the feel of Carlos dick pulsing wildly in his ass.

"Oh, yeah, so good, feels so good," he grunts.

He sprays his thick white cum all over the side of the table. With his dick still in Bill's ass, Carlos reaches around and grabs some of Bill's cum. Carlos rubs it into his chest and into the hair on his belly, then licks the remainder off his thick fingers.

"Ya, it's going to be a hot weekend eh Bill?"

"Yeah, maybe for you. My knees are still bruised from the last trip with you. So watch it, buddy. It's going to be you on your knees this time."

"Oh really, now?" says Carlos "You think you can get that little dick of yours hard enough to fuck my ass?"

"If he can't, I can take care of it!" comes a voice behind them. As the top turns to look, he feels Bill's long arms reach back and pry his ass checks apart. There's a guy coming in off the balcony who must be 6'4, hairy and 300 well-muscled pounds.

"What the fuck?" stutters the open-assed and still bent Carlos.

"This is the customer we're here to service. Looks like it's your turn. Say hello to Ray," Bill grins. As Carlos began to pry himself out of Bill's grasp, a heavy hand fell on his left shoulder from above. A thick cock head (with a ring in it) wedged itself against his hole. A large hairy belly pressed him towards the table. Then both large burly hands were on his hips. Bill pushed his whipped ass into Carlos' wilting dick to further aid in Ray's assault.

"His handle is Bear-Rider."

Bill slipped from beneath him and Big-Ray slammed Carlos to the table. His 10-inch cock began tearing its way into the carpenter's behind.

"Agh! No!" Carlos groaned as Big-Ray pulls back for another punch.

"You liked the rough stuff when you were giving it to your little buddy," Ray growls.

Rays rods slams into Carlos. The table jumps. Carlos screams as Ray continues to push further in. Then the pain is easing as Big-Ray pulls back for another stab at the brown man's ass. Carlos is panting and quivering beneath the massive man.

"Not so tough when you're the bottom!"

Rays rod slams into the ass. The table jumps. The victim screams as Ray continues to push further in. Bill starts to crawl under the table for a better view of the action. Big-Ray eases out.

"I wouldn't crawl under there, little buddy. It might collapse."

The rod slams into the ass. The table jumps. The victim screams. Only this time Big-Ray doesn't back out. His fingers interlace with his gasping victim's. His thigh keeps pressing forward. "Little buddy, help me move this table against the wall." Big-Ray makes the intertwined fingers lift the table and its load. Bill helps him slide the whole table firmly against the wall. The fingers untwine and move to the small of the back, pinning the ass firmly to the now stable table.

The rod slams the ass. The table doesn't jump. The victim doesn't scream. Things are loosening up down there and Ray's python is starting to slide rather than tear in and out of its hole. Bill eyes the whole show in fascination while stroking his peter, then kneels behind Ray.

"Oh yeah, that's what I like, little buddy – a hole for my cock and a tongue for my hole."

Bill was behind him burying his face in the big man's cheeks every time he pulled out in preparation for another thrust. His big butt was wet from the heat and Bill had to pry his cheeks apart to get anywhere near his hairy hole. Each rock of Ray's hips brought him a deeper probing.

"Now my balls. Like my long slapping hairy balls?" Bill obliged and sucked away, licking the golf-ball sized nuts with his wet tongue.

"Can you see my cock going into him from down there? Lick my cock when I pull out." The big guy pulled back until just the head of his ringed cock rested in the bottom's ass. Bill fiddled around beneath the table and then managed a few swipes of the waiting rod.

"Cool!" Big-Ray shouted then the rod slams the ass.

"I'll bet that tool he was beating you with is all tiny and limp now."

Bill mumbled something in reply.

"What?" Big-Ray asked stopping his strokes again.

"No, Carlos is hard."

"You liking the fucking I'm giving you?"

For the first time Carlos spoke. "It's starting to feel good."

Bill mumbled something in the affirmative, and Ray, shaking his head in disbelief, went back at it.

Bill mumbled again.

"What?"

"He said I'm about to come."

Ray eased up and Carlos's legs bent with the first convulsion. Big-Ray caught him as he fell to the floor and guided the still spewing Latino to sit on the bed.

"Oh, gee. Oh, gee!" Carlos moaned as he collapse on the bed and watched his spewing cock bounce around.

"Well, imagine that." Again, Big-Ray shook his head in disbelief. "And I still ain't come yet."

"I can probably help you there." Bill said.

Ray looked down to see his little buddy on all four wiping his chin with the back of his hand. "Really."

Bill rolled out from underneath the table onto his back. Big-Ray went to all fours and began pounding the trail Carlos had blazed so well for him.

Exhausted, spent, bruised, shocked and amazed, Carlos could do nothing but stare at the two men and think, "Yeah, this is going to be one hot weekend!"

A WALK IN THE PARK

As he peed, Joe glanced around the wet woods nervously. His head kept turning till he met my gaze. He shook his dick, took a few steps toward me and said, "Come suck on this thing."

I was finally going to see the whole package. His brown cock began to rise even before the first lick. His balls had shrunken in the chill air. They were surrounded by sparse pubic hair which led to a hairy belly. I threw my coat down near his feet in order to have a place to kneel in the drenched moss.

I slurped his every hardening dick into my waiting mouth and slipped my hand up under his shirt to play with his nipples and keep my hand warm. His cock was rock hard now and he occasionally pushed my head all the way down it. My gag reflex kicked in each time, but I ignored it.

A branch snapped behind me. Joe jumped, pulling his stiff prick out of my mouth with a loud "Plop!" He pulled his pants up and stared frantically into the forest. I rose calmly, and put my coat on. I was chilled. I looked into the old growth. As usual in Southeast, the sky was overcast. This gave a green hue to the light that made it thru the centuries-old canopy. In an ancient rain forest, something is always falling from above. I saw nothing. "Relax, city boy," I assured him, patting him on the shoulder and rubbing his crotch.

Joe pulled it out again as I unzipped and fished my own semi-hard dick out. I returned to sucking, but not on by knees. The position and mossy bog made love-making awkward for both of us.

"Turn around and bend over," he ordered as he pulled a condom out of his jacket pocket.

I bent before him, hefting my shirt and coat up on the small of my back.

He leaned forward. "A little higher," I suggested and repositioned my ass. I braced my torso against my knees with my right arm and started pulling on my dick with my left hand. The tip of his brown shaft was wedged against my bung hole. I wanted to beg him to shove it in. Then I grunted with discomfort.

"Okay," he said more as direction then question.

"Spread my cheeks apart more," I urged him, feeling the thickness of his cockhead just above my twitching asshole.

With that, his thumbs and stubby brown fingers began to knead my butt as he gently rocked back and forth. I knew this was his favorite position because he told me earlier he wanted to pull and push my butt on his cock. As my repeated grunts gave way to groans, he took deeper and deeper strokes until he slipped all the way in. My groan of delight was all it took to send him rocketing my butt back and forth, rising on his toes with each pull to get deeper in. My knees shook with the exertion of holding our position on the uneven, unstable ground. My hand was a mess of pre cum. Joe's breath was becoming labored. In another second, I could feel him dumping loads of lava in my butt. His knees gave out, too, and he leaned his bare brown butt against a black Sitka spruce so we wouldn't fall over. Once Joe's dick slipped out of me, I pushed myself forward on shaky stiff legs and started pulling up my pants.

"No," he said, grabbing for my belt and jerking my pants back down. "I want to see you cum."

So, I started stroking my slimy precum-covered pecker again.

"Grab my ass," I instructed once he'd buckled his pants.

He pulled my ass into the crotch of his jeans and leaned over my shoulder to watch me pound. He leaned so heavily I had to hold us up against the same tree to keep from falling into a nearby muskeg hole. I gasped as my creamy cum shot out on the rough black bark.

I figured he'd drop me at the airport to wait for my plane. Instead he suggested dinner and took me to a place he knew I'd like. He wanted to talk about my life and my wife and my kids. After a few beers we head to the airport. I thought about it a while and then mentioned I'd be passing thru on my way home and would have a motel room the next time.

"That would work." he crowed.

As we pulled up to the curb at the airport, I offered my hand and thanks for a good time. His eyes were wide, he leaned forward in his seat and shook my hand vigorously. I crawled out of his new car and I realized with much satisfaction that Joe had made me cum and made me smile.

A NICE THING

I admired the waiter's ass, broad shoulders and height as he leaned across our table Tuesday morning. He had a wide belly and auburn page boy haircut. A quick glance at his nametag told me he was George. He was having a bad morning and I didn't think propositioning him while standing amongst my co-workers a good idea.

We played phone tag most the day when he could take calls in the restaurant and I could sneak out of my meeting. However, by the end of the day, my pager held directions to his new apartment. I could tell from his voice, it had been one of those days. The taxi driver dropped me right at the front door. Through the open door and curtainless window, I could see him look up from the television and smile. The place was a disaster in the process of being unpacked.

George has a wide round face that blooms when he is happy. He was happy.

I kissed him quickly in case someone walked by. As I took a seat, I noticed he wore a long sleeved t-shirt and boxers. He moaned about his day and touched me as he talked. I kept trying to change the subject and finally succeeded by admiring a big box of unpacked videos.

"Got any good ones?" I asked.

"Yeah."

He put in a video to entertain me while he showered. It starred ludicrously well-hung, muscled fashion models with perfect hair in every scene and bad attitudes, fucking and sucking one another. There was not a condom in sight the studs were fucking bareback.

George made his shower short and returned wearing it seemed nothing but the shirt. He laid his hand across my shoulder and stood behind me watching the television. I reached up from the couch and lifted the hem of his shirt. A black Speedo. Bummer.

"I'd like to do a little more but the curtains are open," I said.

"There's always my bedroom."

"I thought you'd never ask."

I followed him into the litter- and clothes-strewn room. He stopped before the single mattress lying on the floor. I reached up his shirt for his fat boy titties and kissed the small of his neck. He positively purred and pushed the crack of his ass into my crotch while I was kissing and licking his neck. He stretched his neck back and kissed me on the lips in appreciation. When he did, I reached for the Speedos. He was hard. His dick is little and brown.

He usually prefers bottom, but agreed to top for me. As I rubbed his crotch, he pushed his cock into my cupped right hand, then reached behind and unbuttoned my pants. Once he got my dick out he turned to kiss me with his big wet lips and as he stroked us both.

"I want that up my ass," I stated, stripping out of my remaining clothes.

He pushed me to my knees, and after a few minutes of my lips slurping on the head and tongue running up and down the shaft, he pulled me up and headed me for the bare mattress.

"All fours," he directed then spread my knees even further apart to get his wide body between my thighs. He spit on his cock.

As he lined up the head I said, "I've got rubbers and KY."

"Where?" he asked.

I got up on the mattress, turned and stuck my dick in his mouth. After a few reassuring strokes by his pink tongue, I pulled the supplies out of my pants pocket. Assuming the position again, I lowered my ass and shoved. His prick is only six inches and not thick so I was not expecting any difficulties. Maybe because it was sharp, or else I underestimated the amount of damage a big boy can do. But I did not prepare, and it hurt bad as he entered and started to stroke, but I decided to take it like a man. I had to grab the mattress to keep us from falling off as he pounded into me. Eventually my knee hit the floor, repositioning us, so that he went all the way in. I now felt great. I laid there pressed to the mattress as his sweaty chest and sweaty heavy belly. He was grinning away (a very happy boy!) and I was drooling in delight.

When he popped out of me he apologized for being exhausted and unable to keep it up any longer. He put a condom that had been lying on the floor on his dildo and started working my butt as I lay on my back and he pumped his cock. But a dildo rather than a cock up my butt is like jerking off rather than fucking a tight hole. So, I said no thanks. He apologized and lay down next to me. I said I'd gotten what I wanted. No reason to apologize.

"Come here?" he asked and pulled me on top him.

I laid all my 180 pounds on him and returned to kissing and growling in the hollow of his neck, until he convulsed beneath in a fit of giggles and pleaded with me to stop.

Lifting his ankles to his ears I licked up and down his shaft then dry humped until we were both talking about cumming. I braced his ankles on my shoulder and bent over him as we pounded away. He closed his eyes at the moment of climax and opened them to see me coming, too. My copious expulsion of white juice pooled in the crevices above his stomach, slimed his inner thighs, frosted the fuzz on his balls and coated his limp dick. The nice thing about making love to a guy is that afterwards, there's none of that cuddling and talking, to the moans of delight and groans of discomfort coming from the fashion models in the next room, we drifted off to sleep.

WOOD CHIPS

Part One

"Be careful, dear!" my wife called from the front yard.

I was headed out the icy road to get another truckload of wood chips from Jeff Hogg's mill. Jeff had been in the local newspaper's "Police Log" again. This month he'd threatened a contractor who'd leased some equipment from him.

We first read of Jeff three months before. He'd been sitting in the Jacuzzi with his best friend and girl friend. The men were naked. The woman wore a long white t-shirt that did little to hide her large round breasts, dark nipples and patches of pubic hair. Jeff nudged his buddy with his left arm while grabbing his girlfriend's elbow with his right hand.

"How about sucking our cocks?" he asked as both men eased up out of the tepid water expectantly.

"Fuck, no!" she snapped shoving him back.

As his firm hard buttocks bounced off the edge of the pool, he coolly slapped her across the mouth. The police arrived shortly after that. His name appeared among those charged with assault in the next issue of the paper.

My wife and I met him a few weeks later at the office Christmas party. He was in the market for a new girlfriend and started dating a friend of my wife's. That relationship didn't lasted too long, but he and I became friends during it. (He hasn't found a woman in our small town that hasn't been warned about him since.)

He seemed to like me and gave us free wood chips to help with the landscaping of our new house. His portable mill was located out of town nine miles next to the home he was building.

I pulled into the yard where I could see him working alone in the sunshine on the saw. I parked where it would be easy to back up to the snow-frosted wood-chip pile, but not appear presumptuous that he would give it away like usual. Even though he's several inches shorter than my 6'1" and twenty years younger than my forty-five, I always found him a little intimidating.

When I slammed the truck door, he didn't turn around. I stomped loudly as my long legs carried me closer. I did not want to startle him when he had his large hands around the saw blade.

"Bill!" he called with a cock-eyed grin and a rising note that stretched out my name.

"Hey, Jeff," I grinned back.

He kept his head half tilted and body half turned as he put down his wrench and pulled off his gloves. His striped engineer's shirt was unzipped all the way down to the middle of his chest revealing a muscled white body contrasting sharply with jet-black chest hair and the harsh sunburn on his neck. The collars of his shirt were flung wide across his broad shoulders. Red suspenders clinging tightly to his barrel chest held up his narrow-waisted black pants.

The pants did nothing to show off his fine ass, but they did brag up his flat hard belly. Jeff kept his black haircut short and face clean-shaven, in contrast to my salt-and-pepper hair and bristly moustache. His face when not sunburned was as white as his chest in sharp contrast to the deep red blush his cheeks could show. All this above a square dimpled chin. His eyebrows spread wide up and across his forehead to couple above his nose. His eyes (God his eyes!) were baby blue. They could be bright as the sky on a cloudless summer day or cold as the brow of Heaven on a clear, Southeastern winter's morn.

"How's it hanging?" he asked still grinning and extending a clean white hand with large long stubby fingers – the kind of fingers that let you know there's a large long thick dick hanging down the leg of his loose fitting trousers.

"Great! How's it going with you?"

"Good," he said and then mumbled it again, nodding his head and glancing from the truck to Bill and then back again. Some thought replaced the smile on his face.

"Need some more wood chips?" he asked, his eyes not quite so bright, the smile slipped from his face.

"Is that possible, buddy? Got some to spare?"

"I think," Jeff nodded, sky blue eyes on the ground.

"Let's go over here," he said, indicating the floorless shed of rough-cut sweet-smelling cedar he used to store chainsaws, tools, oil, gas, and parts for his mill.

As he set down the odds and ends he carried over from the mill on a plank supported by sawhorses, he asked,

"How many loads you taken out of here, Bill?"

I'd anticipated that question for some time. He turned to look at me. The pupils of his eyes were taut pinpoints of intense passion. He breathed heavily as he stared into my blue eyes. When he turned he found me reaching for my wallet. I, too, breathed excitedly.

"I don't want your money, buddy," he demurred. His powder blue eyes slid down my lanky frame to the sawdust floor. Two fingers of his right hand waved away my wallet as the left closed the shed door a little. He cleared his voice and waited.

"Well, then," I whispered huskily, "How can I ever repay you?"

We stood close and I boldly stared into his rosy face. His glacial cold eyes met and held mine in a harsh stare. He thought a moment, not looking away, not searching my face, but rather searching my eyes.

"Your wife sure is pretty."

I laughed with relief. I could feel the blush rise on my cheeks as my eyes danced merrily before his.

"You like those long legs and blonde hair and big tits?" I asked with a grin. My cupped hands traced her fine figure in the small space between our bellies. Then I patted his left shoulder with my right hand and left it resting there.

"Yeah," he smirked, blushing again and looking down.

So did I.

"Looks like someone else likes her, too!" I pointed out as I let my right index finger ride up the crease bulging out of his trousers. When I looked up, he just kept staring sternly into my face.

"I don't think she'd go for it," I said.

"No?" His left arm came to rest in the small of my back, his fingers rounded as though to pull me closer.

"What if I could find another pair of willing lips and a tight hole?"

"Nearby?" he asked coolly

"You got condoms and "KY"?"

"We don't need that yet."

He looked down at his crotch. So did I. His calloused hand pried the first button on his trousers open, then popped all the others. He stared at me pointedly a moment and then back at his crotch. He then shrugged off his suspenders, grabbed his shirt by the shoulders and yanked it off. Jeff wasn't wearing any shorts. His cock flew out of the open fly. Before I could react, his trousers slid lazily off his small tight ass and dropped to the tops of his heavy leather logging boots. A treasure trail of black semi-curly hair starting between his cold-hardened nipples led down his belly and a small patch of night-like hair kneeling at the root of a thick flat shaft of bruised purple flesh.

I removed my coat and knelt before my woods-god. Sawdust speckled his pubic hair and clung to his tight round balls. He smelled of cedar and the morning chill. I reached for the base of his big dick. His hands spread on either side of my head, clamped down on my ears and bent down my mouth. With a little shake of

his ass and wobble of the purple crown of his manhood, he shoved his cock up through my lips, slid it across the roof of my mouth and started banging the back of my throat.

I gagged a bit, but eased back on the broad shaft, letting my tongue thrum rapidly on his cum-tube and then on the prominent ridge of his cockhead.

"Oh, yeah, Bill. Suck it. Feels so good, man," he groaned.

I took a bit more of the eight-inch monster into my mouth and began a slow in and out movement. I could feel his nearly tasteless precum dripping onto my tongue.

I grabbed his tight muscular ass cheeks and felt them tense further as he pumped into my mouth. He bent his knees, pulled my head down further and soon drove that purple-headed monster in with a steady rhythm.

"Ah, man, I'm close. Fuck. Ready to…." His husky voice drifted off into the cold air. I moved a hand to his low-hanging balls, feeling them slide upward in their hairy enclosure. He shoved hard, pulled my head into his crotch and then grunted loudly: "Oh, oh, oh, it's cumming. Suck it up. Yeah! Take my juice… ah!"

I felt the first spurt hit the back of my throat and backed off to catch another equally plentiful ejaculation on my tongue…salty-sweet with a bitter edge. I gently tugged his balls as several smaller spasms produced more cum.

Jeff leaned down onto the top of my head, gaining his balance by gripping the workbench directly behind me. His cock popped out of my mouth with a loud slurping noise. For several minutes, he hung there panting loudly, his still-dripping organ dangling in front of my eyes.

"Shit, Bill," he said as he straightened up. He wobbled a little. His face was pale and his ice blue eyes iced over. He gulped audibly and then nodded for me to pick up his shirt. "It's cold as hell in here. Let's go up to the house. I need to warm up."

I stood, picked my coat up from the workbench and followed his broad disheveled form up the pathway to his log bungalow.

"Coffee or something?" he asked as we entered the warm kitchen. The blush was returning to his square jawed face, as was the charming smile.

I fidgeted a moment, trying to press my still-erect cock into a more comfortable position. Jeff's eyes followed my hand.

"Forgot, still haven't had yours," he smirked. He reached for my crotch and gripped my cock and balls in his big right hand. He stared at me dead eyed for a cold moment then his arm slid around my waist and we marched down a wide hallway to a sparsely furnished bedroom. We sat down side-by-side on the double bed and he began to unbutton my shirt. I stood and undid my belt and pulled down the zipper of my fly. My cock, still tangled in my white jockey shorts, popped out into Jeff's waiting hand. "Nice one," he said, gripping my six inches that seemed small compared to the thick hunk I recently had between my lips. Jeff didn't appear

to mind at all as he slid my shorts and pants down, poking predatorily at my exposed erection.

He finished stripping me by forcing me gently onto the bed with a shove while he removed my boots, socks pants and underwear.

"Man, you are very good-looking for an old…er, I mean, you have a great body," he snickered, his face reddening at his slip of the tongue.

I laughed, "It's okay, son…you are right handsome yourself for a young virgin."

His grin expanded as he finished undressing himself. I could see his cock was making a surprising revival. He lurched toward me, knelt between my legs and gripped the base of my throbbing prick in the fingers of his right hand.

"Your turn to cum," he said, pushing me back to a lying position. I felt his warm, wet tongue touch my hard dick. He spread my legs wider and began playing with my balls roughly as he expertly tongued the full length of my cock. His mouth slid downward to my balls and he sucked each one hard, his lips pinching the ruffled sack before lifting my legs and pressing me further back on the bed.

"Mmm, a beautiful ass," he whispered huskily his eyes again glazed with passion. His mouth was soon on my asshole with lots of spit and loud lip-smacking. "Like a hot pussy," he said as he lifted his head momentarily. Then he plunged down again, sticking his tongue directly against my pucker. He sucked and licked for what seemed like minutes, but may have been only seconds. "Gonna fuck you," he announced as he stood. He spit into his hand and slathered it onto his cock, now fully erect and drooling precum.

"Condom?" I asked weakly.

He growled in response hefting my left thigh a little higher. I felt the big knob at the entrance to my ass. Slowly, he pressed forward as I tried to relax for his intrusion.

"Oh, man," I moaned reflexively at the initial pain Jeff stood stock still, expressionless for a moment. We were both breathing heavily. I looked up at him and could see sweat moistening his forehead and matting the black hair on his chest.

He looked directly into my eyes, but made not a sound as he shoved forward, lodging about half of his thick rod in my straining asshole. As he eased back a bit, to strike at my ass again, pleasure replaced the pain.

"Oh, that's good. Now. Yeah, fuck me," I moaned.

Jeff didn't need further invitation. Grabbing my cock, which had dwindled to a semi-erect state at the pain of entry, he shoved the rest of his fat prick inside me.

He began a slow, merciless, steady in and out motion, pumping my cock with the same rhythm. Sweat, spit and the copious leakage of his precum did little to ease his rampant prick's dry rape of my butthole. I shoved my ass up to meet his strokes and felt his heavy balls slapping against my dampened ass cheeks.

"Ah, yeah, that's it. Faster, faster, fuck me, fuck me," I grunted.

Jeff's groans merged with my own. "Uh, take it. Take my cock. I'm gonna cum in you…soon, uh, uh, now, here it cums. Ah, oh, fuck, yeah."

I felt his thick man meat twitching and spurting inside my ass. His steady pumping of my stiffened sensitive pecker set me off immediately after the first surge of his hot jizm.

"Mmm, I'm shooting…ah," I told him as my thick white cream squirted into the dark hair of his broad chest and flat belly. "So good."

He literally fell onto me, his elbows down to keep our chests and faces from too intimate a contact, his cock inching further into my still-twitching butthole. We lay breathing heavily, the moistness of our exertions gluing our crotches together. As we caught our breath, Jeff rolled onto his side, staring directly into my eyes.

"I'll get the backhoe and load up the wood chips. You've taken care of two loads." An eyebrow twitched in amusement as his cold eyes continued to stare at me.

I laughed to myself, thinking about how many more loads it would take to finish the landscaping.

Part Two

As the dark winter days settled deeper onto the Southeastern landscape, I saw very little of Jeff. We ran into each other occasionally in town. Once, before the cold snap in December, we got together for lunch and a long, hot afternoon at his cabin out the road.

It was just before the skunk cabbages started poking their yellow heads out of the muskeg that I heard from him again. My wife had taken the kids to the youngest one's first swim meet in a town a hundred miles south of here. The phone rang right after I got home from work.

"Hey, it's Jeff," said the low, husky voice when I answered. "You need any more wood chips? It's getting warm enough to work on your yard again."

"Yeah, it is. And I could use some," I responded. My hand slid automatically to my crotch. Damn, the man's voice was sexy, even in casual chatting.

"Well, how 'bout tomorrow you come out and I give you a load, Bill," he said, a malicious laugh punctuating the double entendre. "It built up some – the wood chip pile, I mean."

"That would be great." My cock began to harden and twitch under my prodding finger. I didn't want to wait that long.

"Tell you what, Jeff. I'm pretty much free tonight if you're going to be home…"

"Hell, yes," he almost shouted. Such enthusiasm. He must have been pussy-less for a long time now.

"I'll be out as soon as I grab a bite to eat and shower, okay?" I tried to keep my voice cool and steady, but somehow the last word came out as a nervous squawk.

A gobbled ham sandwich and performed a lick-and-promise shower. Later, I was speeding long the curving, Sitka spruce lined nine-mile stretch to Jeff's place.

Even in my rush, I remembered to take my digital camera and the "rubber toys" Jeff seemed to like when I introduced them to him back in October. We had shared a motel room in Seattle for two nights and did some major erotic exploration.

It was dark at 7:00 p.m. Only a front light was visible at Jeff's place on the pot-holed gravel road. It was nice for early March, that is the wind wasn't blowing the rain up under your Hailey Hansen raingear. A dog barked at the house closer to the water, a good distance away.

Jeff came out the back door onto the small deck and called to me. He was wearing blue jeans and a white T-shirt. Even in the dark, lit only by the light streaming from the upper windows, I could see his muscular figure was as trim as ever.

"Hi, c'mon in," he said in a very friendly tone, his voice husky.

"Hi, I brought some stuff for you," I said, holding up the plastic grocery bag containing a six-pack of beer, the rubber toys, a tube of lubricant and my camera. We went in through the sliding door to his bedroom, which is always neat and clean. A handmade quilt covered the bed and strange, tacky plaques hung on the wall. A lamp on each side of the bed provided light that not visible from outside through the curtain less windows.

He led the way to the kitchen, a compact area with a nook for a maple dining table bearing gingham design plastic placemats on two sides. The adjacent living room is all glass in the front, sparsely furnished with a large sofa and chair. A huge stone fireplace is at one end with an antique muzzle-loading rifle over the mantle. A nice fire blazes there. No TV set. A long coffee table has a monstrous philodendron with long tendrils hanging out over the ends. You'd expect the plant to be long dead and the place a mess, but the handsome stud has an eighty year old lady friend who stops by to take care of him and the house every Wednesday. It's rumored he takes care of her on the same afternoon.

A huge 10-point deer head trophy is the only wall adornment. As he put my beer in the fridge and retrieved two for us, I noticed he was clean shaven. He had worn a moustache or a beard and moustache the last several times we met. He is ruggedly handsome – a big nose, small mouth, square dimpled chin and dark bushy eyebrows. His ice blue eyes hold no mystery – they are boldly honest. I noticed he had developed a very slight "beer gut" just in recent months, but that would no doubt disappear with the outdoor activities encouraged by the warming spring days. When he handed me the beer, he reached between my legs and squeezed my dick and balls.

I commented about his clean-shaven face, running my hand over his cheek. He looked into my eyes – blue to blue.

"Take your pill?" he asked, smiling.

"Yeah," I said, feeling the heat rise in me while he massaged my growing hardon. I reached for him and found his semi-hard dick.

"Um," he groaned. I leaned into him and could smell soap and a very light after-shave. After a minute of hugging and rubbing, I pulled away.

"We have some time tonight," I said. "My wife is staying in "Tijuana" until tomorrow."

"Good," he said, sitting down at the table and taking a sip of beer.

We talked for a few minutes about what we'd been doing for the past four months. He suggested we go into the bedroom. I agreed and followed him back. He went into the bathroom to take a leak. I could hear his groan of release and the harsh tinkling as I started to undress. I had brought the camera to the bedroom, but forgot the toys. By this time, I didn't care. My pulse pounded and my cock ached to be released.

I watched him in the bathroom across the hall while I undressed. He came into the bedroom his pants undone and his semi-erect dick poking out just as I was taking off my shirt. He had on white jockey shorts and his dark dick contrasted beautifully with them. He stripped in no time and was lying on the bed gripping his hardon – now straining at its full eight inches – while I pulled off my socks and bikini shorts.

I wanted to go right for his dick, but tonight I figured I'd extend our foreplay. I lay down halfway atop him and began licking and nibbling his earlobe while I played with his chest hair. I could feel his very hard cock against mine and his warm balls on my upper leg.

I kissed his cheeks and forehead and eyes, then a brief, soft touch to his lips. Sometimes he turns his mouth away at first, but then lets his lips return hungrily to mine. I went to his chest and sucked his right nipple.

"Oh, yeah," he groaned. "Feels good."

I nibbled the small pencil eraser tip of his nipple and moved to the left one while I lightly fondled his cock and balls. I slid my tongue down his hairy belly and plunged it into his deep navel. He moaned and twisted beneath me. I could tell he was very hot. His cock throbbed in my fingers and his breathing was ragged.

When I got to his dick, I said, "Let me take some pictures now."

He agreed readily, putting his arm across his face to disguise his identity. He knows I may show them to "my friend" on the Internet. I took three photos of him with his hardon poking up. The camera got a little shaky by the time I got to the last one. If my dick was considerably longer, I would have had a tripod. In lieu of that, I set the camera up on the dresser for a timed exposure and got into the picture sucking his cock for two shots.

Then I went to work in earnest on his dick and balls. I held the base of his stiff prong in my fingers tightly and licked at the swollen dark purple head. I eased

back and watched as I pressed my thumb upward on his amazingly prominent cum tube, extracting a brief flow of nearly clear precum. I licked the shaft downward from the wide, drooling head. His cock juice had no taste at all, but the musk of his crotch was like a heady perfume.

I then went to his dark wrinkly ball sack, which is almost totally devoid of hair despite the extreme hairiness of all the surrounding area. His balls are naturally that way. He doesn't shave them, of course. I sucked on the right one which is larger than the left, as big around as a ping pong ball. Then I slurped in the other one. There was no way to get both fat nuts into my mouth.

Suddenly, Jeff began to tug on me, twisting me around in bed so he had access to my cock. His usual love was licking and nibbling my ass checks then tongue fucking my asshole in preparation for drilling me. He has on past occasions tentatively licked and pressed his mouth against my cock and balls. This time he began to work on them in earnest, taking my growing cock all the way into his mouth.

He pulled me off his cock and had me stand on my knees while he sucked noisily on my dick and gently squeezed my balls. Damn, it felt good! Maybe a little too good. I felt pre-orgasmic pressure building rapidly in my nuts, so I pulled away.

"Oh, hold it. I'm ready to cum. I don't want to cum yet," I said. He backed off immediately and I gripped the base of my cock tightly to keep it from going off. But I was too late. My cum spurted and flowed, running down over his hairy chest. "Oh, God, I'm sorry," I mumbled.

Jeff's blue eyes never batted nor did his broad hairy chest flinch at the white whip of cum. He grabbed a tissue and wiped his chest. He then lay face down on the bed, his hard muscled, very white ass cheeks raised slightly and his huge cock and balls poking backward between his dark hairy thighs. I thought about going to get one of the dildos I'd brought, but thought better of it. I decided instead to work on him with my fingers. I put my index finger against his puckered hole and slid it in easily up to the second knuckle. Holding my breath in hopes that this was what he had in mind, I turned my finger so that I was touching his prostate. It was there – healthy, slightly swollen and sensitive.

"Mmm, oh," he grunted. His ass rose higher and I slid in a second finger. "Yeah, oh, oh, Bill," he said.

With my fingers still in his ass, I tugged him up on his knees, lay with my back on the bed and stuck my head between his legs from the back. I licked his balls and then began sucking his cock while I pumped my fingers in and out of his hot ass. He maneuvered himself so that he was standing on the floor and began to pump his cock into my mouth very hard, nearly choking me.

He began growling in a deep voice, "Yeah, motherfucker, suck that cock. Take it all." I feared he was going to suffocate me so I managed to pull his widening prick out of my throat until the broad head rested just inside my cheek. He sputtered

and muttered unintelligibly, still ramming and poking his big rod in and out of my stretched lips.

I pulled his cock out of my mouth and turned over on my stomach to get more control. Without asking or anything, he leaned forwarded, stretched his long right arm across my body and started cramming his fingers in my ass. I jerked back a little in response, but kept sucking on the head while holding the shaft with one hand and squeezing his balls with the other. His left hand came down on my right shoulder. He pinned me to the bed while grunting, groaning, and fucking my face.

"Oh, oh, I'm ready," he finally groaned. He popped his cock from my mouth, gave it two or three quick jerks with his own calloused hand and it began to spew. I held my open mouth over it and caught most of his spurting jizm on my tongue. He gave me four or five good heavy shots, the most I've ever seen from him or any other partner!

One burst of cum he'd carefully aimed into my right eye by twisting my head with his left hand. The part that landed on my tongue tasted bitter but not unpleasant, like the tang of a dark imported beer. I closed my mouth over the throbbing head to get the last dribbles of his juice. A bit of the bluish milky effluent ran down the sides of his dark prick and I licked it clean.

When I looked up at him, his face was like that of a saint transported – his mouth was slightly open and his twilight blue eyes opened and closed rapidly. He staggered and almost fell on top of me.

"Ah, that was great, Bill, just great," he said. I sat up on the side of the bed and he gave me a quick, hard hug. I felt good.

As we started to dress, I thought about the wood chips. But I judiciously kept my mouth shut. I could check on those tomorrow.

Part Three

Bill climbed the wide cedar steps leading to the second floor of Jeff's place and knocked at the living-room door.

Through the cut glass window in the door, he could see the raven-haired man look up startled with the knock, then heard him "Hey!" in response as he hung up the telephone. Bill could see the remains of a six pack on the coffee table and the usual bag of toys, condoms and Vaseline.

"Wanna fuck?" Jeff asked smiling as he answered the door and pulled Bill in with his left hand.

The taller, older man grinned, thinking: "Damn, he's being subtle tonight. Maybe I've used up the supply of wood chips he's been providing me free."

Bill looked again at the muscular stud gripping his wrist. The sky blue eyes that crouched beneath the single black eyebrow lost their twinkle. The haze that replaced their usual mischievous glow wasn't lust either. Bill was late. Jeff was drunk. Very drunk. Jeff's face was puffy and flushed from the hard bottom of his square dimpled chin to the tip-tops of his almost elfin ears.

As Bill kicked off his boots, Jeff struggled the red suspenders off his wide shoulders, whacking the striped blue and grey engineer's shirt twice in the process. The left nipple that got "thanged" twice under the shirt had been hard in the first place. Bill could imagine it stinging sharply as it stood even more prominently from Jeff's well-formed pec.

Jeff unsnapped this black cotton pants with more success and flung them to this ankles where they bunched around the thick grey wool ankle high socks on

his feet. His wide fat eight incher appeared fully erect. Jeff wasn't wearing shorts. Without a word, without removing his Carhart coat, Bill dropped to his knees and stretched his lips over the purpled head. Jeff pulled over his shirt and flung it to the floor.

Bill's right hand stroked the base of Jeff's meat, played with his moderately sized, hairless balls. He tickled at Jeff's asshole where the middle finger found the entrance to be closed even to that moderate-sized digit. He then followed the "treasure trail" from his small triangle of curly black pubic hair to his hairy muscular chest and hard nipples.

Jeff massaged the salt and pepper hair on Bill's scalp, pressing his fellator's head into his crotch occasionally.

"Come here, buddy," Jeff commanded pulling the older man up by his armpits.

"How's this doing?" he asked, groping at Bill's crotch ineffectually. "Take `em off."

Bill happily complied while Jeff staggered and tried to hold the older man by the waist and lick at his six-inch dick.

"Shirt, too!" Jeff instructed while staggering back to enjoy the view.

Still grinning, Bill managed to pull off his coat, sweater and shirt all at once. Now naked except for a pair of wet white socks, Bill reached for his logger lover.

"Up against the wall and spread 'em," Jeff joked with a shout and a stifled chuckle.

His strong arms and stubby fingers forced a willing Bill to comply. Then he stepped forward with bent legs and slipped his knees inside those of the taller man. Flicking his own knees outward sent Bill's feet sliding on the wet floor and lowered his puckering asshole within range of Jeff's raging cock. At the same time, Jeff's left hand slipped under Bill's left arm and clamped onto the bottom's neck.

"KY? Condoms?" Bill asked as he felt Jeff's steely weapon jabbing at his butt. Then he gasped as Jeff pulled him down further with the half nelson.

"We don't need that," Jeff growled. His right hand lined up his hungry rod on Bill's hot ass crack and wedged it into the bunghole.

"Argh!" Bill grunted as Jeff assumed the full nelson.

"How's that?" the top asked as he slammed his cock all the way in. Before the grimacing recipient of his onslaught could answer, Jeff started pounding away with abandon, forcing Bill's face uncomfortably into the wall.

"Like that?"

It was eight rapid-fire strokes later before Bill could honestly answer. As his head continued to slam against the wall and the ache in his hips grew from the forced position he gritted teeth and managed to say, "Yeah, I like it."

"I don't," Jeff snarled. "Let's get you on the coffee table so I can fuck you like a dog."

Bill winced when the thick flat cock flipped out of his butt, partly from pain and partly from the sudden empty feeling in the wake of the huge tool's removal. Limply he stumbled over to the coffee table and tried to crawl onto it. Jeff changed his mind and told him to lie on his back. Then hoisted both his lover's long legs on to his shoulders and drove his dirty dick up Bill's ass again.

"Yeah, yeah." Bill moaned then his hands clapped on Jeff's firm ass.

That was the logger's signal to dig his hairy toes deeper into the shag rug so he could penetrate Bill even deeper.

The beer was beginning to take a more serious effect. Red and puffing, Jeff kept slamming their conjoined bodies into the table as the drool and sweat rolled off his face.

"Yeah. Yeah. There, there!" he yelled as he let a hot load go up Bill's guts.

He's eyes remained glassy as he huffed and puffed above his lover. For a moment it looked like he'd kiss Bill in appreciation. Then he struggled up. "Thanks." he mumbled waving his long cock at Bill, letting the remaining pre-cum and jizm fly off in sticky little lines. "Take care of yourself." Then he collapsed face first onto the couch next to Bill.

Bill was taking care of himself. His right hand stroked his now solid six incher as he admired his hulking, hunky rapist's prone form. A good fucking and Jeff's rock hard belly rubbing against the bottom's cock and balls had done the trick. Bill's ass was already a little sore, but he was still horned up. Suddenly he heard a sound like a small wave crashing on the shore. The "whoosh" of sand being driven up the beach. And finally the tickling and clicking of small shells co-mingling with the debris at the high line mark. Jeff was snoring, dead to the world.

Bill sat up on the coffee table, his knees wide spread. Jeff was laying ass up on the couch, his right leg a little bent which lifted his ass. Bill could see sawdust in the crack of his furry butt.

"Take care of yourself," he repeated, his grin less than even, more than lascivious.

He picked up the Vaseline jar from where Jeff had tossed it on the floor. With a twist he sent the top flying then flipped it over and plopped it onto his cock. He fucked it a few times, straddled Jeff with his left knee on the couch, pressed his cock head between the muscular ass cheeks and firmly against the logger's butt hole.

"A virgin no more," Bill thought, recalling his buddy's firm resolve never to have his macho sanctuary invaded. Bill's slick, precum-dripping prick slid past the tight sphincter with little trouble. The velvety insides enveloped the head of Bill's dick in the warmest sensation its owner could ever remember. "Oh, God," he moaned, feeling rare erotic shivers course upward from his crotch to his armpits.

Long slow strokes merged into bolder, quickening stabs and still the sleeping top remained still, his snoring a counterpoint to Bill's ardent panting. Bill shifted slightly to get a better grip with his feet, pushing his cock fully into Jeff's

tight asshole, his pubic hair tangling wetly with furry ass cheeks. He could feel his balls tighten as he rapidly slid his cock in full strokes into the fleshy pleasure-channel.

"Oh, oh, yeah, oh, I'm cumming," he grunted aloud. Pushing fully forward he felt his cock begin to twitch in orgasm. Just as the first spasm coursed through him, his victim stirred.

"Huh, uh…wha' the fuck?" Jeff snorted as he arose from his beer-induced near-coma.

Bill's second cum shot spurted just as the man beneath him pushed upward. Bill jumped backward, his still-shooting pecker depositing a glob right in the middle of Jeff's back. The two men stood staring at each other, Jeff's face a mask of puzzlement and anger, Bill's sweating with the final tingling of the best cum he'd had in at least ten years.

"Damn you, what the hell do you think…" Jeff's voice trailed off as he raised his fists. His sky blue eyes hazed over with anger.

"Hey, man," Bill said, raising his hands defensively. "I just couldn't resist. You have the cutest ass."

Jeff dropped his fists, running his right hand back to inspect the dripping mess between his recently invaded ass cheeks. Suddenly, he laughed. He laughed loud. Reaching slowly with his gooey fingers between Bill's legs, he gently gripped the softening cock.

"I guess that little thing didn't hurt me much," he blurted between guffaws. Pulling Bill into an awkward bear hug, the big logger said, "Let's go get cleaned up."

They showered together, Bill taking extra care to swab clean his buddy's almost-virginal asshole.

ABOUT THE AUTHOR

Billy Jay Dee feels the most comfortable in a pair of cowboy boots. He has worked in emergency services as a boy scout, volunteer, paid first responder, dispatcher and manager of a 911 office. He's visited five of the seven continents. He's eaten breakfast at Tiffany's. He loves tequila. He's been known to kiss the back of a few hands. This is his second published collection of short stories. He likes his men manly and his girls girly. He can run a chainsaw and drop a burning snag.

www.ingramcontent.com/pod-product-compliance
Lightning Source LLC
Chambersburg PA
CBHW051656260626
47170CB00004B/1531